G000059984

Sunny Disposition

Deanna Grey

Copyright © 2022 by Deanna Grey

All rights reserved. No part of this publication may be reproduced, stored or transmitted in any form or by any means, electronic, mechanical, photocopying, recording, scanning, or otherwise without written permission from the publisher. It is illegal to copy this book, post it to a website, or distribute it by any other means without permission.

This novel is entirely a work of fiction. The names, characters and incidents portrayed in it are the work of the author's imagination. Any resemblance to actual persons, living or dead, events or localities is entirely coincidental.

Editor: Heather Rosman

Beta Reader: Aria J.

Cover Design: Cormar Covers

Contents

Content Notes

This novel includes:

Brief depictions of physical assault.

Discussions of chronic pain, parental neglect and parental death due to cancer.

On-page sex scenes

Glossary

Streamer - game streamers broadcast themselves playing games for online audiences.

Stream Moderator (Mod) – usually a volunteer who helps keep a streamer's chat and/or Discord in order.
They enforce the streamer's rules and help with admin tasks.

VOD – video on demand.

Chapter One

Finn

For the longest time I believed we only got one incredible, life-changing thing in our lives. Hockey was mine. But then, I got lucky. I met her. And everything changed.

I still loved the game. Still would give every ounce of my being to the sport. Except now, I saved energy and time for her, too. Suddenly, there was a life worth living off the ice. And I wanted to enjoy it with her.

Chai03: Nervous but really excited for tonight.

Her message came through as I began suiting up for tonight's game. As I read her words, I brushed a hand across my mouth in a poor attempt to hide my growing smile.

"Are you fucking blushing? Who the hell has you blushing?" Lincoln, our goalie who always ran his mouth like he was being paid, leaned on the locker next to mine. He chuckled when I glared in his direction. If I'd given that look to any other guy on the team, they would've backed off in a heartbeat. But not Lincoln. He feared nothing. He'd laugh in the devil's face if the guy told a semi-decent joke.

"I don't blush," I ground out.

Lincoln threw an arm around my shoulder, shaking me back and forth. "Yeah, you do."

"I do not." I shoved my phone into my bag before he could see the screen.

For now, Chai03 was a secret. My secret. My online friend, turned crush, turned...something more? From the more personal messages we'd been sending lately, we definitely felt like something more. I'd know for sure after tonight.

I had a plan. A) win this game against our biggest rivals, the Crows, and coast on that high to... B) ask her if we could transition our relationship offline.

"Your skin looks like it's on fire," Lincoln continued. "What're you hiding?"

"This." I showed him my middle finger. "Now, fuck off."

He laughed, but at least removed his arm from my shoulder. "Very touchy. Must be important. Are they hot?"

"Who?" The team's star right winger, Henrik, looked up from his seat, where he was pulling on his skates. When his eyes met mine, he smiled and muttered, "Right. Never mind. None of my business."

Unlike Lincoln, Henrik gave a damn what others thought of him. And he knew how to read a room.

"Hey," Sam, our captain, tried to cut through the chatter in the locker room.

A few other guys looked up from their lockers. Most of their conversations continued despite the attempted interruption. Sam called for silence again, only to be ignored. These newbies were ridiculous. Sam's approach to leadership was stern but quiet—I preferred noise.

I slammed my locker and banged my fist against it twice for emphasis. Talking stopped instantly. Gazes turned to me.

"Start of a season isn't an excuse!" My voice was loud and bounced off the walls. "If a captain is speaking, you're shutting the hell up. It's not a hard thing to remember."

Sam crossed his arms over his chest, flashing me a grateful look. It was entertaining to see the guy I grew up with become our leader. I knew how he looked hanging from a flagpole back in middle school. It was hard taking someone seriously after that, but I played along for the sake of balance.

"Get grounded," Sam started his usual pregame speech.

"Leave everything you're worried about in here because, on the ice, it doesn't exist." Sam scanned us all. His gaze lingered on Lincoln, Henrik, and me longer than the rest.

"Let's give them something to rage about on the bus ride home," he finished. The guys cheered in agreement.

Sam pushed through the crowd of our teammates as they started out of the door. "Finn."

I took a deep, readying breath. Dealing with my best friend during game time felt like talking to a parent who was also the school principal.

I shut my locker and pulled on my gloves. "What's up?"

"You got—" he paused, waiting for one guy to squeeze past us, "—the photos?"

I met his gaze with a frown. "Of course. I told you I would."

He raised an impressed brow. "Didn't think you'd be able to deliver."

"Oh, ye of little faith."

Sam snorted. "Get them to me ASAP. I want to verify everything."

"They're large files. I'm going to upload them to a drive later. I'll give you permissions."

"A drive?" His voice hitched, concerned. "That's hackable. We don't want anyone to—"

"Relax, relax." I gestured my hand up and down. "It's under control. Everything's hackable. I get the worry, but what's done is done. We need to focus on the next steps. First of which is getting back-ups."

Sam blew out a breath. "Fine, alright. We'll figure it out."

I nodded. "We will. For now, let's focus on killing some Crows, eh?"

He chuckled, getting back to his usual self. "Right. You ready for it?"

I scoffed. "Am I ready for it?"

"Well..." Sam gestured to his face. "You're a little red."

"I'm fine," I promised in a stiff voice. Damn. I never thought I was this much of an open book when I was excited.

"Better be. I heard Alex Greate's coming for your head."

"Really?" Now, that'd be entertaining. Alex Greate was a Crow legacy. A fourth-generation player from a line of pro-players. He was one of the best defensemen in the league. One of the most dangerous too, with a temper that matched my own.

"Really." Sam gave me a curt nod. I heard my phone buzz in my locker. My fingers clenched. I resisted the urge to respond, which was difficult because I knew it was her.

"I can handle him," I promised.

"Good." He pointed to my locker. "Mentally, let's leave whatever that is in there."

He was talking about the photos. But if he knew about Chai, he'd warn me against her, too. I nodded, watching him go.

"Is it a someone?" Henrik asked.

He'd been so quiet, I forgot he was still in the room.

"Remember that thing you said about it being none of your business?"

Henrik smiled and stood from his seat. "Right. I just thought you'd like to tell at least one of us. Secrets feel heavier on the ice. Lighter loads mean easier wins."

I stared at him for a moment, considering. "Yeah. It's a someone."

"Do I know her?"

"I've never met her... not in person. That's happening tonight." My stomach clenched hearing myself say it out loud. Shit. None of these nerves were about the game. They were all for her.

"Congrats," Henrik said, sounding genuine. "Let's make sure you get to meet her in one piece."

"You heard that nonsense about Greate?"

Henrik snorted. "Everyone has. Stick tight. None of that renegade stuff you play. At least not when you want to make a decent first impression. Showing up to a date with a black eye's kind of a red flag."

I nodded. "Yeah, you're right." Chai knew only a little about hockey. Explaining a black eye to her while also asking her to take our relationship to the next level would be awkward and challenging.

"I'll make it as clean as possible," I said.

Henrik laughed in disbelief. "You playing clean? Oh, this should be good."

I took a spot in the penalty box. There was blood on my tongue and sweat in my eyes. We were still in the second period, with ten minutes left on the clock.

Henrik was right. Playing clean and I didn't quite fit. I'd shoved Greate against the boards as soon as I could because, in my book, it was better to strike first. Well before his skates touched the ice, I understood he was determined to be my personal nightmare. So, I was determined to show him two could play that game.

I felt his gaze on me from where he stood across the ice. He was waiting for my clock to run out, so he'd get another chance to swing. Since I took the first shot, it didn't sit well with him.

Sam blazed past the box with the puck at the edge of his stick. I could tell by the slight tilt of his shoulder he was waiting for Henrik—who wasn't as fast but was far more tactical in getting close to the net.

Henrik was on the opposite end of the rink, doing his best to bulldoze his way through defenders. I knew he'd score before his stick touched the puck.

The point put us in the lead. As soon as the penalty timer was up, I rejoined them.

"Clean, huh?" Henrik grinned, slowing as he moved by.

"He was asking for it," I said.

"What should I make for your funeral?"

"Crepes," I suggested. "My sisters love that shit."

That got a laugh out of him and before moving on, he said, "I'll see what I can do."

Sam stopped for a moment to say, "Nice work. Target on your back's doubled in size."

"Gonna help me out?" I raised a brow at his smile.

He slapped my shoulder pad before starting off. "No worries. I got it under control."

Sam kept his word. His success shocked me to no end. Greate and I didn't have any other run-ins. At least, not in the rink.

Post-game victory celebrations started in the parking lot. I weaved through the crowd, politely declining requests for signatures and photos from kids with dreams of playing hockey in college. Sam protested when he saw a familiar look on my face.

"Come on!" he called after me. "Party starts at nine on Chester Street."

The anxious guy he'd been pre-game seemed like a mirage. Currently, he had a beautiful girl in one hand and a beer in the other.

"Busy," I called back with a shake of my head.

"The photos?" he asked in a moment of seriousness.

I flashed him a thumbs up. "I got you."

"My man!" He raised his beer in my direction before pulling his girl close for a deep kiss. I snorted at the sight.

"Hey." Lincoln caught up to me and walked backward. He had a level of energy one shouldn't be able to maintain after playing an intense game. I don't think the guy ever ran out of steam. "You sure you don't want to join us tonight? Think it could be good seeing as the new guys on the team think you're a rage demon we've summoned from the ashes."

"Imagination running wild, huh? Drafting stories again?"

"Actually, I do have this new idea I want to run by you—"

I held up my hand. "That wasn't an invitation, Link. I have somewhere important to be tonight. I can't be late."

His eyes lit up, and I regretted the feeling I'd put into my words.

"Do you need company? A bodyguard? You know those Crows love a good fight out of the rink, too."

"I'll be fine..." When he gave me a disbelieving look, I added, "Promise. If my important meeting goes well, you'll be the first to know."

He nodded, more hyped than I ever thought someone could get over something unseen. I'd never admit it out loud, but he wasn't the worst friend a person could have.

"Be careful," he warned. "Don't do anything I wouldn't."

"Yeah, yeah. Go enjoy the party."

He gave me a fist bump before heading back toward the crowds. I continued through the parking lot. The walk to my van wasn't long. By the time I got there, my phone buzzed with a message. Her username flashed on my screen and my smile was back.

Chai03: Heading out now. I'll be the girl shaking with nerves. See you soon!

I chuckled at her honesty and quickly shot her a confirmation text. Dots appeared on her end. She was typing. I waited, but before the response came through, something hard and cold slammed against my jaw. My mouth tasted of iron in an instant. I recovered fast enough to set my gaze on Alex Greate. Without padding he was still a large guy with angry eyes and burning red skin.

"Doesn't feel too hot, does it?" he asked, voice rough like he hadn't used it in ages. "Getting knocked out of nowhere."

"No teammates or referees to get between us this time," I warned when I stood my full height again, straightening my back and cracking my neck.

"You're damn right. Sucks for you, asshole," he said before winding up for another punch.

I rarely got the chance to do stuff like this off the ice. Sure, I had somewhere to be, but this would only take a minute. And God, it was going to be satisfying.

Most people frowned upon aggression outside sports. I understood that. Respected it. But it never felt right.

What felt right was my knuckles connecting with Greate's nose. My knee shoved in his gut. The crook of my arm around his neck. Hearing his voice strained as he begged me to stop. Feeling his blood on my skin as I tightened my grip a little more.

I'm not sure if I would've stopped if the other guys didn't show up. But once they did, everything went south in a heartbeat. In the end, I was the one gasping for air. Like me, they had little taste for mercy.

I understood that. Respected it.

Two of them shoved me into a broken stone bollard. My spine connected with a sharp edge. There should've been more pain, but I couldn't feel much of anything at that point.

Once my head hit the concrete and a crack sounded, the painlessness felt permanent. My understanding waned, along with everything else. For a second, I stared up at the sky, listening to faraway voices panic about blood. And then, everything was dark. I couldn't maintain focus long enough to keep my eyes open. Only one thought ran through my brain.

After all that, I'm still showing up to this date with a black eye.

Chapter Two

Finn

On day seven post-op, I got my hands on a phone. According to my sisters, my original one got damaged in the fight. They'd brought me a new one with almost everything re-installed. It was large and shiny and unlocked whenever I held it up to my face.

My hospital bed sheets felt scratchy, and the buzzing of nurses constantly walking through the halls kept me up. I needed a decent distraction. The phone seemed like a perfect one.

As I scrolled through the device, I felt like I was invading someone's privacy. Occasionally, my amnesia allowed me to remember small, mundane things. I knew my name. How to tie my shoes. Fix a cup of coffee the way I liked.

I hadn't known my sister's names were Denver and Anna. My parents had divorced. Dad worked a lot. Mom moved to England to be with her girlfriend. My friends were hockey players. I was one, too.

I decided it would be wise to make a list of the things that felt unfamiliar, so I could ask questions about them later. On the notes app on my phone, I made two categories: things I remembered and things that confused me. There were only three in the familiar column. The confusion column got longer every day.

After minutes of trying to come up with something familiar, a notification ding distracted me from my list-making. The message came from an app I haven't had time to study yet.

Chai03: Hi, just checking in...again. I feel like these messages might be annoying if you're seeing them. But if you are seeing them, please let me know if you're okay! I'll leave you alone if I know you're okay.

I frowned. The username didn't ring any bells, so I added it to the confusion column. I scrolled through the message thread to see how long I'd been talking to this person. Unlike my text messages, I didn't set this app to auto-delete threads after a certain amount of time. There were months' worth of conversations.

My heart hammered as I read through the messages. None of the words triggered a full memory, but while reading, a warm feeling moved over my body. I knew this person. Not only knew but was close to them. From the direction of some messages, I think I had a crush on them.

I noted the dates and time stamps. We spoke constantly. Every day for almost a year. From what I gathered, I moderated her game streams. She trusted me with secrets she hadn't told her best friend. We planned to meet up for the first time...the night of my accident. The night I forgot everything important.

My stomach dropped when I read the messages from that night and after. Chai started out worried, then confused, hurt, pissed, and now, was back to worry.

Chai03: Please, I need to know you're okay.

Please, was her most common plea. The more time passed, the fewer messages she sent. But they still came in. The messages were no longer angry—she'd apologized about those. Instead, they were sad and my heart ached for a relationship I couldn't remember. It wasn't just an ache; it was longing. For what we had, what we were becoming, and everything between.

A wiser person would have started with an explanation and ended with an offer to meet up. But I was in no state for first impressions. Not only because I didn't know who I was, but my injuries left me looking and feeling like a mess. I needed to get my stitches removed from my chin, at least. Wait until some of my swelling went down, too.

Instead of explaining, I apologized. It took me an hour to come up with something I thought was worth sending.

MidQuest: Hi, Chai. I'm okay. I've only now read all your messages. Thank you for checking in on me. I'm sorry for how I left things. That wasn't part of the plan at all...I know it might take a while for you to trust me again, but I'm willing to do what it takes to earn it back. I'm going to do what I can to make this up to you and hope you can forgive me.

I pressed send and held my breath. This person, whoever they were, meant a lot to me. Reading their messages was the first time something felt right after waking up. I didn't want to lose them. Sure, I didn't know Chai, but somehow, the possibility of ending this relationship made my stomach twist in discomfort.

It took a few minutes—which felt like eons—before I got a response.

Chai03: I nearly choked on my relief! You're back? And responding? You're an asshole for going dark, but I love you, so I forgive you.

My heart pounded at the phrase 'I love you.' I'm sure it held little weight to Chai. After all, they were messaging a user named MidQuest—who was only me by a technicality. They probably did love me, whoever I'd been. I wasn't him—that person—anymore. Those words weren't for me. Still,

I felt sadder about that than when I couldn't remember what house I'd grown up in.

Chai03: Don't you dare think this means you're off the hook!

I smiled at the angry GIF they sent. Chai quickly remedied it with a sweet, heart beating one to make sure I didn't take her anger too seriously. This exchange felt familiar. It felt good. I would do whatever it took to hold on to it.

Chapter Three

Naomi

I smelled like someone threw up on me because...well, they had. In a secondhand sort of way. Celeste frowned when I explained how someone could throw up on a person secondhand. As I spoke, I wrung out my uniform shirt over an industrial sink. We'd found a quiet janitor's closet on the hockey arena's storage floor so I could wash up and recount my horrible night to her in obsessive detail.

"You need to quit." Celeste hugged a bag of fresh clothes for me to her chest. She sat on a lopsided metal chair, trying to balance her weight so it wouldn't topple over. "This place is toxic."

"It's a seasonal gig," I reminded her, and myself, for the millionth time. "One more week and the wonderful paychecks stop rolling in."

My current bank balance was laughable. Even the bank thought so because they'd charged me for not having enough. So hilarious.

"This will be the third time this week something's gone wrong," she noted.

I looked up from my washing in time to catch the worry on her perfectly plucked brow. As per usual, she'd come in her armor: a face full of makeup. She'd braided her kinky hair into a crown, with no wayward strands in sight.

"Sorry for bothering you this time." Guilt washed over me as I remembered her anxiety in public spaces. "I can usually thug it out, but the smell was getting to me, and there were only old scrunchies in the lost and found. My boobs are small, but not that small."

"No, it's fine. I don't mind helping. I needed to get out of the house."

Celeste would gladly stay locked in her room until the sun burned out. I often fantasized about being right next to her. I wanted our heaven to be her cozy room packed with every gaming console known to man.

"Check my phone real quick?" I used a baby wipe to clean my arms for the fourth time.

"Waiting for a message from MidQuest again?" Celeste gave me a disapproving look, but still retrieved my phone from my bag.

I shrugged, watching her through the mirror. "Not particularly...I just have a stream tonight and want to know which mods are showing up."

Lies. I only wanted to know about one mod.

"Sure, sure." Celeste chewed on her lip to hide a smile as she typed in my password. I wanted so much to throw a look in her direction, but couldn't hold back my smile, either.

"So?" I asked when the anticipation got too overwhelming.

Celeste cleared her throat before reading in a voice deeper than her own. "I fixed your panels. Look when you get a chance. Also, don't rush too much tonight. Everyone will understand if you're running a little late. You need to prioritize yourself."

I rolled my eyes and laughed. "He doesn't sound like that."

Celeste raised a brow. "And how would you know?"

My mouth twisted to the side as I tried to think of a comeback.

"How long has it been since he...you know?"

"Since he stood me up and ignored my messages for weeks?" I filled in. "You can say it. I won't curl up and cry."

Though, I had wanted to when it first happened.

Celeste held up her hands, pleading innocence. "Hey, I wasn't trying to make him sound like a complete douche, but if the shoe fits."

"It was five months ago. I've forgiven him," I informed her. "And he had a reasonable explanation."

There'd been an accident, and he'd been in the hospital. He didn't go into too much detail, but I trusted MidQuest, weirdly enough. We hadn't met face-to-face, hadn't spoken outside of my streams. He knew what I sounded like and vaguely what I looked like—I used an illustration instead of a camera for streams. But I had nothing more than his screen name. Despite that, I only needed his word, and I was satisfied.

"Over a year of knowing him and not meeting yet, you're still checking for this guy?" Celeste unzipped my bag and tossed a thin T-shirt in my direction.

"We're friends."

"No, *we're* friends." She gestured between herself and me. "He's an online acquaintance who's probably catfishing you."

I snorted. "Mid's not catfishing me."

"Excuse me if I find it hard to believe a guy on the Internet."

I laughed. Celeste had a point—she always did. I was usually more cautious when investing my time in people. I had little to waste. I was a broke, orphaned college student who'd still be living in her car if her best friend didn't catch her trying to use dry shampoo on a week-old twist-out.

"I agree with one sentiment this guy has," Celeste said. "You need to prioritize yourself. Stop taking shitty jobs like this one. You know my parents and I got you."

My smile came easily. The Able family had my back. Saved me from being homeless for the past year. Offered me more than food and shelter, but a safe place where I could explore hobbies like streaming. And earlier this week, offered to rent me a room in one of their houses near campus, so I could get a traditional college experience.

The T-shirt I pulled over my head ruined my baby hairs, so I pulled on the Einstein Arena cap to hide the chaos. "I know, Celeste. You guys have been the best, and I'm forever grateful."

"So, why are you pushing yourself so hard?"

I needed to learn to stand on my own. No handouts. No aids. If growing up with my mother taught me anything, it was that people who knew how to do shit on their own survived in this world. I wasn't always going to be lucky and find people like the Ables. People wouldn't keep saving me. I'd have to learn how to save myself.

I didn't tell Celeste this, of course. I gave her my trademark wide smile and said, "You know I love a challenge. Plus, this is a cool venue. I got to see *Disney on Ice* and some Olympic skaters for free."

"At what cost mentally?" Celeste nudged my puke-stained sneakers with her own bright white pair.

"I'm also building character and new skills." There was a bright side to my situation. I always found a bright side because I couldn't afford to do the opposite. I wouldn't have made it this far if I did the opposite.

"Come on." I finished buttoning up my uniform shirt. It was wet and wrinkly, but it'd have to do. "I'll get the girl working concession to sneak us some soft pretzels."

Celeste sighed but followed. "I can't turn down carbs. It's against my moral code."

"That's the spirit," I cheered, and grabbed my mop and bucket.

The hall to the storage room got little traffic in the middle of events. So, when I swung the door open, I didn't think there'd be someone on the other side. The crash and sound of someone cursing debunked my assumption in a blink of an eye.

I covered my mouth when I saw two guys standing on the other side of the door. One bent over, holding onto his nose. The other tried to keep a straight face as he asked his friend if he was okay.

"Oh, my God." I held out a hand but didn't touch the guy. Even bent over, I could tell he was as tall as me. The hard muscle of his arms contrasted with the softness of his core. His brown curls reached past his ears, covering his face as he tried to recover from my unintentional attack. I caught sight of the bright red on his hand when he finally stood upright and tilted his head back.

"You good, man?" the friend asked. He was slimmer but as long-limbed as his companion. His skin was russet-brown, and his black hair cut close to his scalp.

"I'm fine," the bleeding guy said in a clipped tone, waving off his friend.

"I am so sorry." I scrambled, trying to find something to help clean his bleeding nose. "People aren't usually down here."

"So you go around throwing open doors?" Bleeding Guy asked, eyeing me with a deep-set frown.

I nervously smiled back, trying to lighten the mood. "Sometimes it's fun to pretend I have Herculean strength."

He didn't look amused, but his friend chuckled and said, "Doesn't look like you need to pretend. I think you do."

Celeste offered me my bag without making eye contact with the guys. Instinctively, I stepped in front of her. My mistake shouldn't force her to interact with them.

I pulled out a baby wipe and handed it to him. "Here."

The guy glanced at it before he turned his gaze to me. I stood my ground, trying my best not to be intimidated by his dark eyes. There was scarring on one side of his face. The skin had long ago healed, leaving soft, pink lines stretching across the pale skin. His jaw did that clenching thing guys do when they're holding back or trying to hide something. My stomach flipped at the sight.

He was hot in an 'I'm not sure why this look works for you, but damn it does' way. I didn't usually go for guys who don't smile at least once in the first few minutes of interacting. So, it came as a surprise to me when the scowl he wore made him more appealing.

"Thanks." Bleeding Guy's friend was the one who took the wipe. "Sorry about my buddy. He's not used to getting whacked by non-athletes. A bruise to the ego he'll have to endure."

Bleeding Guy snatched the wipe from his friend. "Shut up."

"We should go," Celeste whispered in my ear. Her voice was shaky. I grabbed her hand and squeezed it.

"Again, my sincerest apologies, kind sir," I spoke quickly and tugged Celeste forward. The guys blocking our path moved when I bulldozed through.

"Kind sir?" Bleeding Guy sounded confused. And maybe even offended? Huh. I suppose I'd get aggravated too if someone called me something I wasn't.

"There's a first aid kit at the end of this hall." I pointed over his shoulder. "And if you want compensation for your injuries, please...take it up with management. Or, come by the concession stand after hours. I got a hookup."

"I don't need a hookup," he said, voice matching his dark expression.

"Well..." My eyebrows raised at how his deep voice sent a wave of warmth through my body. He didn't need a hookup, but my body was telling me *I* did. "I suppose we're done here."

"We are." He sounded so dismissive. As if he were a boss and I, his employee. Despite being surprised—and annoyed—I flashed another smile in his direction and waved. "Enjoy the rest of your night."

"Unlikely," he replied, gaze still cold and still locked on me. Seemed like the sweetness I put in my voice gave him a worse headache than the door.

His friend laughed and tried to smooth things over with, "We will. Thank you..."

The lull happened because he wanted a name. And not just mine. His gaze strayed to the still anxious and still avoiding eye contact, Celeste.

"You're welcome," I said, instead of giving him what he wanted.

I tugged Celeste after me, and we hurried down the hall.

"The big one was rude," she mumbled once they were out of earshot.

"I'll say," I agreed with a shake of my head. "Those looks are wasted on that personality. Crying shame."

Chapter Four

Finn

The pain in my spine dulled when I heard Chai's cheery 'hello.' Her stream's chat had already come to life with messages from her usual group of viewers. A handful of newbies was in the mix, so I welcomed them and highlighted the chat rules.

It was inconvenient to moderate the stream on my phone, but I'd do my best to make it work. The guys and I were supposed to spend the last week before school at Sam's family cabin. A tradition, according to the three of them. I pretended to remember as they packed my van earlier. Unfortunately, my brain still failed to reboot memories labeled 'tradition.' I didn't tell them that. The last time I confessed to not remembering something important, I received teary looks from my sisters.

No part of me was a people pleaser. At least, I didn't feel like one post-accident. Still, I wanted to minimize those looks as much as possible. The easiest way to do that was to pretend like I remembered. Pretend like the amnesia resulting from the fight wasn't as big as it actually was.

We were currently waiting in Henrik's driveway—our last stop before we headed up the mountain—while he figured out which textbooks to bring for the trip. He wanted to get ahead for the semester and only I looked confused over his declaration.

Was he always like this? I wanted to ask Sam or Lincoln. But Sam was too busy making out with a beautiful blonde outside, at the back of the van, for me to question. And Lincoln was too busy rambling about my 'stiff personality.' I needed to escape them as soon as possible.

"We need to get you back out there," Lincoln said as he adjusted the passenger's seat to recline. "I can't have my main wingman scaring women away."

My forehead wrinkled. "Main wingman?"

"Sam outshines me, and Henrik likes to discuss intellectual shit." He studied me. "And people seemed to like our quiet guy, loud guy dynamic."

I huffed, disbelieving, which didn't count for much.

"How would you feel about a sub-a-thon, Mid?" Chai's voice sounded through my earbuds. "Next month, maybe? Feel free to say 'no.' I've heard they're brutal, but they always seem fun."

I typed into the stream chat, **If that's what you want, that's exactly what we'll do.**

She squealed with excitement, and my shoulders relaxed at the sound. For the past couple months, my life had been about recovery. I reacquainted myself with the life I once had and my friendship with a girl I've never met face-to-face.

Resuming conversations with Chai was the easiest thing I've done since getting out of the hospital. My body's response to her laughter felt like sinking onto a couch after being on my feet all day. Nothing else gave me that feeling. And for all I knew, nothing ever had.

"We'll get you back out there, bud," Lincoln continued like I gave a damn. "At least you learned your first lesson: when a beautiful girl accidentally wrecks your nose, you at least ask for her number."

I sighed and touched the band-aid on the bridge of my bruised nose. Some girl from the arena knocked the hell out of me a few days ago. Lincoln thought she was a riot. I thought she needed to slow down. She'd spoken so fast that I could barely keep up.

"Hey, do you have any—"

"No," I interrupted before he got the chance to make the mistake of asking.

Lincoln slouched. "Liar."

"You should charge him. Make a side hustle out of it." Sam appeared at my window and gave me a knowing smile. The girl he'd been rubbing up against was heading toward Henrik's house, needing a bathroom.

"He can't afford it," I said. They both laughed because, yeah, the comment was ridiculous. It didn't take me long to learn of the four of us, only I came from a family that didn't have money to spare.

"Name your price, Mid," Lincoln teased.

"Don't"—I took a breath so my tone wouldn't appear too clipped—"call me that."

"What's this about?" Sam looked intrigued. I couldn't catch a break.

Lincoln jerked his chin at my phone. "Some girl on the other end said that, and he scrambled to put his headphones in."

"Ah." Sam tried to look over my shoulder, but I pulled the phone to my chest.

"You ever mind your own business?" I asked.

They laughed like that was the most ridiculous thing they'd ever heard.

As far as I knew, my gamer tag and moderating for Chai were things I kept from my friends. I don't know why, but for now it felt nice to have something of my own. From how much the guys called me up to hang out, I understood we spent copious amounts of time together. We weren't just friends. From all the photos I had in my house of teen versions of us, we were more like brothers. How did you tell your brothers you barely remember their names and didn't trust them for shit?

"Fine, fine," Lincoln gave in. "I'll leave you alone…if you sell me two pills. I got a fifty."

"I'm not selling my drugs. I don't take them for recreation."

Sam's brow wrinkled, and he stood up straighter. "I thought you said you didn't take them at all. You didn't need them anymore."

"I need them." My mouth was a firm line. As if to prove my dependency, my lower back warmed with a familiar ache.

"I see." Sam's jaw clenched, concerned. "Are you in pain right now?"

"Yes." I turned my gaze back down to the phone, checking on Chai's chat to make sure everything was okay.

"Should we tell Coach before training starts?" Sam asked. Gone was his carefree attitude. I'd seen him flip like this often in the last few days. It was an impressive trick. "Are you able to be on the ice again?"

"There's no need to tell Coach," I said without hesitation. I only knew two things for certain: I wanted to hear Chai's voice and I needed to be on the ice. As soon as I put on skates, muscle memory kicked in and I wasn't pretending to be someone else.

"I'm fine. The doctor cleared me," I assured.

Sam didn't look convinced and stared at me for a beat before saying, "Alright. I'll take your word for it."

"Good. We'll leave it at that," I said, hoping my words would work as a manifestation of sorts. But from the look Sam exchanged with Lincoln, I knew any manifestation I tried wouldn't be strong enough.

Thankfully, Henrik exited his house before our conversation could continue. His amount of luggage stole the spotlight from me. I breathed a sigh.

"You're quiet today, Mid," Chai was saying. "The chat's going on a proper rant about our favorite squadmates in *Mass Effect* and you're not saying a thing. Are you okay? Can't have my mod slacking on his sworn duty."

She was teasing. A couple of others chimed in on the chat, repeating familiar jokes about my sudden disappearance months ago. I winced, feeling guilt at the reminder.

MidQuest: I'm here. Not going anywhere.

"Good. I missed you too much last time," she said. That sentence sounded effortless but left me with a bundle of nerves. Happy nerves. MidQuest was more real than Finn Howard at this point. And our relationship was more real than anything I tried to rebuild with people offline.

Chapter Five

Naomi

"**I** know this isn't exactly what you were expecting." Celeste placed her hand on my shoulder. "But it's going to be great, trust me."

My friend chewed on her lip as she watched me stare at the house in front of us. The blue paint peeled from years of neglect. The mailbox kissed the sidewalk and the window framing the front door looked cracked.

"Go on." I kept my encouraging smile intact. Even though this wasn't the house or the neighborhood where her parents originally said I'd be living, it was better than nothing.

"The Chester Street houses went up in popularity since last semester. The school's basketball and baseball teams like the row. My folks couldn't pass up the opportunity to jump on the hype and raise rent prices."

"Right, of course." I waved my hand. "Totally get it. Capitalism. Got to play the game or get left behind."

Celeste blew out a breath and pulled out the house keys. "I promise, it looks better inside."

I kept the pep in my step as we made our way up the walk. This house was about twenty minutes away from campus. Nothing like the five-minute walk Chester Street would've afforded me. But I had a car. It was a clunker, but it still worked...on the days it wanted to. When it didn't, I could easily take the bus. The commute to school would give me time to mess around on some games Celeste gave me for my Nintendo DS.

"Do you know where the closest bus stop is?" I asked as we tackled the stairs. They misaligned a few panels during construction, otherwise, the porch felt sturdy enough. Plus, it faced the west, which meant it'd have a great view of the sunset every evening. Perfect for lounging.

"Um...a few miles away." Celeste sounded apologetic.

I waved my hand. "That's fine. It's a Plan B sort of thing."

"Since your car's been giving you so much trouble, take mine for the semester." She unlocked the front door and let me walk in first. "You know I don't use it unless it's an emergency."

"Nah. It's good you have it in case you decide to be spontaneous." When we made eye contact, we laughed. Celeste being spontaneous? I'd sooner grow horns.

"Come on," she said once we recovered. "I'll give you the grand tour."

True to her word, the place didn't look too terrible on the inside. The Ables had freshly painted each room. The furniture was old but cute. They were going for a warm, earthy feel, using browns, greens, and blues to decorate the place.

Celeste pointed above. "The guys will be upstairs."

"Right." I eyed the ceiling warily as if they were already there. "The guys."

Celeste heard the apprehension in my tone. "You don't have to do this, you know? My folks are completely fine with you staying with us. Plus, you know I'd prefer it. You're the sister I'll never have. I enjoy ganging up on the boys."

"Thanks." I laughed, thinking about the times we won movie night arguments against her brothers. "But it's time for me to stand on my own. I need to keep my adulting skills fresh."

"I get it." Her shoulders sagged. "I don't like it, but I get it."

I gave her a side hug. "It'll be fun. An adventure. I've never lived with strangers before. Especially not guys."

"Dad said to call him immediately if they cause trouble." Celeste pointed her finger at me. "*Immediately.*"

"It's going to be fine. I know how to stand up for myself." I playfully shoved her hand away. "Speaking of keeping my skills fresh, where do you keep the cleaning supplies?"

A part of my deal living here was being the cleaner. Not a glamorous position, but I had experience from my gig at the arena. The Ables knew that and offered to split my rent in half if I cleaned up the place. I think the addition of a live-in maid added to the appeal of this house once they offered it to their renters. What college student didn't want someone around to pick up after them?

"There's some in the garage and the bathroom upstairs. Did I mention the bathrooms are only upstairs?"

My face must have fallen because Celeste chewed on her nail. Bathrooms upstairs only where four guys lived? Well, that was just great.

"It's fine." That'd become my motto as of late.

"Let me show you your room." She hurried through the kitchen and opened two glass doors. "It used to be a dining area, but my mom converted it into a bedroom. There are curtains for privacy. The door's a little flimsy, but I can get my dad to install a lock. For now, you could shove a box against it to keep it closed. Also, the heating doesn't really work in here during the winter, so it's going to get pretty cold...God, I'm sorry, Mimi."

I was in the middle of the room now. I spun around to take in the floral wallpaper, gorgeous bay windows that faced the backyard, and the adorable desk and bed set. It looked like a room in a 90s movie about a perfect girl who grew up in the suburbs and didn't know how lucky she was. This room was just like the ones I fantasized about when sleeping on a blow-up mattress in a studio apartment when I was younger.

"What are you apologizing for?" I still spun, marveling at how, for this semester, this was all mine. My chest warmed and my throat tightened.

"It's small and cold and the door doesn't even work," Celeste explained.

"It's perfect." I looked at her and she frowned, not understanding. I didn't blame her. She'd grown up in the same two-story house all her life. Her lights were never out, her fridge was never empty, and she always had the chance to go wherever she pleased. She had parents who cared about things like stability and consistency. Her mother didn't give her paychecks away, hoping to win it back tenfold in lotteries. Her father stuck around to make sure she was home at night.

"You sure?" my friend scanned the room, trying to see what I saw. "I should bring some of my things down. We'll fix it up."

"Celeste." I shook my head and pulled her in for a hug. She froze for a moment but eventually wrapped her arms around me in return. "This is more than I could ever ask for. Thank you."

She tightened her grip around me. "You can always ask for more. I'd give you the world if I could."

I laughed. "We're such saps."

"We are." She pulled away with a wide smile. "So, I promised my folks I'd do a quick walk around before the other renters show up. They're supposed to be here later tonight."

"Of course." I nodded. "Go ahead. Do what you need to do. I'll start bringing my stuff in."

"Once I'm done, I'll help, and then head out. Do you mind giving them the run-down I gave you?" She winced at having to ask the question.

"Consider it done." I squeezed her arm.

Her smile was back. "Thanks."

My phone buzzed as soon as Celeste left the room. I unlocked it to see a new message from MidQuest.

MidQuest: Sooo, how's the place?

I'd been so excited about moving that I talked to him about it in our private chats. He was as pumped as I was since he knew the story about me having to move in with Celeste's family. I leaned against my bedroom wall as I typed my response:

Chai03: Not what I expected, but better somehow. What about you? How's your new digs?

He was moving back to his school's campus, too. We'd spoken about it a few nights ago, and he admitted he was nervous. It was the first time he'd ever sounded afraid, and I stayed up all night trying to distract the anxiety away with memes.

MidQust: Digs? How old are you again?

I snorted. **Old enough.**

He sent a laughing emoji. I smiled widely, trying to imagine what his laughter sounded like. I couldn't imagine what he looked like going off of his name alone. Whenever I tried to think up an image, my mind painted a picture of a guy no taller than my six-foot frame. A little chubby around the middle because most avid gamers were. And he had a calming voice. Something deep. He probably held his stomach when he laughed, too. Like all cute guys did.

MidQuest: My place fell through. It's fine though. My friend found another spot not too far from the last.

So, he had people he could count on, too? Good.

Chai03: Yay! I'll probably be all moved in by tonight. You?

MidQuest: Same. Does this mean the stream's still on?

Chai03: It's a go. You'll be able to make it, right? I promise not to stay up too late. I know how much you like to channel your inner old man.

MidQuest: I'll be there. Promise.

I smiled at the response, pushing away the annoying voice warning me he could go MIA again and I shouldn't get too attached like before.

I slid down the wall, sending him a heart in response. Once he sent one back, I placed my phone against my chest and stared at the room.

Keep smiling through it all. No matter what happens, no one can take that away.

I nodded to myself, making a promise to not let the bad distract me. If I kept pushing, I could make sure things stayed good.

Chapter Six

Naomi

Earl.mai: Oh no! Someone sounds tired...

    ChaoticNeutralGood: @Chai03, you're making me sleepy, and I just woke up, LOL.

I laughed around what felt like my hundredth yawn of the night. "Sorry, guys. Today was moving day for me. I guess it tired me out more than I thought."

After Celeste left, I got to work cleaning my room from top to bottom. I only had two boxes of stuff, so getting my things in order didn't take long. After that, I tackled cleaning the rest of the first floor. The house smelled stale from being shut in and a layer of dust covered most surfaces. Before the stream started, I disinfected all the countertops and opened the windows to welcome the breeze.

MidQuest: Break for the night? You should get some rest.

"I think you're right, Mid." I sighed with a small laugh. "Even though I don't want to, I'm going to end a little early, guys."

There were a few teasing protests. I almost let them talk me into staying another half hour. But my eyes were too heavy to take in the screen for much longer. I promised to be back for an extra-long stream tomorrow. A weekend with no work at the arena meant I wouldn't have many other obligations.

My stomach grumbled when I turned off my laptop. Now that the distraction from gaming was gone, my body pleaded for attention. I'd only brought water and a few fruit cups to the house. I'd have to go grocery shopping as soon as the arena deposited my next check. Celeste told me her parents had stocked the pantry with ramen and canned peaches, the essential college student meal. I got out of my seat and pushed back the box I'd shoved against the door to keep it closed.

I paused, listening to the house before I stepped out of the room. The renters were supposed to be here a few hours ago, according to Celeste. But, so far, the house remained dark and quiet. If I hurried, I could make a bowl of ramen and use the restroom without a run-in. It felt too late in the night to be meeting my roommates. I didn't want to change out of my comfortable shorts and oversized tee to get presentable. They'd have to meet 'put together' Naomi tomorrow because tonight, I wanted to chill with my legs out.

When I flipped on the kitchen light, it flickered a few times before staying on. I found the ramen and put a pot of water on top of the oven's eye. Instead of waiting around, I used the restroom. Going up and down the stairs was probably going to become a nuisance—especially with four other people in the house. So, I needed to take advantage of any and every opportunity the house was empty. I didn't enjoy making small talk when I needed to relieve myself.

I hurried up the creaky staircase, skipping one step at a time. This second floor desperately needed cosmetic renovations. The hardwood floors looked scuffed when I turned on the hall light. And the bathroom door needed a good shoulder shove to close it all the way. Once inside, I noticed the strange choice of wallpaper: portraits of old, gray-haired men lined up on a pink backdrop. I eyed the designs as I washed my hands, getting freaked out by the weird shape of their eyes.

"What the hell?" I pulled out my phone and snapped a few photos to send to Celeste. I needed answers—and solutions—because I didn't think I could shower in here without feeling like I was being watched.

Once I sent my message, I tugged on the door. It didn't budge. I tried again, putting my back into it. Nothing.

The eyes of the portraits seemed a little more alive as I started to panic-yank at the knob. I couldn't be stuck in this cursed-looking bathroom.

I continued to tug and shake the handle, groaning when it didn't do its one and only job.

"Think, think." I knelt to investigate the crack of the door to see if there was something wrong with the lock. Maybe I'd turned it by accident? But no. I couldn't see anything hindering the door from opening.

My tugging soon turned to banging, as if my fist could do more work at loosening the jammed handle. Between bangs, I heard a voice. It was faint at first, so I pressed my ear against the wood to listen closer.

"Hey!" I called when I heard the voice again. "Come upstairs!"

It was the roommates. Had to be. Or random people who came to rob me. Either way, I didn't care. They could have the ramen and peaches if they got me away from these beady-eyed bastards who were staring like I didn't have any home training.

I continued to bang, forgetting I wasn't exactly presentable in my short shorts and headscarf. But hell, I needed out. The air in here was feeling hot and heavy.

"Hello?" a deep voice asked on the other side of the door.

"Here!" I called. "I'm stuck. The door won't open and I'm on the verge of a panic attack because the color pink makes me claustrophobic."

"Okay, calm down," he said. A shadow appeared at the bottom of the door and the knob wiggled on the other side. "Did you lock it on accident?"

"Oh, gee, I don't know. Let me have that be the last thing I check," I said, tone clipped.

"My bad." He stopped wiggling the lock.

"Sorry." I pressed my hand to my forehead. "Usually, I'm not this snappy. I'm tired and hungry and freaking out."

"It's fine." He was quiet for a moment, presumably thinking. "Stand back from the door."

I glanced behind me. "Standing back is like one foot away from the door's radius. It's not an enormous bathroom."

"Well, do your best and get ready for the door to swing open," he said.

"Okay, tell me when—" I didn't get to finish because the guy went barreling forward, forcing the door open with his momentum. I yelped as the wood almost hit me and I lost my balance, nearly falling on my ass. He reached for me before I toppled over, grabbing my wrist to pull me upright.

"Jesus!" I gasped and could hear my racing heart in my ears. "You could have given a girl a countdown or something. It's common courtesy, you know? Have you never saved someone trapped in a bathroom?"

My joke went over his head because he gave me a flat, "No."

As my fear of almost getting killed by a swinging door faded, I realized the guy standing before me looked familiar. That dark hair, those pink scars, and an annoyed glare...

"Holy shit," I breathed and laughed a little.

"You're the girl from the arena," he said, recognizing me, too.

"I guess karma's a bitch," I joked. When his forehead furrowed, I gestured to my nose. "You know... I almost ended you with a door and now you've done the same."

"Right." He didn't look amused. He looked pissed. "I told you to stand back."

I snorted. "Well, whatever. We're even, and apparently we're roommates."

"So, it seems."

"Aren't you the conversationalist? I'm going to have a hard time keeping up." I pressed my lips together to keep from laughing at his angry expression. Oh, boy. This was going to be a long semester if he couldn't get my sarcasm.

"I'm Naomi." I went to offer my hand for a shake but noticed he was still holding onto my wrist. His fingers were cold from the outside and hardened with callouses. I could tell he was holding back his strength. The guy held me like I was the handle of a teacup. When he realized what he was doing, he snatched his fingers away.

"Finn." He barely opened his mouth as he spoke.

"Nice to officially meet you. Once again, I'm sorry about the door thing." I winced a little. "Didn't mean to assault and flee. I was on the clock and my friend needed a soft pretzel stat so..."

"It's fine," he said, sounding like he wanted me to shut up.

"I cook a mean ramen," I offered. "Too late for an apology meal?"

"I don't need a meal."

"Oh, come on." I moved, squeezing past him to start to the stairs. For a moment, our bodies were mere centimeters apart. Finn smelled like what I dreamed the perfect man would. Like wood and spice and a burning flame. I bit my bottom lip to bring myself back to reality.

Focus.

Crushing on a moody roommate who probably already hated me wasn't productive. Besides, I had unfinished business with Mid. It'd feel weird liking someone else.

"Let me at least say thank you for saving me from dying in front of those creepy illustrations. I owe you my life." I beamed at him, hoping my smile wiped away any sign I'd nearly gone feral over his scent.

"That's dramatic," he noted, following me out of the bathroom.

I shrugged. "What's life without little theatrics here or there?"

"Simple."

"Boring," I corrected with a wink.

He frowned, pausing on the top stair while I continued down.

"All good?" I called to him over my shoulder.

His response was a grunt, and he resumed making his way down the stairs. I'd take it as his version of a 'yes.'

Chapter Seven

Finn

That voice. There's no way that's the same voice.

I tried to come up with some logic on why my new roommate wasn't the girl I've been anonymously messaging. As I panicked, she rambled on and on about a house tour.

It couldn't be her. No way in hell the girl standing in front of me was Chai. Her voice sounded similar, yes. But out of the billions of people on this planet, there was bound to be someone who sounded like her. Out of those billions, the probability of us renting the same house in the same college town was slim to none.

And yet...this is happening.

The guys were still outside, unloading their things from my van. So, I only had a few minutes to recover from realizing the girl before me drew out her vowels in a familiar singsong way.

She introduced herself as Naomi. I met her a week ago when she nearly knocked me to my knees. Naomi sent my head spinning so I couldn't concentrate on the obvious similarities between her tone and Chai's.

Like at the arena, the first thing I noticed was how tall she was. It was especially difficult to ignore her height now, because she wore a large tee that barely went past her ass. She moved like a graceful dancer as she walked around the kitchen, showing me where they kept the appliances. Naomi's smile lit up her brown eyes, and I felt a clench in my chest whenever she looked in my direction.

What the hell was wrong with me? I didn't get this way around people IRL. I didn't want to avoid eye contact and also be close enough to feel the heat of someone's body. My doctor said the medication I was taking could have side effects. Nervousness and heart palpitations were on the list. I'd have to discuss readjusting my dosage as soon as possible.

"Which flavor do you prefer?" She gestured to the pantry. Someone had filled the shelves with dozens of ramen packets.

I opened my mouth to answer but got distracted when she reached into a high cabinet. Her fist curled around the edge of her shirt, trying to make sure it remained in place. The fabric still edged up a little in the back and... fuck. Her ass looked incredible.

I went over to help get down the bowls. No matter what my body was feeling, my brain told me the sooner she stopped holding onto her shirt, the better. Especially since I could hear the guys at the front door.

"Thanks." She smiled when I handed her the bowls. Her fingers felt like a summer morning when they brushed against mine. I noticed how she maintained eye contact with me, not straying to my scars like most people did when I got this close to them.

"Well, well, who do we have here?" Henrik's voice made Naomi break eye contact. I should have been thankful for the interruption. Instead, my jaw clenched at Naomi's transfer of attention. I was going to have to share her. That shouldn't have annoyed me.

She gave Henrik the same smile she'd given me. "I'm Naomi. Roommate, live-in cleaner, and semi-functional human."

Henrik was a better man than me. His eyes didn't stray from her face once when she shook his hand. The same couldn't be said for Lincoln or Sam.

"Didn't realize this place came with art," Lincoln teased.

I scoffed at the line. Naomi didn't seem to mind, though. Her posture straightened ever so slightly when she laid eyes on Sam. In the past few months, I've spent time around him, I understood most women usually felt shy in his presence. Sure, Lincoln was the flirt, but Sam had something I couldn't quite understand. And that something worked wonders on women. Naomi was no exception.

She seemed his type, too. Sam liked women who shined. And right now, Naomi was the sun. She stood in the center of the room, trying to balance conversation with guys who unabashedly (and, in my case, awkwardly) wanted her attention.

"Warning, the bathroom upstairs is a death trap." Naomi pointed up. "Finn saved me from a night curled up in the fetal position."

"How heroic." Lincoln winked in my direction. "What's that? The second time this guy's been on the other end of your door. Must mean something."

Could he be more heavy-handed? I shot him a glare that I didn't wipe away quick enough. Naomi glanced at me and her smile wavered for a second. Damn, I think she took my response the wrong way. Her hand was back on her shirt, tugging at the hem as she stirred the boiling noodles. It didn't take her long to recover. Someone who wasn't paying attention wouldn't have noticed. But I was paying too much attention, trying to read through the lines of her smile.

"Do you all go to Mendell?" she asked.

"We do," Henrik confirmed. He was the only one who brought in something useful from the car, a box of kitchen utensils, and was currently unpacking as he spoke. "Third year for us."

"My second." She smiled, directing it only toward Henrik. "Well... it's my first on-campus. I feel more official now. I took classes online last year because I was working a lot."

"So that means you haven't experienced everything Mendell has to offer?" Lincoln sounded like he had a terrible plan. Naomi laughed, obviously not of the same opinion.

"I suppose not," she said as she started filling the bowls. I handed them to her, one by one. Our fingers didn't touch once. I couldn't tell if I was the one being more careful this time or if it was her.

"We're going to have to change that." Lincoln sat on the counter closest to her.

Naomi made a face that was supposed to look silly but damn if it didn't make her even sexier. "I'm not much of a party person if that's what you're getting at. I do like to watch people get drunk, though."

"There's way more to Mendell than just parties," Sam spoke up. He had his phone out, only half interested in the conversation.

"He's right. But, the parties are usually the highlight," Lincoln said. "We'll convince you to come to at least one. It's a college essential. Along with weird date nights, tail-gating, and random road trips."

Naomi's eyes shone with excitement. "Well, I am a sucker for a good road trip."

"Who isn't?" Henrik agreed.

"Finn?" Sam's voice tore my attention from the conversation. I hadn't realized how hard I'd been staring at Naomi until my gaze moved to him.

"Help me?" He gestured over his shoulder to the front door.

I cleared my throat and nodded. While I'd been watching Naomi, at some point, Sam stared at me. Since he knew more about me than I did of myself, it didn't bold well for my hopes of keeping life simple this semester.

He said nothing until we got to the back of the van. The lights from the house cast a warm glow onto the dark driveway. I pulled out a few suitcases. As soon as the last one hit the ground, Sam said,

"We haven't had time to talk one-on-one since you got out of the hospital." Instead of moving luggage, he took a seat in the open hood. I hesitated for a second as I tried to figure out how to maneuver out from this conversation.

I avoided one-on-ones with most people because it was harder to pretend to be Finn with one person. Figured that out weeks ago when I was stuck at home, recovering while surrounded by my family.

"Yeah, things have been busy." The comment felt safe enough.

Sam nodded. "I thought I'd check-in. You haven't been saying much lately."

"Do I usually?" The question slipped out because my curiosity got the best of me.

"You do. At least around us. Me." Sam shrugged like it was no big deal. I noticed how he poked his tongue against the inside of his cheek. He did that after the girl he'd brought to the cabin ordered a Lyft, ending the vacation early in a huff. They had a loud argument. He didn't talk about it with the rest of us, continuing as if it didn't happen.

"Been more tired than usual, you know?"

He nodded. "And in pain."

My shoulders relaxed. So, this was what he wanted to discuss. "It's being managed. Got a great doctor. Few physical therapists. All thanks to you, right? My dad said yours hooked us up."

I nudged his arm with my elbow on instinct. It felt like the right thing to do.

"Of course. Everyone wanted you to have the best." Sam crossed his arms over his chest and tilted his head up to the sky. It was cloudy tonight, so most of the stars remained unseen.

"I have the best," I agreed. "All the more reason for you not to worry. I'll be back on the ice and better than ever."

He turned his gaze to me. "You think I'm worried about the ice?"

I frowned. "Yeah...I mean...it's an important year for you. For most of the guys on the team, right?"

Sam tilted his head like I was speaking a different language. I replayed what I said but couldn't find the issue. God, picking apart things was exhausting.

"What?" I asked when the silence stretched.

"You remember what we talked about? At our last game against the Crows?"

My stomach twisted. "Vaguely."

"Why are you lying?"

I stuffed my hands into my pockets. "I...It's taken some time to get everything back. I'm still working toward full capacity."

His brow wrinkled. "What percentage are you at now?"

"At least eighty." More like ten on a good day.

"*Really?*"

I glanced back at the house to make sure no one else joined us. "Keep this between us, alright? I can't have the guys slipping up and saying something when I'm on the phone with my folks. Or around Coach."

Sam looked unsure. "Why are you keeping it a secret?"

"I don't like the poking and prodding," I said, letting some of my truth slip through my façade. "My dad started taking me to psychics. He believes almost anything people tell him."

He chuckled. "Tell me about it. He used to go on and on about mysticism—something I'm guessin' you also don't remember. It's the reason he's not welcome to dinner at my place. My mom hates that kind of talk."

"Well, you should know I had a bad reading and it left him thinking I might be possessed."

Sam's smile fell. "What the hell?"

"Some lady said I was... What was it?" I massaged my temple, trying to remember. "A shell? Someone new. Freaked him the fuck out for a few days. Understandably, but still, I didn't like the reaction. I don't want to make people feel weird around me."

He hummed. "That's different. The Finn I knew doesn't care how people feel around him."

I let out a breath, building up the courage to say what I wanted to next. "Until I remember everything, I want to be someone new."

"You sure? Struggling with your memories seems like a big thing to hide. Especially from doctors. What if something abnormal is going on, and they can fix it?"

I shook my head, determined to get him on my side. "There's nothing to fix. My scans are fine. It'll come back. Tons of stuff already has. For now, I want to be someone new. Different. Possibly better."

What I wanted was to bury old Finn in that parking lot. He already felt like a ghost. It freaked me out to think maybe I took his body. I kept that fear to myself.

"I could try to jog your memory," Sam suggested. "We could go on a victory tour of sorts. I—"

"No," I cut in. "I don't want that. I want this to stay between us."

Sam sighed. "That's the thing. The stuff that used to be just between us is now something only I remember."

My brow furrowed. "What do you mean?"

He paused for a second to think. "You know, they say ignorance is bliss. Maybe the memory relapse isn't so bad. You deserve a break from the stress."

A part of me wanted to hear more, but before I could ask, Sam clapped my shoulder. He looked ready for the conversation to be over. I knew that feeling well.

"Look, don't worry about it. Forget I said anything. Focus on your recovery. Until then, I look forward to getting the old Finn back."

I nodded, feeling guilty when I thought, *don't hold your breath.*

"Let's get this stuff in. It's getting cold." I nudged my chin to the luggage.

Sam smiled. "Couldn't agree more."

Chapter Eight

Naomi

After meeting my roommates, I decided living with four guys wouldn't be as awkward as I originally thought. They seemed fine and even friendly. Mostly.

Finn didn't like me, plain and simple. I've gotten used to people not taking to me on principle alone. Streaming for a year opened me up to criticism. After being hate-raided many times, I'd grown what I'd consider a thick skin and 'fuck 'em' attitude. I knew how to keep a smile on my face while interacting with trolls. Doing it in real life would be harder.

"There's a perfectly good deck out back. We should have the newbie welcome party here," Lincoln suggested.

Once I'd dished up our food and the guys put their luggage in their rooms, we'd gathered in the living area. The guys wanted to plan a get-together for their team. All four of them played hockey for the school. I knew absolutely nothing about the sport—something that appalled them. Despite being a janitor at the arena, I never took much interest the games. I preferred the ice shows. Hockey rules went over my head the first time I tried to watch.

"We'll make you an expert by the end of the semester," Lincoln promised. He was by far the most energetic of the group. The guy couldn't sit still, he even stood when he ate.

"It's not as difficult to understand as it might seem," Henrik had chimed in. "I couldn't remember all the rules at first, too. It gets easier after you've seen a couple of games. Even easier when you play."

Henrik spoke in a calm voice. Unlike the rest of the guys, he wasn't a large presence. Not in stature or in personality. He was always the first person to say, 'thank you' or 'excuse me.' He was polite in how he spoke and how he maintained his appearance. He slicked his brown hair out of his face. His neatly pressed black dress shirt was tucked into a pair of gray slacks. He looked like he belonged in a boardroom, not on a college campus. His skin was even paler than Finn's and his eyes darker.

Sam smiled at me. "We should get you on the ice, Naomi. Who knows, maybe you'll show up some rookies on the team. Heaven knows we're going to need the help this year."

Unlike his friends, Sam didn't mind talking over people. It was safe to say the others looked up to him, glancing his way for the final say when everyone threw their opinions around. His clear, dark skin and perfect smile gave me pause upon first meeting him. Sam reminded me of a dashing hero in an otome game. I didn't think people like him existed outside of a computer screen.

"Fat chance." I laughed at the suggestion. Me better than athletes on the ice? "I can barely stand up on skates."

"Something we should remedy immediately." Sam gave me a charming smile. I returned it.

At that moment, my gaze strayed in Finn's direction. He hadn't said a word since we sat down. The guys tried to include him in the conversation many times, but he brushed them off.

He was staring down at his phone. It didn't take long for him to sense me looking at him. When we made eye contact, my cheeks burned. Despite the feeling, I didn't turn away. He raised a brow, silently asking if I wanted to say something. I didn't. Or maybe I couldn't because my tongue felt heavy under his gaze.

The guys' conversation faded into the background as Finn and I continued to stare at one another. I couldn't figure out what we were doing. He leaned back in his seat, pressing buttons on his phone's screen before placing it face down on his knee. My phone buzzed in my back pocket, but I didn't reach for it.

Finn rested his chin in his hand, studying me. It surprised me I didn't feel self-conscious under his gaze. Something about how Finn looked at me said he wasn't judging. He was taking me in and trying to figure out the same thing I was: why was I interested in him? Out of the four of them, he was the most standoffish and intimidating.

Another vibration in my pocket made me forfeit our staring match. I dug my phone out to read the screen.

MidQuest: I was thinking about you. How's your night going?

My heart hammered. *This* was the type of guy I should focus on. Someone who didn't mind checking in. Though I just met Finn, I could tell he wasn't the 'texts you randomly because he was thinking about you' kind of guy.

Chai03: I'm good, thanks! Getting ready to turn in soon.

While I waited for him to text back, I looked at Finn. He was distracted by his phone again and stayed that way as I resumed staring.

MidQuest: Hope you get a good night's sleep. I'll talk to you in the morning.

I sent him a heart back and pushed off the couch, announcing to the guys it was well past my bedtime. Everyone except Finn protested. I argued with their pleas, reminding them they also had their first day of class tomorrow. Apparently, we were all unfortunate enough to have classes scheduled before ten AM on a Monday.

They decided to be responsible and turn in early at my suggestion. For one night only, according to Lincoln. We said our goodnights and headed to our rooms. I waved at them before closing my door. The box I used to hold it shut slid into place. I crawled into my bed and stared at the ceiling. My stomach buzzed with nerves of excitement for the semester ahead.

I woke with a crick in my neck. My mouth felt like cotton and my head pounded with a headache. As cute as my bed looked, the mattress felt like bricks. Anytime I rolled over, I woke up from the sheer discomfort.

As I reached over to turn off my alarm, I glimpsed the time. According to my screen, I'd pressed snooze five times this morning.

Shit, shit, shit.

My first class of the day was in forty minutes. I was supposed to be on campus a half hour ago to get a parking pass. Without the pass, I could kiss getting a decent space goodbye.

I regretted my refusal to buy an electric scooter as I tugged on a plain, gray, long sleeve shirt and jeans. I sprayed on a cheap body mist that reminded me of middle school.

Usually, I didn't wear make-up, but Celeste had taught me a ton in the last year. And it'd suck for all her work to go to waste. Plus, I heard the guys' voices already outside. I wanted to look at least somewhat presentable.

With a quick swipe of eyeliner, mascara, and some blush, I grabbed a jacket and rushed out the door. In my haste, I almost forgot to switch out my satin night headscarf for my daytime cotton one. It took me another few minutes to get the scarf to look the way I wanted. I tugged down a few curls to frame my face.

Relax, I urged myself as I closed my bedroom door.

Henrik and Lincoln were already in the driveway when I got outside.

"Good morning, sunshine," Lincoln said, looking all bright and awake.

I smiled and gestured at the yellow van he was leaning on. It looked like a taxicab with its decals peeled off and its brightness increased by one hundred percent. "Morning. If I'm sunshine, what the hell is that? I'm pretty sure satellites from space could pick that thing up."

Henrik laughed. "It is quite the sight, isn't it?"

He pushed off the van to meet me on the front walk. Both his hands were full of to-go mugs. One of which he offered to me. "I was hoping we'd see you this morning. You're not allergic to ginger, are you?"

My smile widened. "Not at all. This is for me?"

Henrik nodded, eyes twinkling at my excited response. "It is. Wait a few minutes before drinking. I've found the optimal time is seven and a half."

I raised a brow, amused, and impressed. "Is that so? Did you run trials or something?"

His cheeks turned red. "I did."

"Henrik extensively researches anything he does and says for the sake of effectiveness," Lincoln noted. "He even forages for the ginger himself. Under the cover of nightfall, because it's most optimal to harvest by moonlight."

Henrik shot him the most clean-cut glare I've ever seen. I didn't know 'shut-the-hell-up' could look so respectable.

"He's joking," Henrik turned back to me. "Partially, I mean. I run trials for fun. But I don't forage ginger by moonlight—that would be ridiculous. I've only foraged once in my life."

"Oh, only once?" I nodded and chewed on my lip so I wouldn't grin too wide at his shy look.

"So, I'm supposed to keep track of how many times you've gone foraging?" Lincoln teased.

"Yes, if you're going to go around making declarations, you should have your facts straight," Henrik said.

"Hey," a deep voice interrupted them. "Relax. It's too early for back and forth."

We all looked to Finn, who was currently struggling to get his key in the front door's lock. He grumbled something about the cracked windows as he wiggled the key. A duffel bag with two hockey sticks hanging out of it rested on his shoulder. I tried to focus my gaze on the equipment and not on how broad his shoulders looked underneath his sweatshirt.

"You good, boss?" Lincoln remained lounging on the hood of the van as we all watched Finn struggle.

"Fucking hell," Finn cursed under his breath and snatched his key out in defeat.

"Don't worry about it." Henrik waved his hand. "Sam can deal with it."

"He's still asleep?" Finn frowned and glanced at his watch. "Doesn't he have a morning class?"

"Yeah, but he'll bite your head off if you try to wake him. Best to leave sleeping giants lie, you know?" Lincoln asked.

Finn's expression clouded. It was an 'if you blink, you miss it' type of moment. I tilted my head, curious about its quick appearance. Finn started down the porch steps. He didn't once look in my direction, but from our strange exchange last night, I expected as much. Greetings didn't seem to fit his vibe.

"Hurry and get in." He gave Lincoln a pointed look. "We're running late."

"Need a ride, Naomi?" Henrik offered before joining his friends.

Finn's gaze finally turned in my direction. His jaw tightened at Henrik's words. Nothing subtle about that. Was it strange that I appreciated how much of an open book he was? I liked knowing what I saw was what I got with him.

"I'm good, thanks. That's my car over there." I pointed toward the edge of the street. My beat-up car earned me a low whistle from Lincoln.

"Glad you pointed that out," Lincoln said as he leaned against Finn's ride to stare at mine. "I was about to have it towed last night. Sam was complaining about it being an eyesore."

Henrik made a disapproving noise. "Lincoln."

"What?" Lincoln held up his hands. "I was."

"No worries." I shook my head because honestly, I would have thought the same thing, too. My ride was an eyesore, but it got me through hell and back. I'd slept in it after we lost our apartment when my mom was in the hospital. It was my home until the Ables took me in. I wouldn't give it up for anything, even if I had money to replace it. I felt like I owed the little hatchback so much.

Henrik continued to scold Lincoln in a low tone as I walked to my car. There was a trick to get the front door open. I had to twist the handle at a weird angle. When it clicked into place, the door opened with a noticeable squeak. I felt the guys watching but didn't look back. I knew their eyes would fill with pity or shock if they saw the inside. My leather seats looked like they were coughing up cotton, so I never offered people rides. The front windshield had a crack reminiscent of a frozen lake melting.

I placed my key in the ignition, and the engine sputtered. This was to be expected. Three more turns—four tops—and it'd come to life. Or, at least, that's what usually happened.

On my sixth attempt to start the engine, there was a knock on my window. The glass shook underneath the hand. My automatic window system broke a long time ago, so I had to open the door to answer.

Seeing Finn standing in front of me came as a shock. I raised a brow, and he peered down at me with an unreadable expression. His hand folded over the top of the door, opening it wider. A gust of wind left his hair in slight disarray and blew some of his spicy scent in my direction. My body buzzed, much to my dismay.

"You need a ride." It didn't come out as a question, but as a statement. Like he wouldn't even entertain the word 'no.'

"It's just my battery. I have an EverStart jump starter that works like a charm."

Finn shook his head. "This car looks like a death trap. The battery's the least of your worries."

I blinked. "Sure, it's a little rough around the edges—"

"Hurry and grab your things. You'll ride with us," he said, simply. "Be prepared to show up late because I still need to stop for gas on the way."

"I..."

He started back to his van before I could voice another protest. I sighed and grabbed my bag. There was no point in arguing. Not when it'd take me a good twenty minutes to jump my car, and that was if I could get my hood to pop and stay up during the process.

"Welcome aboard." Henrik opened the passenger's door for me. I smiled and whispered a 'thanks' as I slipped into the seat. As soon as the working heat of the car hit my face, my shoulders relaxed. It'd been so long since I sat in a car with a functioning seatbelt. It felt odd to click something around my waist.

Finn slipped into the driver's side and didn't even look my way when he asked, "Do you have a preference?"

He fiddled with the radio's volume. I blinked, confused. Henrik translated, "The music."

"You've never in the history of ever asked *us* if we wanted to listen to something other than your podcasts," Lincoln complained as he settled in the middle seat. I'm not sure why he sat in the middle since there were only two of them in the back. Henrik seemed equally perplexed. I watched him through the rearview as he frowned, but didn't tell Lincoln to move over.

"If that's true, it's probably cause your taste in music annoys me." Finn put the car in reverse. "Podcasts are neutral ground."

"Neutral ground my ass," Lincoln grumbled. Henrik offered him a pair of earbuds, which were begrudgingly accepted.

"I like podcasts. This one's a favorite," I said in a soft voice.

Finn kept his eyes on the road. For a second, I didn't think he heard me. Eventually he offered me a curt nod. I smiled because it seemed approving.

Chapter Nine

Naomi

We stopped at NicMart, a gas station right outside of campus. Lincoln and Henrik hopped out of the car to grab a few snacks while Finn pumped the gas. I tried not to watch him through the side mirror, but my gaze kept straying his way. He hadn't said a word on the ride as Lincoln and Henrik grilled me with questions.

Finn's brand of quiet left me wanting more. I used to sit next to the quiet kids in school—it's how Celeste and I became friends. In class, I was a motor mouth. My teachers had the same feedback during parent-teacher conferences: talks a lot, huge distraction.

Celeste was the first person who didn't complain. She was a good listener. I enjoyed making her smile. I was the person she was most comfortable with, and it felt like an honor.

On the one occasion I got insecure about talking her ear off, she assured me she enjoyed hearing my voice.

"I like when you talk because you never force me to," she'd said.

When Finn reentered the car, I decided I'd take this approach with him. I'd simply talk and maybe he'd appreciate it. Maybe I could crack through the stone wall he had up. It might take some time, but I had a bit of hope he'd open up to me. Maybe I'd learn to interpret each of his looks. Not for romantic reasons, of course. I wanted to be close with all the guys. Each one of them was worth getting to know.

"Hey," I said when he slipped back into the driver's seat. The air smelt of gasoline and his cologne.

Finn didn't respond. He reached for a travel-size bottle of disinfectant and rubbed the gel across his palms.

"I'm curious about how long you've been playing hockey?" I asked, doing my best to tone down the cheer in my voice. 'Happy' scared people sometimes. Celeste warned me my energy could be a lot for people who just met me.

He looked at me, expression blank. I waited, chewing on my lip, trying my best to remain patient.

"Since I was a kid," he said and then pulled out a chunky brown knit beanie. It mashed his thick hair down as he tugged it on. The fabric looked so fuzzy and cute. I wondered if a girlfriend gifted it to him. It seemed like something a partner would want a guy like him to wear. God, how did someone pull off adorable and sexy all in one go? And why was I taken aback by it?

It's a damn beanie, girl. Pull yourself together.

I cleared my throat when he started drinking from his water bottle. The bob of his Adam's apple made my skin heat. I turned my gaze to the outside world. Enough swooning over Finn Howard doing mundane things for now.

The gas station looked packed. I could see Lincoln already in line with arms full of junk food. Mountains framed the view behind the station. The thing I loved most about Mendell's campus was how they built it in a valley between the mountains. Coming out of class felt like stepping into the pages of a Tolkien novel. When I toured the school with my high school class, I imagined campus in the winter. The snow-capped mountains never disappointed me. Even without the snow, the changing colors of the fall leaves made the place look like a Bob Ross painting. When my life felt like it'd gone to shit, I always felt better looking up at those mountains and remembering I lived here.

"Must be fun to play hockey in a place like this. Especially when the lakes freeze over. Bet there are tons of places to practice," I noted.

"I suppose."

"You all must practice a lot," I tried. "I heard our team's good. One of the best in the league."

"We're alright." His comment sounded flat, the definition of disinterested.

"Alright? Lincoln was bragging about you guys qualifying for championship games. What's 'good' to you?" I teased.

"Being undefeated."

I stuck out my bottom lip, considering his words. "You must be the tough one to please on the team. It's always nice to have an unsatisfied teammate. I used to play soccer in middle school and our captain was a stickler. Total badass who led us to victory. I had the biggest crush on her. Serious people do that to me...not that your seriousness is...um, what I'm trying to say is it's admirable that you're not easily satisfied."

God, I was rambling my ass off. How did I start talking about what made me attracted to someone? And why did I draw a line from *him* to that attraction?

Throughout my word vomit episode, Finn remained silent. I dared to look at him again. He was fiddling with his phone. Maybe he hadn't been listening too closely? I could still salvage this conversation. I needed to pause for a minute and come up with the perfect segue. Something not hinting at what kind of person I liked to date or that he might be that person.

I pulled on the edge of my headscarf, trying to find another topic which could entice him into responding. As I opened my mouth to probe him on his interesting choice of vehicle—who in the world wanted to drive an out-of-commission taxi van—Finn opened his door and stepped outside. He closed the door behind him without saying a word.

My mouth remained open for a second longer. I leaned back in my seat and let out a confused huff. Finn didn't move toward the store like I expected. Instead, he went to stand at the back of the car. He'd rather stand outside in the wind than sit inside with me? Well, hell.

I felt a twinge in my belly. Sure, I could respect his preference to endure the elements, but was I so unbearable by comparison?

Instead of inwardly worrying about my potential faux pas, I decided to get a second opinion on the matter. MidQuest was my only other friend who had his shit together.

Chai03: Morning! Quick question: Have you ever had someone hate you on sight IRL?

MidQuest: Good morning...and, yeah, probably. I don't pay attention unless it's certain people. Why? What's up?

I chewed on my bottom lip and peeked in the side mirror to make sure Finn was still there. He leaned against the van now, with his back to me and shoulders hunched.

Chai03: My roommate hates my guts. Could be the fact I nearly broke his nose with a door...but it looked like it was healing up fine, so I don't think it's that.

MidQuest: ...

Chai03: It was an accident, BTW. I wouldn't purposely draw blood unless threatened. You know that.

MidQuest: Do I?

Chai03: Haha, hilarious. I'm being serious right now. I need your advice.

MidQuest: Fine. But I don't think your roommate hates you.

Chai03: You don't see how he looks at me.

MidQuest: No, but you're a very hard person to hate.

Chai03: You're sweet. You're biased, but I'll take what I can get at this point.

MidQuest: Don't jump to conclusions. Whoever this asshole is, he's probably nervous or shy or dense. Maybe all three. Whatever it is... It's. Not. You.

Chai03: It. Probably. Is.

I smiled at his eye roll emoji. Despite my insistence, Mid was making sense. There could be a long list of reasons Finn gave me the cold shoulder.

MidQuest: Repeat after me: *I don't care what this guy thinks. It doesn't matter what he thinks. Because I'm incredible, and better than him. He'd be lucky to have me as a friend.*

Chai03: I don't care. I'm cool sometimes.

MidQuest: Eh, close enough.

Chai03: LOL, it was too much to type. Sorry.

I heard Henrik and Lincoln's voices nearing. Finn moved closer, too.

Chai03: I have to go. Talk to you tonight, right? Community Minecraft? I'm excited about finishing our house.

MidQuest: Wouldn't miss it. Enjoy your day. And message me if you feel nervous about your likability again. I'll pull you back over the edge.

Chai03: Thanks. I can always count on you.

Chai03: You know you can do the same? Message me if you're on the edge. Anytime. Day or night. Rain or shine. Maybe we could even try voice chatting sometime? If you're comfortable, of course. I just think it'd be easier to talk.

I felt a little lightheaded as I anticipated his response to my invitation. The guys all got into the car and Mid still said nothing. I clicked on my seatbelt as Finn turned on the engine. Instead of trying to jump back into conversation with him, I turned to look outside. I'd give talking a break for now. Mainly because I was now anxious about my message.

Mid and I never discussed meeting up after he went dark. Mostly because our first failed attempt embarrassed both of us. He felt awful for standing me up and I felt awful I waited for him until the sun came up. We didn't bring up IRL things. Even voice chatting was off the table for him. Before the failed meet-up, he was open to the idea. But afterward, something changed. He wouldn't say, and I never pushed. Now, my last message felt a little pushy.

The vibration of my phone in my lap made me jump. My stomach twisted as I unlocked the screen.

MidQuest: Sure, I'll think about it.

Chapter Ten

Finn

There was no question about it. Naomi was Chai, and I was already fucking this up. I needed to get better at this talking thing and fast.

After my accident, I had to start over in more ways than one. Each day felt like I was re-learning something that came naturally to most people.

In the beginning, I tried to watch those around me and imitate how people interacted. I couldn't read them well, though. The things I heard weren't the things they meant. And what I saw was rarely how people felt.

I needed to push myself harder because I needed to be honest with Naomi. Sooner rather than later. She deserved more. She deserved a friend who could tell her she was great to her face.

First, I wanted to feel stable, so I could explain why I'm not the person she befriended online.

My appointment with the team's physical therapist seemed like a decent place to test the waters of honesty. Aden Martin was an ex-NHL player who had to end his career early because of a bike accident. He'd suffered a brain injury that left his doctors convinced he'd never walk again. Not only did he make a full recovery, but he went back to school to get his Master's. And from what I gathered from his desk lined with family photos, he moved on to live the life he wanted. I still felt like mine was on pause. He was the perfect person who could tell me how to press play.

"How's the back pain today, kid? One through ten," Aden asked as he sat in front of me.

We went through our usual routine. Small exercises. Stretches. And now, questionnaire time. I've seen five physical therapists since my accident. None of them experienced brain injuries themselves. And none of them checked in like Aden did. He never pushed me to give him more than I wanted. I enjoyed not feeling pressured.

I settled onto the leather couch across from him. "Six."

He nodded and made a note in his folder. "You good with that, or are we looking to up your dosage?"

"Maybe a bit." I accepted, long ago, that a completely pain-free life would not be in my cards. Numbing it was the best we could do.

He smiled at me. "Sounds like a plan."

We watched one another for a moment. He tapped his pen against his mouth. It took me a few sessions to understand his silence was purposeful, giving me the opportunity to elaborate. Today would be the first day I took him up on the offer.

"Can I ask you about your injury and recovery?"

He didn't miss a beat. Aden leaned back in his chair, crossing his ankle over his leg like he had all the time in the world. Like I was his only patient.

"I'm an open book. What do you want to know?"

I rested my elbows on my knees, leaning closer because a few of the guys from the team were walking past in the hallways. Aden's door was only partially closed.

"You said you had memory loss, right?"

He nodded. "Yup. Strangest thing I've ever gone through. Like reaching for a cup that isn't there. Someone told you it exists, but you can't remember setting anything down."

I sighed, shoulders relaxing because he got it.

"You still struggling to regain some of your lost time?" Aden raised a brow when I nodded. "How much?"

I cleared my throat. "Just...some personality stuff. For example, Lincoln asked me what flavor ice cream I wanted the other day. I said, strawberry. According to him, I hated strawberries. Small thing but it got me wondering, how much of me is..."

"Lost somewhere?" he filled in.

"Yeah." I chewed on my inner cheek. The more words spilled out, the more I realized how scary this felt. "We're our memories, right? And because I don't know what I lost, I don't think I'm the same person. If I'm not the same person... What should I do? Try to get him back? Become him?"

Aden pressed his lips together, considering. "Humans are in a constant state of evolution. Most of us don't remember who we were when we were three years old. People past seventy probably don't recognize their twenty-year-old selves."

I rubbed my temple. "No, of course, I get that, but..."

"You've lost your building blocks." Aden nodded. "I understand."

"I don't know the guy I see in the mirror," I said. "Literally couldn't tell anyone what I looked like."

"It's up to you to figure out who he is today. You don't have to figure out who you were. You can build him. Who do you want to be, Finn?"

I shook my head. "Sometimes, I want to be who I was because people liked him. But I can't help thinking maybe I should start over. New town, new friends, new everything. It'd be easier. Simple."

"If that's really how you feel, you should. Except, from the way you sound, I don't think you want to lose the people you have."

My jaw tightened. Aden sensed my frustration.

"You don't have to figure everything out in one day. It takes a lifetime to become who you're meant to be. And even that's not long enough."

I unclasped and re-clasped my fingers, considering his words. He waited patiently as I tried to build my courage and confess one more thing.

"A part of me is afraid of becoming anything again. I don't know if this makes any sense," I cut myself short, getting insecure about voicing the fear that'd burrowed itself deep inside me.

"Doesn't have to make sense," Aden insisted. "It's okay to ramble."

I almost smiled. That sounded like something Naomi would say. It was definitely something she did on a daily basis. One of my favorite things about her. She was good at it. I was learning it wasn't as easy as she made it look.

"I'm afraid of forgetting again." As I spoke, I watched the ground. "Forgetting someone important to me. I've already done it once."

"Why do you think you'll forget again?"

I shrugged. "It was so easy the first time. One wrong head bash and I became no one."

Aden gave me a warm smile. "You're not 'no one.' And I don't think it's productive to be afraid of something that is statistically unlikely to happen. We're working toward making you stronger. And you're doing your part to stay out of trouble...?"

I nodded.

"Great, then I don't see you having another brain injury soon. If you do—by some odd, cosmic happening—forget again, you'll always have people to remind you," Aden said. "Like Lincoln, with the ice cream."

He chuckled, and I tried to smile. The expression felt strange though, so I gave up.

"You have a great group of friends," Aden continued. "They've supported you through this every step, right?"

"They have," I agreed, taking a deep breath. And here I was, being so goddamn ungrateful.

"They'll do it again. And I'm sure whoever you're scared to forget will also support you."

I wanted to believe those words. Truly. But something about them didn't stick. If Naomi knew me, *this* me, would I really be enough?

"You're right, we are our memories. But I choose to believe we're something more. Some core part of us remains after we've experienced trauma. You might not recognize who you are, but the people who care about you do. They always will. Keep letting them remind you until you recognize yourself and who you want to be."

Chapter Eleven

Naomi

As I walked to my last class of the day, I was bombarded by students promoting their campus organizations. The first day back to school was prime time for welcome back totes and plastic-wrapped cookies from groups recruiting. It took a huge amount of willpower not to stop at every table to grab a pamphlet and chit-chat. Instead, I snapped photos and sent the interesting ones to Celeste. She was enrolled here too, but preferred the low-stakes environment of hybrid night classes.

Me: Wanna join something with me? We could rush! Or learn how to build train replicas!

I could picture the wrinkle of her nose when she responded.

Celeste: Do you really think we could keep up with rushes? And we're more of airplane model girls...IMO.

Me: You right, you right. Though you would be great in a sorority.

Celeste: I love you for making up and believing lies that make me sound cool. You're a real one.

I laughed and shoved my phone back into my pocket. My wide smile remained in place as I walked into my economics course. A professor I've only interacted with through a computer screen sat on the edge of her desk to welcome students. As soon as I introduced myself, her eyes lit up with recognition.

"Naomi Lewis?" Professor Blake's eyes brightened. "From my online course last semester?"

I beamed. "You remembered?"

"Of course. Your contributions to the discussions were some of the most engaging I've received. I don't get students like you very often. It was exciting coming to class knowing someone would have a question to ask."

Perfect. Exactly what I'd been going for. I was good at school but better at making teachers remember me. And if I wanted to get into an impressive graduate program, I needed to stand out.

"Plus, you were the only student who showed up during my office hours." She laughed, but the sag of her shoulders hinted at disappointment. "It's lovely to meet you in the flesh."

"Likewise. I'm excited to be on campus this year."

"Oh! Seeing you reminded me of a comment you made last semester." She turned to grab a flyer off her desk. "My fiancée runs the student lab in the library. They're looking for more peer tutors. There's an open position for someone who has experience with statistics. I remember you said something about teaching. This could be a great way to gain experience."

My eyes widened when I saw the hourly rate. They were offering almost double what the stadium paid me. Because the Ables sliced my rent in half, I planned to coast doing odd jobs this year. But with a tutoring gig, I could finally start stocking up on nice groceries. No more canned goods for each meal. Hell, I could splurge on takeout now and then!

"This is so perfect." I held the flyer to my chest. "Thank you for telling me. It means a lot."

She waved her hand like it was no big deal. Her expression was like Celeste's when she showed me my room. I know these were small things to people who were used to abundance, but it meant more than they could imagine to me.

"No worries. I'm just happy I can recommend a capable applicant," Professor Blake said.

I grinned and sat at an empty desk in the front. My leg bounced in anticipation of going to the student lab and filling out an application as soon as class was over. This year was in the running to be one of my best yet.

The student lab was on the first floor of the library, right next to the coffee shop. I tinkered with my essential oil necklace, trying to get a whiff of the lavender as I waited near the unmanned front desk.

A willowy guy with a nose ring and a thin brown cardigan finally rounded the corner just when I was ready to move behind the desk and peek my head in the back room.

"Yes?" the guy asked in a scratchy voice.

"Hi." I smiled widely, doing my best to rid of any lingering impatience in my expression. He stared back at me, eyes blank and mouth in a straight line.

"May I help you?" he spoke slowly, like he'd rather not offer at all.

"I was told there's a tutoring position open," I said while bouncing on the balls of my feet. "I'm interested in applying."

He still wore a blank expression. "A tutoring position?"

My excitement continued to fuel my tone. "Yes, Professor Blake told me one was available and there's a sign."

He raised a brow. "A sign?"

"Yeah...um, right in front of you." I pointed to the small, handwritten sign that read, *Needed: Student Tutor.*

The writing was bold, neat, and unmissable.

"Is it?" He didn't turn to look.

My smile wavered. "It is."

"Hm."

I blinked, confused. He stared back like I was the one with the problem. I tried on my smile again, but it felt a little tight.

"Michael." A curvy woman with short black curls and winged eyeliner appeared from the back room. Her arms were full of hard textbooks, which she deposited into the guy's arms without asking. "What did I say? You can't hold job positions like library loans for your little friends."

"He'll be here in two minutes," Michael promised. His demeanor flipped from off-putting to meek in a blink of an eye.

"You said that an hour ago. Being late for an interview is a red flag. Tell your buddy he missed his shot." She shooed him away. Michael groaned, disappearing into the back.

"Sorry about that," she said with a shake of her head. When she met my gaze, I marveled at the piercing blue of her eyes. She laughed, seeming to know exactly why my expression changed.

"They're only contacts. I'm a cosplayer and got excited when I got them today. Tried them on at lunch and didn't have time to take them out."

"Cosplayer, really?"

She shrugged. "Never too old. At least that's what my mother used to say when she dragged me around to *Star Trek* conventions."

"No, I didn't mean...I never met someone who cosplays in real life. Not anyone who admits to it anyway," I confessed. "I wanted to get into it but it's pretty intense." Money wise.

"Oh, totally," she agreed. "But it's worth it. Start with something small and super low pressure. I promise you won't regret it once you start. Fair warning, it's quite addicting."

"I bet."

"So, you're here for the tutoring position? You're the first person who's shown up for an interview, and I don't even have you on my schedule."

My shoulders relaxed because if I was the first person I'd be more likely to end up with the position. "Yeah. Professor Blake recommended I apply. I'm a second-year but I've taken stats classes since high school. I finished my first year here with a 4.0."

"Well, you sound more than qualified," she said. "But I still have to put you to the test."

I nodded, more than willing to jump through hoops if it meant getting a job on campus.

She moved to retrieve a thin workbook from under the table. "Do you have an hour or two for a test and then a shadowing session?"

"Definitely. I don't have any classes for the rest of the day so I'm completely free." I had wanted to catch the guys for a ride home, but the bus would have to do.

"Wonderful. Follow me." She beckoned me behind the counter. "What did you say your name was?"

"I'm Naomi. Naomi Lewis." I offered her my hand.

"It's nice to meet you, Naomi. I'm Lettie Majors."

She set me up at a desk across from a pensive-looking Michael. I gave him a friendly smile before settling into the cushioned desk chair. Lettie gave me a workbook with ten problems. It'd probably take me forty minutes to get through them. Lettie insisted I take my time. There was no rush and the average applicant usually got through the problems in an hour and a half.

As soon as she left me, I pulled out my pencil and got to work. It was quiet sans the occasional clearing of Michael's throat or turning of his book page. I could feel his eyes on me, but I remained focused on getting everything correct. I couldn't miss one, not if I wanted to make the impression I needed.

Thankfully, there weren't too many word problems to overwhelm me. My nerves didn't get the letters jumbled up in the way they usually did. In the end, it only took me thirty minutes to complete the test. I reread the problems and checked my work twice, just to be sure I wasn't missing anything. But I wasn't. It felt like a cakewalk.

Michael raised an eyebrow when he saw me stand. "Lettie wasn't just being nice. You *can* take your time."

"I know." I nodded and continued to where I heard Lettie's voice.

I waited while she helped a student schedule a session. When she turned to me, she said, "Oh, did you need extra scrap paper? There should be some near the filing cabinets."

"Nope, you gave me more than enough. I'm done."

"You're...done?" She looked like Michael had, and I silently wondered if maybe I should've feigned working on the problems a little longer. But she'd said there would be a shadowing part of the interview too and that'd take time. What was the point of pretending I had more work to do when I was done?

I handed her the workbook, and Lettie tried to fix her expression back to something neutral. She pulled out another book to check my work. Like me, she checked everything twice. She even got out her own pen and did a problem herself. Once she was done, the grin on her face made her blue contacts shine brighter.

"Well, Naomi, this looks perfect. And in record time, too. Very impressive."

I breathed a sigh of relief. The tension in my fingers dissipated. I could feel the air in my lungs once more. The problems were easy, and I knew

I got them right, but a little part of me thought maybe I was being too cocky.

"Now, we shadow. Well, I shadow, and you tutor." She scanned the large space. The sparsely placed tables were mostly empty because of how early it was in the semester. There were a few people here and there, curled over books and scribbling on paper.

"I have just the student." Lettie motioned for me to follow her. "He came in a few minutes ago. Riley, our other specialized math tutor, is scheduled to work later. So, I had asked him to wait. Now, he won't have to."

I'm not sure why I didn't recognize him before we weaved through the tables. It wasn't like Finn blended in. He did the exact opposite with his large frame and dark hair. When our eyes met, my heart sped up. His eyes were apprehensive, like he was praying we weren't coming in his direction. When Lettie stopped in front of him, I saw his lips part with a sigh. She smiled, probably thinking it was a sigh of relief. From what I knew of him, I'm sure relief was nowhere close to what he was feeling.

"Hello, Finn? Was it?" Lettie pulled out a chair for me.

"Yes," Finn said. Hey, at least, I wasn't the only one who received one-word replies from him. It was nice to know I wasn't special.

"This is Naomi." Lettie rested her hand on my shoulder. "She's interviewing for a position as a peer tutor today. If you're still in need of some help and are comfortable with me supervising, we can get to work."

When he didn't answer immediately, Lettie continued, "I can assure you, you're in skilled hands. Interview or not, I'm positive Naomi's going to be one of our best and brightest. She just knocked my socks off on her evaluation exam and I'm not easily impressed."

My cheeks warmed. I could barely meet Finn's gaze. He wasn't easy to impress, either. And probably still wouldn't be, even if I did a handstand and started reciting the Declaration of Independence backward.

"What do you say? That work for you?" Lettie asked, sounding a bit more hesitant than before. Finn was as still as a stone wall. A marbled column. An oak tree in the middle of the woods. Steady, solid, and silent.

He looked at me. I couldn't avoid eye contact without things getting more awkward. I stared back, and it was like we resumed the stare-off that began at home. As time stretched into something almost mind-numbing, he said, "Sure, that works."

Chapter Twelve

Naomi

Finn had a simple question about regression analysis. He explained his issue in a steady, low voice. I nodded as he spoke, thankful he took the time to explain the issue, so I didn't have to read it from the textbook myself.

Finn talked with his hands, fingers moving in the air as he tried to make sense and shape of numbers. I listened, structuring my plan of action while simultaneously admiring how kind he looked up close. Freckles trailed down his neck, disappearing underneath his shirt. We were sitting close enough for me to get a whiff of his cologne. It'd faded from this morning and mixed with something far more appealing. More natural. My body ached to lean closer.

Don't do this to yourself. Not with the one guy who clearly doesn't like you, I pleaded. Naturally, I understood I would develop crushes on some guys in the house. I was a sucker for pining. Crushing was fun and one of my favorite pastimes. I hadn't been able to do it in person in a while, so I planned to indulge in a brief fantasy. But not with Finn. Swooning over him would be a poor misuse of energy.

Finn paused for a moment. I cleared my throat, realizing it was my turn to speak. Lettie's eyes were on me too, expectant.

"Um, may I?" I held open my hand for his pencil. He glanced down at my palm, studying it for a second before handing the pencil over. The tips of his fingers were rough and cold as they brushed against my skin.

"So, you're not taking into consideration the outliers in your data," I started as I used the edge of an index card to draw a graph. "And by doing that, your results won't be as accurate."

Finn rubbed the base of his neck, listening to my explanation. He didn't say a word as I spoke, though the wrinkle on his brow got deeper every second.

A phone buzzed, and we glanced at Lettie as she fumbled to get it out of her pocket. She looked down at her screen.

"You two keep going." Lettie sounded distracted as she studied her phone. "I'll be back in a second."

We watched her walk away, probably looking like children being left at daycare for the first time. I recovered before Finn, straightening my back, and looking at the graph I made.

"Is this your first economics course?" I asked.

He shook his head, staring down at the graph as he answered, "No, not really."

I glanced in his direction. "Not really?"

"I had to drop this course last year," he explained, still looking down. I followed his line of sight and realized he wasn't looking at the page I'd written on at all. He was looking at my fingers gripping the pencil.

"Are you an Econ major?" I kept my distance, though I wanted to lean closer to hear his low voice.

"English Lit."

I tilted my head to the side and my mouth made an 'O' shape. Like Mid. I smiled, entertaining the idea that the guy before me had something in common with my online crush. Yeah, I definitely had a type.

Finn looked at me as if sensing something was off. I wanted to poke and prod a little now that I had him as a semi-captive audience.

"You have an interest in stats?" I asked.

"I hate it."

I laughed, thinking he was joking. But Finn didn't crack a smile. In fact, his eyebrows knitted, confused by my laughter. Was Finn capable of taking a joke? "Why are you taking such a hard course when you don't need it for your major?"

He shrugged. "The professor makes it interesting."

"Who do you have?"

"Jefferson."

I gawked. "*Jefferson*? For Economics?"

"That's who I said, yes." Finn didn't look concerned in the slightest. Econ students dubbed Jefferson the Grim Reaper. Students discussed horror stories about his breakneck teaching style. Professor Jefferson graded on a curve because in the fifteen years he's taught here, no one could get higher than fifty percent on his exams.

I'd been lucky and got a spot in Professor Darcy's course. It took staying up all night and registering as soon as the clock struck twelve for me to get a spot in her class, but I did it. Everyone wanted Darcy and only a handful of us were lucky enough to get her, considering she only taught two courses a semester.

Finn watched me closely. "I take it from your tone I'm supposed to be...alarmed."

"Um... no. No, you should be fine." I gave him a calm smile, trying to smooth things over. I'm sure they'd frown upon panicking in front of a student when I was the tutor. He was here for hope, not hysteria.

"You think so?" He raised a brow, and for a split second, I was getting something from him that wasn't stiff and short. He was asking me a question and there was curiosity in his eyes. Why did my stomach jump knowing he was waiting for an honest answer?

"Yes, of course. You'll do great. Whenever you have an issue, you can come here. The tutoring lab's open until eight. And even after that, I think there's an online chat…"

I turned, looking for Lettie, or maybe a sign that could confirm my information. She was still on the phone with her back turned to us. And the only posters on the wall were encouraging quotes and common equations.

"I'll double-check on the online chat thing later," I promised when I turned back to him.

"Okay." He still watched me, looking like he expected me to say something more. I stared back, wondering what else he wanted me to do. I let out another nervous laugh. He frowned, not getting the joke because there wasn't any. I just needed to make some sort of noise.

"So… I see you have another problem." I directed my gaze to his page. "This one's real simple—"

"I'm good, actually." He closed his book. The air from the pages created a breeze that kissed my face.

"Oh, um, are you sure? We haven't been working for long. I'm not even sure I explained the outliers issue fully."

"I'm good," he repeated, finality in the words.

"Okay, then." My stomach churned with embarrassment. I felt like I failed some sort of test. Not just the tutoring test, but something more. Ever since I met this guy I'd been failing it. My uncertainty morphed into annoyance as I watched Finn pack up his belongings. Questions boiled to the surface so quickly I couldn't hold back.

"Hey?" My voice was steady.

Finn met my gaze with a frown. He stood up from the table but kept his feet planted, waiting for whatever I had to say.

I stood up too, not wanting to talk while he towered over me. "We're probably going to see a lot of each other this semester."

"I don't plan on coming here after today," he said with no emotion in the words. "So, I won't be in your way."

I let out a dry laugh. "I'm not talking about here. At the house."

He didn't look like he understood what I meant. "It's big. You live downstairs."

"Yeah, but... I'm going to clean, use the common areas, and hang out with the other guys sometimes. My point is, maybe we should discuss your issue with me. If it's still the nose thing—"

"Issue? I don't have an issue with you. I don't care about what happened at the arena." He looked honest enough. His body turned to me completely, as if he was ready and willing to receive whatever feedback I offered him.

"Really? Because you left right in the middle of our conversation in the car earlier," I reminded him.

He scratched his jaw. "I...I didn't realize you were still wanting to talk. It was quiet for a while, so I thought you were done."

"Fair." My shoulders sagged. Perhaps I had been reading too much into that moment. I was taking things too personally, but for the sake of my sanity, I needed to be sure I hadn't stepped on Finn's toes. "How about now? You clearly need more help, but you're refusing it because they paired you with me."

"I don't need more help."

"All semester? You said you don't plan on coming here again. That's a little unwise since you're in one of the most difficult courses at this school and it's outside of your major."

"I'll manage. Your explanation was sufficient."

I scoffed. "Sufficient? Sufficient enough to help you for an entire semester?"

"Yes." He gave me a one-shoulder shrug. When I frowned, he added, "I don't have an issue with you, Naomi. Promise."

There was a silly flutter in the pit of my stomach from the way he said my name. How did he make it sound so...new? Obviously, my name's been worn out over the years. People called it beautiful, but the thing about having a beautiful name was that the magic was lost on you. My name sounded as common as the word 'school' or 'car.' But not when he said it. On Finn's lips, something common sounded like magic for the first time.

"Do you have an issue with me?" His question seemed like a challenge. A dare. Like he wanted me to be the one with the problem. I would not let him off that easily. If he wasn't going to show his hand, I sure as hell wasn't showing mine.

I crossed my arms over my chest. "Not really."

Something flickered in his eyes, like he could sense I was holding back. I raised a brow, a dare to ask.

"That's...okay." Finn readjusted his bag on his shoulder and opened his mouth to say something else. I braced myself for the impending question, but he cleared his throat instead.

"Okay?" I asked, trying to prompt him.

"Yes. Okay." Instead of elaborating, Finn brushed past me and started toward the door.

I pressed my fingers to my temple, frustrated I'd let him get under my skin. My hands dropped in a blink of an eye when I heard his heavy footsteps return.

"Naomi," he said.

I took a breath and turned to him, fixing my face to my usual welcoming expression. "Yes?"

"We stay after ten on Mondays for practice. If you need a ride, we'll be in the arena parking lot. I...we'll wait for you if you need some extra time to meet us." The explanation was simple, straight to the point. I marveled at his ability to move forward from our weird moment seconds before. I suppose I'd follow his lead and ignore it too.

I nodded. "You guys won't have to wait, I'll be there on time. Thank you. I appreciate it."

He gave me a curt nod and started back toward the exit. I watched him disappear. He didn't look back once.

I replayed our exchange again and again to make some sense of things. Finn claimed not to have an issue, but something about our conversations felt off. He planned to avoid the lab because I was here but seemed to feel guilty, so he came back to offer me a ride. He was so freaking annoying and yet still, my mind kept replaying how my name sounded coming out of his mouth.

"Sorry about that." Lettie appeared at my side with an apologetic smile. "Did the student leave?"

"Yeah, he said my help was...sufficient." I shrugged, repeating the word. Who the hell talked like that?

Lettie looked pleased. "I'm sure it was. What do you say about joining our team? I know I didn't get to shadow you for long, but I can already tell you're going to be a wonderful addition."

My annoyance with Finn was replaced with excitement in an instant. I forgot all about my grumpy roommate as I accepted Lettie's offer. Forget Finn. I was going to be the best tutor in this building and by the end of the semester, he'd be begging me to *sufficiently* help him.

Chapter Thirteen

Finn

Muscle memory was a gift. In a sea of impossible, I stayed afloat because my body knew how to handle itself with a hockey stick in hand. I didn't even have to think. Weaving through my teammates was like a steady inhale, slow and safe. Handling the puck was like an excited exhale, hopeful.

I never worried when I skated. I left every awkward, over-thinking action in the locker room. Because hockey didn't require words. It didn't look at me with beautiful brown eyes. It didn't feel warm or sound like a dream. Tonight, I needed cold and pain. The ache in my back continued to spread, but I ignored it for a chance to be on neutral ground for once. To not think.

"Here," I called, trying to get Henrik's attention. He struggled to keep up with me tonight. Getting him to execute a clean pass felt like pulling teeth. When he gave the puck to Sam instead, my jaw tightened.

"Finn!" Coach Haynes waved me over to where he and a few other guys were sitting on the bench.

I let out a heavy breath, annoyed at having to break my focus. One guy on the bench stood to take my place in the drill we'd been running. I paused in front of the boards where Haynes stood.

"All good?" I asked, hoping this would be some quick note.

Coach Haynes was a large man with a close-cut graying beard. The red knitted beanie he wore sunk back on his head, revealing his balding scalp. He looked cold as he crossed his arms over his chest. The red on his nose was made worse by his constant rubbing it with tissues.

"I was going to ask you that," Haynes said with a smile. "How's it feel to be back?"

One of the other guys who was sitting with him joined us. He was younger than Haynes by at least a decade. The black polo he wore was tucked into gray dress pants. We made eye contact, he nodded like he knew who I was.

"I feel good," I said and then decided I needed to give a little more if I wanted to make a decent impression. "Strong."

Haynes looked pleased. "Glad to hear it. I was telling Stoll about your recovery story."

The man in the black polo nodded and said, "It's impressive. We're glad to have you back, Howard. You're an important part of the team."

I raised a brow because something about that sentence seemed familiar. "Um...thank you. I'm glad to be back."

"You look good out there," Stoll continued. "Fearless, despite everything that's happened."

I shrugged. One pro of having amnesia was I didn't remember my fears. There was nothing to fear unless I got bad results. Or unless it had to do with a certain bright-eyed girl.

"Spoke to Aden today and he said you're on the right track." Haynes nodded in approval. "As long as you keep up with your appointments with him and your primary care doctor throughout the week, you'll be cleared to play during game time. I don't want to hear about you skipping any check-ups."

"Understood." I didn't let it show on my face, but the idea of having to check in with my doctor in addition to Aden throughout the week felt excessive. After coming back to campus, I'd hoped my interactions with poking and prodding doctors would be limited. I could handle Aden. The rest would be difficult.

Haynes cleared his throat, hesitating before continuing. He glanced at Stoll, who seemed to give him a nod of approval. My back stiffened, pain heightening as I braced myself for the bad news.

"Everything good?" I asked.

"Whitfield's starting left wing this year. O'Brien's in the second line and the other two are also full." Haynes crossed his arms over his chest like he was bracing for some sort of pushback from me. "I don't see that changing this season. There were a lot of guys vying for a starting spot. If you want time on the ice, you'll have to work for it. Whitfield's hungry, though. He won't give it to you easily."

Jack Whitfield was a cocky, loudmouth. I'd run into him in the locker room and quickly learned he liked mind games. That was useful as a hockey player but a nuisance from a teammate. I refused to let an ass like him beat me.

"I'm hungry too, sir," I promised, squaring my shoulders. "I'll work for it."

"Just what we wanted to hear." Stoll clapped my shoulder. I stared at the spot for a second. Who the hell was this guy? And why did it seem like I've had this conversation before?

"Coach," Sam interrupted us, stopping right next to me. "Ready for us to switch out?"

"Oh, right!" Haynes whistled, getting the attention of the guys already on the ice.

"Mr. Stoll." Sam nodded to the man and turned to ask me, "Ready for me to show you that play?"

What play?

I didn't show the question on my face. I simply nodded and followed him.

"What was going on there?" Sam grabbed a puck and dribbled it as he spoke.

"Coach wanted me to know I'm not going to start any time soon." I had to hold back the bite in my words. The decision made sense. I respected it and would have done the same if my player was in recovery, too. But that didn't mean I had to like it.

"And Stoll?" Sam passed me the puck. I didn't know what to do with it, so just dribbled.

"Who is he?" I asked. Since Sam knew about the extent of my memory loss, I didn't feel too embarrassed about asking him to fill in the blanks.

He looked a little confused at my question at first. "Warren Stoll's the athletic director. Real chummy with Haynes and the rest of the hockey department."

"You say that like it's a bad thing." Having an AD on one's side could come in handy. Especially when it came to budgeting. From what I knew, our team was good, but there were plenty of programs at Mendell that were better. For one, the basketball team were state champions for five years in a row. Lincoln wouldn't stop comparing our record to theirs during warm-ups.

Sam chuckled. "Could be depending on who you ask. He said you were out for the season?"

"Yeah, Whitfield," I said simply.

"Whitfield." Sam laughed again. This time it didn't sound humorous. "God, that's rich. Perfect, really."

84

"What?"

"Look." He moved closer as a few of our teammates blazed by doing a sprinting drill. "This season's big for us. For you, too. Our team isn't full of rookies anymore. I know you can handle being out here. Coach knows that too. But... no matter how hard you work ice time is probably out of the question. Haynes might have you thinking you can get it if you work hard enough. If I were you, I wouldn't get my hopes up. I'd start thinking of other options for the sake of my career."

I frowned. "Why do you say that?"

Sam sighed and stretched his neck. He looked tired. He always looked tired, but something about the weight in his eyes seemed uniquely heavy. "I keep forgetting about you forgetting. Just...sometimes, the people in charge look for ways to make a quick buck. And we pay for it. You and me, we were going to change that until you got your head cracked open."

I winced at the phrasing.

"Sorry. Bad choice of words."

"It's fine." I didn't like to talk about that night. Didn't like to linger because it was over and done. In the past, where it belonged.

Sam didn't seem as willing to let it go. "I've been meaning to apologize."

"You already did." All the guys had. As soon as I could take visitors, Sam, Lincoln, and Henrik were there. They regretted not finding me sooner that night. Wished they'd urged me to stay with them longer.

"I know, it just never felt like enough." His jaw tightened. "Finn, I feel like—"

I shook my head. "You don't have to say anything else. If you really think you have something to make up for, then help me get my spot back."

He let out a breath. "That's not going to be easy. In fact, it might be impossible."

"I need this, Sam. It's all I have left." Besides Chai, of course. But if my confession didn't go over well with her, hockey would be my only thing.

Sam studied me. He could see the determination in my eyes. Without him, I'd find another way. When push came to shove, I was going to play. I was going to rank again. I was going to be the best or die trying.

"Fine, I'll see what I can do," Sam said. "But I need something from you first."

My shoulders relaxed at hearing he was willing to help. "Of course."

"I need to borrow your phone later. I have someone who might be able to retrieve deleted data."

"What for?"

"Before your accident, you were going to send me something about Stoll," he explained.

"This is the stress you were keeping from me," I figured out.

"More or less."

I nodded. "I'll get you my phone. But I want to know what this is about. I can handle it fine."

These blind spots felt like they were piling up. I couldn't stand them. From now on, I wanted to fill in the gaps.

"I get the data and you get the story," he promised. "If not, we're both in the dark. Because I only had speculation. You had hard facts."

The sky was alight with stars. Despite Tinsel being a busy college town, when I looked up, I felt like I was back in the quiet safety of my small hometown. If I blocked out the noise of rushing cars and lights from the town center, I could pretend I was home. I didn't miss being there, but I missed the idea of it.

Naomi broke my focus. She stood leaning against the passenger door of my van. The light from her phone painted her face. She smiled at whatever was on the screen. As soon as my eyes landed on her, my footsteps hesitated.

The guys were still in the locker room, taking their precious time. It'd probably be another five to ten minutes before they made their way to the parking lot. Not a lot of time, but for some reason, it felt like a century.

She looked up from her phone, possibly sensing my presence or maybe hearing the heavy beating of my heart. It was freezing out here. She clung to the edge of her jacket. There was a faint smile on her face when our gazes met. Her eyes were as bright as the stars above. I wanted to trace her skin like I would trace the constellations in the sky. Would she feel as satisfying as those myths? She sure looked as wondrous.

"How was practice?" Naomi sounded upbeat for someone whose day had been as long as mine. She didn't seem at all stuck on how I acted before in the tutoring lab. I felt lingering bits of embarrassment about how nervous I'd gotten around her. There was a point where I could barely speak because she continued to impress me. The girl was a genius when it came to math. What the hell couldn't she do?

"Fine." I pulled out my keys. "Why are you..."

She raised an eyebrow, waiting patiently for me to continue.

"Out here? It's cold," I finished.

Naomi's smile faded. "I had a phone call and needed some air. It can get pretty loud in there."

I frowned, thinking about how far she had to walk from the arena to the van. She hadn't known where it was parked since I moved it earlier, so it must've taken time to find.

"Get in," I ordered.

Her smile disappeared as she obliged. Once we were both inside with the doors closed, I turn on the heat and adjusted the vents so they'd filter in her direction. Naomi hummed at the feel of warm air. I watched her hold her fingers to the vents. Her eyes stayed closed as she soaked in the much-needed warmth.

"You should wear more layers. The cold's only going to get worse," I noted in a gruff tone. I didn't mean to come off as harsh. Her lack of clothing and decision to stand in the cold bugged me far more than it should.

"Tell me about it," she murmured.

I couldn't pull my gaze away from her. My eyes kept straying to her parted lips. Her exhales were heavy, as if she would willingly drown in relief. My jaw tightened when she brought one of her hands to her cheek. Her fingers were long and graceful as she brushed them across her dark skin.

Stop it, I willed myself. She's your friend. Once you tell her you're Mid, she'll stay your friend because you can't lose each other. What we have is important. Too important to fuck up.

I opened my mouth, ready to start the conversation I'd been dreading. Ever since I bolted from the lab, I rehearsed how I wanted to tell her the truth. Naomi beat me to the punch with, "So, I saw you out on the ice and you're amazing. Far more graceful than I expected from a guy your size."

"Graceful," I repeated with a grunt.

"Sorry, is that offensive?" Her eyes were open now and locked with mine. She looked so concerned.

"No. It's fine." I looked away. Eye contact with her for too long made my palms burn with the desire to replace her hand with mine on her cheek. I could keep her warm.

Damn it. Stop.

"Since I can't even stand up on skates, I suppose any forward motion is graceful to me," she said with a light laugh.

"I'm really surprised you don't skate." I grew up on the ice and so did most people in the surrounding towns. It was hard to avoid skating rinks or hockey fans in Tinsel.

Naomi shook her head. "I tried and failed once. Never went back. The blades on skates freak me out. I watched a *Myth Busters* episode about the blade being able to slice into someone's neck and vowed to never again get that close. Obviously, one would have to be doing something intense to result in an accident of that level, but with my luck, anything's possible."

My mouth twitched. I almost smiled at her rambling. Of course, she would think of the most impossible scenario when it came to trying something new. "It's not that bad once you get used to it. I could..."

Teach her? No. That'd be weird. She seemed busy, and I wasn't in any shape to spend more than a few minutes socializing. Besides, she needed to know who I was before we spent too much time together.

"You could...?" She tried with a raised brow.

I shook my head, ready to bury the idea. "Nothing."

We went quiet. Once the silence settled, she pulled out her phone again. I trained my eyes forward and tried to keep my expression unbothered when I felt a buzz in my pocket. I waited a good minute before pulling out my phone to check the notification.

Chai03: So, I'm doing my best with the roommate but, no dice. Think Imma give up. Being likable is exhausting.

My heart sunk. I stared at the message for another second and then turned off my notifications before she got suspicious.

My fingers combed through my hair as I tried to figure out how to salvage the conversation. But nothing felt right. Just blurting out I was MidQuest would probably do more harm than good now. She was nice. Naomi would feel bad for just sending that message, and she shouldn't. I was the one who should feel embarrassed. I wasn't anywhere close to the guy she'd come to depend on. She was right. Trying to be likable was exhausting.

Chapter Fourteen

Finn

The house was quiet enough for me to hear every creak of wood or cough from the guys. Someone was having sex. My room was at the end of the hall, so I couldn't figure out who. It'd been going on for almost an hour before Lincoln complained in our group chat:

Lincoln: This is getting ridiculous.

Me: I'll say.

Henrik: Boohoo. Lucky you two aren't right next door.

I chuckled. Of course, it was Sam. When wasn't it?

Lincoln: He's either really good or really bad at getting this girl off. Either way, I hate I'm wondering which it is.

Henrik: He's good. No need to wonder.

Lincoln: Good Lord, I'm ordering earplugs.

Now, that sounded like a smart investment.

Me: Get me some too?

Henrik: Three.

Lincoln: Consider it done.

I pushed out of my bed and exited my room. There was no point in chasing sleep with Sam testing the bounds of his stamina. I did my best to keep my footsteps light as I headed down the stairs. The girl's moans mixed with Sam's muffled words followed me down into the foyer. I wanted to be more annoyed but honestly, I felt jealous. Lonely, too.

The kitchen was empty and semi-lit from a lamp in the adjacent living room. I paused in the doorway when I saw Naomi sitting on the living room floor, surrounded by hordes of craft supplies. I haven't had a one-on-one conversation with her IRL since our exchange in my van. That was a week ago. We'd become experts at using the guys as buffers. She did it because she'd given up on getting to know me. I did it because I wanted to practice talking to less intimidating people.

For the past few days, I've gone out of my way to interact with people other than my friends. Approached teammates, classmates, and even a few random people at the student center. With each conversation, I pushed myself to figure out how to keep the words flowing. And how to be less... grumpy sounding, as Lincoln would put it. It wasn't easy and never felt natural. I was getting the hang of it, though. And now, I needed to put what I'd been practicing to the test.

It's just like hockey, I tried to pump myself up. *Not going to be perfect until you flub it up a few times.*

With a deep breath and a quick run of my fingers through my hair, I moved closer. Naomi looked up at the sound of my feet on the floor. The small smile on her face didn't quite reach her eyes.

"Hey." She straightened her back, so she wasn't leaning over whatever she'd been making.

I stuffed my hands in my pockets. "Hi."

Silence—save for my racing heart. Naomi stared up at me and I stared back. When she started chewing on her lip, I asked, "Couldn't sleep either?"

"No... um... Got some stuff on my mind and there's, you know." She gestured upstairs.

"Yeah." I nodded and moved a little closer. "Do you mind if I sit?"

Naomi's eyes widened. She scrambled, trying to clear up space on the floor for me. "Oh, yeah, go for it."

I claimed a spot next to her on the rug. There were a good couple of feet in-between us, but I could still smell her floral scent. She wore a robe that was tied tight enough to highlight the curve of her waist. There was length to the fabric, but not enough to hide her legs. I urged myself to focus on what she'd been doing and not think about untying the bow holding the fabric shut.

"Are you..." I'd been going to fill in my own blank but couldn't manage to once I got a glimpse of the material on the ground. I couldn't figure out what she was making exactly.

There was a towel rolled out on the floor. On top of it, she'd lined up colorful balls of clay. Sharp instruments and flat pieces of glass were scattered around the towel edges. Some objects looked like cookie cutters, shaped like hearts and diamonds. At the head of the towel sat a half-painted crate. The wood looked old even with the sage paint doing its best to brighten it up.

"Making something?" I finished.

"Jewelry." She nodded, eyes shining a little as she reached for her phone. "I'm trying to make something like this for my friend."

I leaned in when Naomi turned her phone to me. She moved closer, knees pointed in my direction.

"It's nice." I nodded, taking in the bear earrings. There were chunky brown circles layered on top of one another to create the friendly-looking creature. "Have you done something like this before?"

"I do it all the time," she said. "Usually when I'm having problems sleeping—which is why you've probably seen a ton of aluminum foil lying around."

I had, but I assumed it'd been the guys leaving their stuff out like usual.

"How does the crate fit into the gift?" I wondered.

She waved a dismissive hand in its direction. "That's my door stopper. I'm trying to make it look cute. My weakness is making my surroundings as cute as possible."

"Doorstopper?" My eyebrows wrinkled.

"I don't have a lock." She shrugged. "And the door swings open if nothing's blocking it."

I frowned. "Have you told the Ables? I'm sure they'd fix it."

"I have, but I think they forgot." She shook her head. "It's not a big deal. Not like the window on the front door or the issues with the toilet upstairs. Those take priority."

"They still should fix it," I insisted. Having a door that locked would make anyone feel more comfortable. Especially someone who was living with four guys. None of us posed a threat to Naomi, of course. But that small bit of security could go a long way in helping her feel like she had a safe space at the end of the day.

I knew parts of Chai's past from reading our old messages. She moved a lot with her mother and rarely lived in the safest neighborhoods. The instability left her mind hyperactive at night. From the timestamps of our old messages, I knew that talking to her until the sun came up wasn't a rare occurrence.

I hadn't met the Ables—Sam had taken it upon himself to secure our housing this year. But from what little I knew, they weren't great landlords. I'd heard Sam saying something about Naomi being friends with their daughter. So, perhaps, that's what made her more forgiving.

"And since we're on the topic..." For the first time, it felt easy to not overthink in Naomi's presence because the subject of her comfort made all other issues feel trivial. "The heating's terrible down here. The kitchen barely gets any warmth and since your room's right off of it, I'm guessing it's even worse."

"That's what blankets and socks are for." She smiled, completely unaware of what it did to me and for me. I'd drive in the middle of the night to the hardware store and pick her out a lock for her door if she asked me to. I'd learn how to fix the heating system, even if it took days. Weeks.

"You should remind them," I said. "I'll remind them."

Naomi laughed. "I promise, it's fine. Why are you... I'm sorry, I'm confused. You seem so worried about...I don't know."

You. "I don't like the idea of someone paying rent and not getting their money's worth. You work here, too. And you do a good job. At the very least, you should have a working lock on your door and a warm place to sleep. It's annoying to see someone not get what they deserve."

Naomi stared at me, blinking with surprise. I'm sure this was the most I'd said to her in one go since we met. And my response was loaded with more opinions than I've ever voiced.

"You're not wrong," she said, recovering from my words by reaching for a ball of clay. "I should say something. I *will* say something."

I nodded and made a conscious effort to soften my features. This conversation wasn't supposed to be scolding in nature. All I wanted was for her to smile and mean it. Naomi's mood was infectious, but I knew her happiness wasn't always natural. She knew how to manufacture that beautiful smile so it shined bright. I hated the thought of her trying to do that around me.

"For now, I'm going to do what I can," she said with a determined nod of her head. "And that's distracting myself by making something nice."

"May I help?"

She raised a brow. "Of course. Um, it's not as hard as it looks. I could teach you some techniques I've learned in the last few hours. I'm a big believer in trial and error. No tutorials."

When I realized she was referring to the earrings she was making, I shook my head. "No, the door stopper. I thought I could finish painting that. It'll need time to dry and it's already late. It'd be nice to have it ready for you by tomorrow."

"Of course, sounds good. A more responsible approach." She laughed. "Here I was prioritizing earrings."

"There's nothing wrong with your priorities."

"And there's nothing wrong with you making earrings, too. If you want," she teased.

"I know." I nodded. "My hands just don't seem built for small details, you know?"

"Oh." Naomi leaned back against the couch and studied my fingers. "I think they're fine. They seem steady enough. Half the battle's believing you can do it."

Something about how she continued to study my hands triggered a warmth in my belly. My jaw tightened when she pulled her bottom lip between her teeth before looking away. If I was Lincoln or Sam, I'd figure out a way to get her to tell me what was on her mind. Hell, even Henrik's polite personality could probably pull something out of her. Unfortunately, I couldn't figure out how to flirt without cringing.

"They've become steadier from knitting," I said and could practically hear my friends telling me to shut up. Sure, knitting wasn't a common pastime for college-age guys. But it was surprisingly fun. My therapist suggested I pick up something new to help with my recovery. There'd been a knitting circle at the hospital and the women there were kind and patient. They even gifted me a set of needles when I left.

Naomi's head popped up, studying me as if she didn't catch what I said. "Knitting?"

"I do it to relax. Kind of like you do this, I suppose."

Her smile was back, cheeks round with sheer pleasure. I'd done that. Just by saying something honest. Mundane. A feeling of pride warmed my chest.

"That beanie you wear? Did you make that?"

I nodded. "My first project. Didn't turn out like I wanted—"

"It's perfect!" She seemed determined not to hear an objection. "Like adorable. The color looks great on you."

"Thanks." I raised a brow when she looked away for a second. The lighting was so bad in here, but I think I saw a shadow of shyness cross her face.

"Does it help?" she asked.

I tilted my head to the side, wanting her to elaborate.

"With relaxing, I mean. Making jewelry is nice, but I think it's lost its edge. I'm in the market for something new."

"What's bothering you?" The question came naturally because I felt like I was talking to Chai. I *was* talking to her, but not as a friend. I was her awkward roommate who knew nothing about her.

Her face fell a bit at my question. I cursed myself for skipping a few steps too soon. She asked for tips on knitting and in turn, I asked for her to share something far deeper.

"You know, usual school stuff." Naomi molded the clay into an unrecognizable shape. "And—please, don't tell the guys this—but my birthday's coming up."

I knew that. A few of us in her stream Discord were planning a surprise. And I'd ordered her something special from her wish list.

"You don't like your birthday?" I asked. She never mentioned disliking it on the stream. Not in private chats, either. If anything, she always sounded neutral about it. Not now, though. Her shoulders were slumped and her fingers fidgeting.

"It's a day." She paused so long I thought we were going to leave it at that. But with a deep breath, she finally added, "I don't celebrate anymore. Not after my mom died."

The flash of sadness across her face made my throat tighten. I itched to reach for her, to place my hand on hers, and press our shoulders together. I dared to move closer so she could at least feel the heat of my body. It wasn't much, but I hoped it helped her feel less alone.

"We never celebrated or anything." She brushed at her cheeks even though there weren't any tears. "It only got hard because Mom loves attention. Even in death."

I raised a brow, waiting for her to continue. Naomi picked up one of the jewelry-making instruments that had a sharp edge. She carved designs into the clay as she shared a secret with me that she hadn't told Mid.

"She's going to send me an email. Or, she already did." She laughed humorlessly. "She used a scheduling service before she died. Lined up emails for my birthdays when she realized she wasn't going to beat cancer."

"And you don't want the emails?" I watched her struggle to find words. Naomi resented her mother. She never said as much, but I could read between the lines in messages. Her smiles and joy were products of her upbringing. I could see how much she pushed herself not to be angry.

"I've only got one so far," she said. "Didn't read it. I couldn't... I... sorry. The last thing I want to do is bring someone down."

"You could never bring me down," I said without thinking. My cheeks burned.

"That's sweet of you to say." She laughed a little. "But you don't have to. You don't have to pretend."

"I'm not pretending. I have a hard time doing that. Especially around...well, people like you."

She sat up straight like my words were a needle prick. It took me a moment to realize that she *had* been pricked. Not by me, but the thing she'd been using on the clay.

"Shit." She dropped the clay when a bead of blood formed on her index finger.

"Hang tight." I pushed off the floor and hurried to get a first aid kit. There was one underneath the kitchen sink. By the time I made it back, Naomi was applying pressure in an attempt not to stain the carpet.

"Let's see." I reached for her hand, and she let me take it.

"I'm a klutz." She winced when I urged her to straighten the finger, so I'd be able to clean it better.

"Nah, I shouldn't have been distracting you." I tore open a disinfectant wipe packet with my teeth.

She stared at me as I wiped her finger. "True. This is half your fault."

"I'll take the full blame. It's the least I could do."

Naomi laughed, sounding surprised at my willingness. "God. And to think I was lightheaded over how you say my name. Now you go take responsibility without protest."

"How I say your name? Have I been pronouncing it wrong?" That seemed improbable, but knowing me, I'd find a way to mess something like that up.

"Uh..." She blinked and shook her head. "No. I don't know why I said that. You missed a spot. There."

Naomi pressed her lips together and pointed to a small dot at the base of her finger. I cleaned it, still curious about her comment, but I left it alone.

"And there." She pointed, looking earnest. I didn't see a thing but I followed her directions. "There, too."

Again, no spot. I cleaned clear skin and once I was done, she pointed at another blood-less area.

"Are you fucking with me?" I asked, feeling amused.

"Maybe." Her smile widened. "It's a little fun. You frown so much, I just kind of wanted to see if it worked the other way around."

"I smile."

She hummed and gave me a knowing look.

"Sometimes," I corrected and tossed down the wipe to grab a band-aid. "When it's necessary."

"Necessary," she repeated in a deep voice in her attempt to imitate me. It was cute. She was cute. And her hands were warm. And her legs were more exposed because she'd moved positions. The robe crept up her thighs. I wanted to press my fingers on her skin and pull her closer until she sat on my lap.

I kept my eyes on hers because I didn't want to miss a moment of her happiness. This wasn't a forced kind of happiness. It was alive and real. For a second, we felt like something that could be real.

Her lips parted with a sigh when I finished wrapping the band-aid. I didn't let go, even though I was done. Instead, I pretended to inspect my handy work.

"How does it feel?" I wanted to drag this out as long as possible. Touching her seemed as close to heaven as I'd ever get.

"Stings a bit." She watched me examine her. "Thanks for cleaning me up. You did a great job."

I met her gaze then. She'd leaned closer, pretending to be curious about the finger. Her eyes strayed to my mouth. I pressed my back teeth together, failing to relax. I couldn't kiss her. Not here. Not when I still had so much to say and needed time to learn how to say it.

My brain said one thing and my body did another. I leaned in. She didn't move. Not toward me, but not away either. I paused when I could feel her exhale on my lips. Naomi tilted her head slightly, gaze still stuck on my mouth. I used the hand not cradling her injured finger to touch her cheek.

She felt far softer than I'd imagined. The back of my fingers brushed her cheek, and she leaned into the touch. My chest tightened when she closed her eyes as I made small circles on her skin.

Damn, I want this woman in every way imaginable.

"Naomi," I whispered. A shiver ran through her, and I frowned. "Are you cold?"

She shook her head, eyes half-open now. "Only a little. Your...your hand is kind of cold."

I pulled away, and she frowned.

"Sorry," I breathed. "I didn't..."

"It's fine. I..." She paused and was the one to pull back this time. Someone was coming down the hall. I turned around in time to see Sam's guest padding into the kitchen, dressed in one of his T-shirts.

She smiled and waved at us. "Hi, sorry. Didn't mean to sneak up on y'all."

"It's fine." Naomi smiled too and began straightening up her things.

I watched her pile her supplies into a plastic bin. The girl lingered in front of the fridge, trying to decide on what to drink from the near-empty shelves. I swallowed a frustrated sigh, praying she'd decide on something soon, so Naomi and I could be alone.

Naomi didn't seem to want that to happen. In fact, she looked determined to avoid it. My stomach twisted when she said, "I should go to bed. Think sleep's finally calling."

"Okay," I said, watching blankly as she pushed off the ground and walked toward her room.

"Good night," Naomi said, her voice sweet and normal as she waved at the girl and me. My skin felt like it was on fire from touching her. I don't think I could stand yet.

"Have a good night," the girl called at a volume a little too loud for this late.

Naomi's door clicked shut, and I heard her shove something against it. I sighed and leaned on the couch with my head tilted to the ceiling.

"You two are cute together," the girl said with a water bottle in hand.

I grunted in response as she gave me a smile before retreating upstairs.

God, I felt pathetic. I wanted Naomi so much it hurt. I'd thought maybe she could feel the same. Except, she bolted, and I think trying to kiss her was a mistake.

Talk about a damn flub up.

Chapter Fifteen

Naomi

I'd been staring at the band-aid on my finger for almost five minutes before I snapped out of it. With a shake of my head, I finished drying the last dish. Today was a deep cleaning day and I wouldn't get through half my list if I didn't remain focused.

My brain only allowed a few minutes of productivity before returning to what it deemed more interesting: Finn.

He'd been so different last night. First, the willingness to stay in my presence, then asking questions like I was interesting enough to listen to, and he...well, I think he was going to kiss me.

That's ridiculous.

But what else is someone doing when they lean into someone? Count eyelashes? No. Finn was going to kiss me.

Or maybe he hadn't been leaning in at all? Maybe the leaning was all me?

Last night, I'd been feeling the effects of my poor sleep patterns. Pair that with loneliness and you'd get the perfect recipe for questionable decisions.

I filled a plastic spray bottle with cleaning liquid. As I coated the counter with suds, I replayed my birthday confession. I'm not sure why, of all people, I told Finn about my birthday. Not even Celeste and Mid knew about my mother's emails. I kept that to myself, along with most things about my relationship with Mom. Lately, my secret had been boiling to the surface, practically begging for release.

A sigh fell from my lips as I scrubbed the granite. I suppose telling a stranger something personal was easier than telling a friend. Finn and I would never get closer than roommates. Hell, he probably already forgot what I said last night. There was no need to panic because he knew something about me.

He hadn't been leaning in, I decided. I had. It was definitely me. A small moment of vulnerability I wouldn't let happen again.

Hot water burned my skin as I washed the soap from my palms. When I turned off the sink, I heard a creak on the stairs.

I turned with a smile, expecting to see Lincoln or Henrik because they were usually the first up. My expectations were shot when my gaze met Finn's. His dark hair stuck up in a few places, giving him a softer, more approachable look. He wore a pair of black-framed glasses and was shirtless. I swallowed. *Oh, my.*

No washboard abs. Just thick muscle and fat. He resembled a boulder, and I couldn't help but remember how gentle his fingers felt on mine last night. Finn could crush a man, but while cleaning my skin he'd been incredibly gentle.

It took a lot of willpower not to stare at how his thick biceps curved, painted with visible veins. His chest was bulky enough to withstand a head-on collision. In the end, it was the hair trailing from his belly button down into his pants that made my breathing shallow. If he was this thick in every visible part of his body, then it only made sense that...*damn it.*

My smile felt wobbly as my mind wandered into dangerous territory. Finn didn't seem like he was fighting with the same battle. He wore his usual solemn look, complete with an unbothered brow.

"Good morning," I said, sounding a bit too cheery even to my own ears. Instead of waiting for his response, I resumed scrubbing the already sparkling counter.

Finn lingered in the doorway for a moment. "Morning."

I could feel his gaze tracking my movements around the kitchen. Should I say something about last night? A joke to smooth things over? *I was so exhausted last night, I might have dreamed you tolerated me enough to kiss me?* No. Absolutely not.

As I struggled to start a simple conversation, Finn moved to the refrigerator. He pulled out a carton of orange juice and yogurt. I expected he'd move into the living room or back upstairs, but he lingered at the island.

"It's early for cleaning," he noted in that deep voice that touched my core.

I raised a brow and glanced over at the clock above the microwave. It read, six-thirty. "I guess. I like to get a head start on weekends. Got a lot of stuff to do before tonight's..."

I clamped my mouth shut. I'd been about to say stream. Finn studied me, waiting to hear the end of my sentence.

From our talk last night, I doubted Finn would judge me for streaming. I expected an ambivalent response. Still, I wanted to keep my streaming life to myself. It was too special for me to share with too many people in my everyday life.

"Studying," I said with a shrug. Finn was completely unaware of how close he'd been to getting another one of my secrets. He wasn't even trying, and he was good at making me feel comfortable. Yeah, that was it. Last night was the first time I felt comfortable around him.

Finn nodded at my response and absentmindedly flicked the plastic flap of his yogurt's lid. I pressed my lips together when I noted how steady the tip of his finger looked. How consistent and firm his movement was against the plastic's edge. *Holy crap.* When was I ever this horny? It was settled. Next paycheck I was going to invest in a vibrator.

"I was wondering if—" Finn began to say, but stopped short when Henrik and Lincoln's voices filled the hall.

My shoulders relaxed, realizing we weren't going to be alone much longer. Finn's jaw tightened when he saw his friends, which I found strange. He was usually as relieved as I was to have them interrupt our alone time. I forgot about his change in demeanor as soon as Lincoln greeted me by taking my sponge. He grabbed my hand, urging me to spin around once. I laughed at the impromptu dance session when he dipped me. Henrik looked equally impressed and offered applause as he told us he was making us pancakes.

"You shouldn't be up this early, sunshine. Let alone cleaning." Lincoln chucked the sponge into the sink. It made a sad smack when it hit the steel.

"It's kind of my job," I reminded him with a smile.

"Take a break. This place is in pretty good shape," Henrik insisted while unloading the pancake supplies from the refrigerator. He was cooking them from scratch. My stomach grumbled in excitement.

"We shouldn't get in her way," Finn said, voice firm with warning.

"We're not. We're helping by entertaining." Lincoln picked up a barstool for me and placed it next to where Finn stood at the island. I plopped down at Lincoln's insistence. "It's Murder Mystery Saturday. Remember?"

My forehead wrinkled. Finn shook his head like he didn't want to hear another word.

"Murder Mystery Saturday?" I asked.

Finn brought a stool to sit beside me. He took up so much space that I could feel the heat of his body against my arm. And to think, he'd been even closer than this last night. He'd been touching me last night.

I kept my eyes trained on Lincoln and Henrik, doing my best to ignore the cartwheels in my stomach. Why did he have to be shirtless for this long? Didn't his parents ever teach him manners? And why was he sticking around? He never stuck around for long when his friends gave him a decent excuse to leave.

"Lincoln fancies himself a mystery writer," Henrik explained as he organized his ingredients. "Most of us weren't allowed to watch TV in the mornings as kids. So, instead of Saturday cartoons, we got Murder Mystery Saturdays. Lincoln was always the host. Kids in our neighborhood ate it up."

"You're going to love this," Lincoln insisted as he lifted himself onto the counter and pulled out his phone. "Should I wait for Sammy?"

"Just wake him," Henrik said.

Finn shook his head. "Let him rest. He needs it."

Lincoln snorted. "Oh, I'm sure he does."

"And miss bacon with a side of nonsense?" Sam leaned against the kitchen's entrance. Like Finn, he was shirtless. Unlike Finn, he wore an untied bathrobe that covered most of his upper body.

"Never." Sam retrieved a vape from his pocket. The air smelt of weed as he shuffled past Finn and me, asking Henrik to put him to work.

"Alright, are we playing teams, or is everyone a part of the same precinct this time?" Lincoln questioned with an excited grin.

"Wait, I'm confused." I held up my hands for him to pause. "I thought you were telling a ghost story or something."

"Nope. Murder Saturday is where I describe a fictional murder or disappearance. I give you all the clues and you guys have to solve it before we finish eating," Lincoln explained. "It's like dinner theatre but for breakfast."

Sam blew out a small cloud of smoke. "If we don't solve it, he gets to ask for a favor from the losers."

"Which is why I never lose," Henrik explained. "You should be on my team, Naomi."

I laughed when he winked.

"Hey, don't try to charm your way into getting a new member. It's not fair," Sam protested. "Let her decide on her own that the superior team would be my team because I have the most experience."

This earned him a snort from Finn.

"What do we get if we win?" I asked.

"Same thing. A favor from whoever you choose." Sam smiled, looking as if he had something devious planned. "They can't refuse."

"You don't have to play." Finn's voice made me tear my gaze away from the guys. There was a surprising gentleness in his tone. "It's a silly game."

Sam chuckled. "Says the guy who took extensive notes last time we played."

"It's wise to keep track," Finn said. "Lincoln likes to lie, and he's barely good at it."

"What? I do not." Lincoln scoffed, appalled at the accusation. I laughed at the dirty look he threw at his friends. "I occasionally change points in the story. But only when you all started complaining about predictability. It's near impossible to tell a mystery to a live audience."

"Yeah, yeah." Sam moved his hand back and forth, impatient with the excuses. "Let's get this show on the road. I want to claim my win before we leave for the community center."

Lincoln's smile vanished. "We're still doing that?"

"A promise's a promise," Sam said.

"Yeah, but we weren't exactly in on the promise when you made it." Henrik turned on the stove. He placed a skillet on top and drizzled on the oil.

"What's at the community center?" I asked.

"Volunteer hours. We're tutoring or something," Sam explained while Lincoln let out a heavy sigh. "Oh, come on. It looks good on resumes.

Coach thinks it's great for a few of the players to get involved with the community, and—most importantly—I told the Ables we'd show up. Do you know how many applicants they had for this place? I needed something to help us stand out."

My eyes widened, excited to hear new people joining the program. "I volunteer there sometimes on the weekends, too. It can be pretty rewarding. I'd be happy to join you guys and pick up an hour or two."

Sam gestured to me. "See. It'll be rewarding. Thanks, Naomi. Your company would be appreciated."

"It's free babysitting," Lincoln noted in a flat voice. "I should know, seeing that my mom dropped me off at a similar program every weekend without fail. And then, proceeded to 'forget' to pick me up."

"Huh. Is that where your abandonment issues stem from?" Sam pretended to be thinking hard.

"No, actually, but you're on the right track," Lincoln said. Henrik shook his head, laughing at them.

"Hey, come on," I interrupted. "Don't write off the center just yet. I promise it's way more fun than you'd expect. Soon enough, it'll be your favorite part of the week."

"You hear that?" Sam asked. "It'll be our favorite part of the week."

"Okay, repeating everything she says isn't going to make it more appealing," Lincoln told him.

Sam, Henrik, and I laughed at his complaint. For some reason, my gaze strayed to Finn. I didn't care about what he thought, I just wanted to see his reaction. I expected he'd look aloof as usual, but was surprised to find his eyes already on me.

When we made eye contact, Finn turned away almost instantly. He ran his fingers through his hair like he needed something to do. I turned back to the guys, shaking off the warm feeling creeping into my cheeks.

He was probably lost in a daydream.

I pressed my lips together, determined to resume focus on the conversation at hand.

Chapter Sixteen

Finn

Post breakfast, I went on a run, hoping pounding pavement would get my mind off Naomi. I was only twenty minutes into the run when I realized it wasn't going to help. My persistent thoughts about how incomparable she was wouldn't fade because my lungs hurt.

I stopped in the middle of the sidewalk and rested my hands on my knees, trying to get rid of a stitch in my side. My back pain made steady breathing more difficult. As if sensing my struggle, my phone vibrated with a call from my sister, Anna.

"Everything okay?" was her greeting.

I straightened up to speak. "Everything's great."

"You sure...you sound winded." There were voices on her end. Dad and Denver were in the background, whispering questions I couldn't fully make out.

I winced at a few familiar phrases, 'take it easy' and 'don't think he's ready.'

"I was on a run," I said.

"A run?" Denver gasped, and suddenly, her voice was the main one filtering through the speaker. "Are you sure that's a good idea?"

"I've been on plenty of runs in the last week," I explained, trying to keep my tone even and calm. There couldn't be a repeat of my first, and only, outburst when I got out of the hospital. My anger almost got me sent to a recovery center. I much preferred the freedom of school.

"With other people, right?" Denver asked. "Like, your hockey buddies or whatever?"

"Or whatever," I joked in a flat tone. Of course, it didn't land. My delivery needed work.

"This is serious." Anna held the phone once more.

"So, I've heard." I covered the receiver for a second and let out a sigh. Conversations with my family always went this way: I updated them on how I was coping, they gasped in horror at everything and preceded to tell me how I'd have never done stuff like this before. We barreled to an inevitable end in which they expressed their hopes things would start feeling normal again. Translation, normal for them. They didn't like the new Finn. They'd never tell me that to my face, but I heard it in their voices. I wasn't enough for them.

"We just want you to get better," Anna said. "We're not trying to make you feel like you need to be careful of every sharp object."

"But do keep an eye out," Denver added.

"Okay, ladies, could you..." Dad took over the call. "Look, champ."

I winced at the nickname. "Hey, Dad."

"Pops," he corrected and continued forward. "Your sisters were having one of their 'feeling moments.'"

"It's called intuition," Denver corrected. I could imagine the roll of her eyes. "And it worked all the other times."

"They thought you were in trouble," Dad explained with a chuckle.

"I'm fine. But thank you all for the concern." They weren't exactly wrong, but my issues with Naomi weren't something I wanted to share with them.

I needed to figure out how to hang up before I said something prickly that I regretted. It was a shame I'd never know if my family was always like this. I'd asked the guys how their folks affected their mood and their responses were similar to mine. Yet still, I felt like something was off. My reactions to speaking with family felt ten times as emotional and difficult to maneuver than they needed to be.

"Well, that's good to hear," Dad said. There was a lull where I'm sure I was supposed to say something. When I didn't, he continued, "So, does this mean we can expect you home next weekend?"

I gripped the phone as I forced out my lie. "No, actually, I have a big paper coming up soon. I need to stick around campus. Plus, with our first game around the corner, things are going to get hectic."

"Understandable." He didn't sound disappointed. In fact, he sounded relieved. The psychic's comment about me being a shell was probably still rattling in his brain.

"You're still helping me with my stats course, right?" Denver asked. "In a few weeks? You'll make time, right? You always made time."

"Denver," Dad warned.

"Yeah, sure," I spoke before I knew what I was saying. Apparently, I'd been the one to tutor my sisters through most of their subjects since we were kids. Math wasn't my strong point but they seemed to trust me with it and I couldn't bring myself to be the bearer of more disappointment. At the beginning of the semester, I tried to refresh on some concepts but gave up because of frustration... and because Naomi's presence in the tutoring lab made me anxious. I suppose I could try again.

"Perfect!" Denver sung. The joy in her tone made me feel a tad less guilty. Damn, I wished I didn't feel like I was on the outside of their bubble. As a whole, they seemed like fine people. Excessively superstitious, but even superstitious people had their moments.

"We'll let you finish your run," Dad decided with amusement in his voice. Denver was probably doing her happy dance. "Don't push yourself too much. Remember, everything will start feeling like normal, eventually. You'll be the same again."

"Right." I nodded, even though he couldn't see. "Normal and the same, eventually."

"Exactly, champ. Talk to you later."

"You too..." I hesitated before adding a "Pops."

But by the time I said it, he'd already hung up.

I hopped in the shower after my failure of a run. I'd hoped the hot water would relax me for a few minutes. But even a shower couldn't distract me today. My mind was determined to entangle itself with wanderings of Naomi and now worrying about my family. The water turned cold quickly, and I shut it off.

Out of us guys, I was the one to pull the short straw for bedrooms. That meant I had the only room upstairs without a bathroom attached. So, I used the one Naomi got stuck in during our first night here. I shared it with her, and quite a few of her shampoo bottles littered the shower caddy. I did my best to ignore how much her familiar scent surrounded me as I wrapped a towel around my lower body.

My feet left small puddles as I made my way down the hall. Sam called from somewhere downstairs, telling us to be ready in ten minutes to head out to the community center. My shoulders stiffened at the reminder. No part of me wanted to drive across town to spend the day watching kids.

Every part of me wanted to sink back into my bed until I mustered the energy to head to the rink and get in a few drills.

I didn't realize someone else was in my room until after I closed the door. My back was to her at first, so I removed my towel without a second thought. I went to the closet to grab some pants and a shirt. My eyes locked with hers in the mirror hanging on the closet door.

We both froze. Naomi had a vacuum in hand. She wore headphones with small, deer antlers on the top. I got those for her... well, Mid did. They'd been on her wish list for her birthday last year. I watched a VOD where she gave me a watery 'thank you' over stream when she realized how many items I'd sent over.

"I..." Naomi shook her head as if the movement would turn back time so neither of us would make this awkward mistake.

My towel was close to the door, so I couldn't backtrack without turning to her and giving her a full view of what I had going on. Through the mirror, I watched her gaze travel down my back to my ass. Her eyes widened and she let out a heavy breath when I moved toward my dresser. Embarrassment looked cute on her. Naomi pulled her bottom lip between her teeth and fumbled with the vacuum's cord. It was stuck on something under my desk.

As she struggled, I opened a drawer and retrieved a pair of boxers. With them on I hoped the air would feel a little less heavy, but that wasn't the case.

"I was cleaning." She gestured around the room, doing her best not to make eye contact. "I thought you were still out. If I'd known..."

I nodded, hoping my calm would transfer to her. "Don't worry about it."

"I wouldn't have come in here," she continued. As Naomi spoke, she refused to meet my gaze. "Maybe we should have a schedule for when I clean stuff so that this doesn't happen."

"You don't have to clean in here," I decided. The rest of the guys were used to being picked up after, but having a maid was uncomfortable for me. Especially since I knew how hard Naomi worked in every other facet of her life.

"Oh, no, I still can. We should just coordinate, is all." Her eyes finally met mine. My stomach flipped at how her smile, even when hesitant, lit up her face. Even through the awkwardness, she still offered something. How did she do it so easily?

I didn't realize I was frowning at first. It was more of a habit. The clearing of her throat brought me back to the reality where we were still technically strangers. I was supposed to know nothing about how she couldn't stand the quiet.

"I should go." She gave me another smile, but this one wasn't as bright. A few seconds in my presence did that. "Let you get ready in peace."

I nodded, watching her leave. I wanted to call her back. Ask if she'd slept well. Or maybe talk about our almost kiss and how I was sorry if it made her uncomfortable. Words refused to leave my lips. It was for the best.

As soon as the door clicked behind her, I fell back onto my bed. With my hands covering my eyes, I groaned.

How the hell was I going to get Naomi to like me as much as she liked Mid? I wanted to make some type of good impression so it'd at least soften the blow of my confession. I couldn't keep this secret from her. The longer I stayed quiet, the more it'd hurt.

I'd give myself a deadline. By the end of the week, we'd talk. I'd be honest, open, and real. As real as this version of me could get. She'd know and whatever she decided, I'd accept. I'd quit moderating for her. I'd leave the

Discord. Whatever she needed, whatever made her happy, I'd give it to her. Even if it was a life without me.

Chapter Seventeen

Naomi

My mind was still racing from seeing Finn naked. I knew his large thighs would be mind-numbing underneath his clothes—he was a hockey player, for heaven's sake. But I never expected to break out in a cold sweat.

Being this turned on, by looks alone, was a rarity for me. I needed a little more than an attractive body to get me in the mood. I suppose Finn possessed that little more in some way. Who knew the secret to getting me hot and bothered was grouchiness and speaking in one-word sentences ninety percent of the time?

On the ride to the community center, I opted for a spot in the back. There was no way in hell I'd be able to sit next to Finn and not think about how the muscles in his calves gave me fantasies I didn't know were possible—who fantasizes about calves? And don't get me started on how large his dick looked in that closet mirror. He wasn't even erect. How would it look when he was ready to get to work?

I sighed and fanned myself at the thought. Lincoln and Henrik sat on either side of me, discussing the mystery story from breakfast. I gripped an arm across my chest, careful not to brush against either of them while I imagined their friend throwing me over his knee.

Lincoln and Henrik's discussion soon broached argument territory. Sam egged them on from the passenger's seat, playing devil's advocate for both sides. Finn was his usual quiet self. When I dared to glance at him in the rearview mirror, his gaze remained trained forward. He never looked away from the road, even when his friends tried to bait him into an argument.

"Point is, Finn won." Sam gave a one-shoulder shrug.

"Even if he helped craft the story?" Henrik asked. "That hardly seems fair."

Lincoln groaned. "For the last fucking time, I asked him one question about story structure. He's read more books than all of us combined. I'd be a fool if I didn't use him as a resource."

"You basically retold an episode of *Sherlock*. Didn't seem like you were using any other resources besides that," Henrik said. "Of course, Finn would detect your 'subtle nuances.' The guy loves Sherlock."

"Why are you using air quotes?" Lincoln mocked the use by curling his fingers. "My subtlety is real."

"Link, there's nothing subtle or nuanced about anything you do," Henrik explained.

"You are quite the exclamation point," Sam agreed with a chuckle.

"What? I could be a period, if I wanted," Lincoln insisted and then turned to me. "What do you think?"

I shook my head, not expecting to be included in the conversation. After spending so much time with them, I'd accepted they spoke too fast and moved around each other with such familiarity that I'd struggle to get a word in if I wasn't willing to work for it.

"I wouldn't know what punctuation mark you'd be." I laughed. The conversation was ridiculous.

"But, if you had to guess," Lincoln probed, not willing to let this go.

I shrugged and thought for a second. "Ellipses, maybe?"

He tilted his head and leaned back in his seat to think about it. "Huh. I kind of like that."

"It's cause he's never finished yapping, isn't it?" Sam grinned at me.

Henrik snorted. "I'll say."

Lincoln shot them a death glare.

"No, it's because he never seems ready to be done. And that's not a bad thing. It's like a consistent string of new beginnings," I clarified. The more I spoke, the more it made sense. I liked Lincoln's energy. Whenever he was in the room, things felt more alive.

"What about me?" Henrik asked.

I studied him. "Hm...probably a period."

The smile on his face lit up his brown eyes. "Why?"

"You're straight to the point. What you see is what you get," I explained. "Very respectable."

Sam laughed. "Oh, Naomi. So innocent and naïve. If only you knew."

I tossed a glance in his direction. "What do you mean?"

"He's messing with you," Henrik insisted, though, from the way his smile faltered, I considered otherwise.

Henrik's brush-off seemed to pull Finn out of his world. He glanced at Henrik in the rearview and the two exchanged something unspoken as Henrik said, "Do Sam."

"Alright, let's hear it." Sam motioned his hand for me to continue.

"You're an exclamation point," I said.

Sam raised a brow, looking pleased. "Sounds like a compliment to me. I'll take it. Now, what about Finn?"

My smile faded. I dared to glance over at him. His eyes were back on the road.

"Uh..." I wanted to say, question mark, but couldn't decide if that was terribly offensive or not. Maybe I could pretend to not have one in mind? But that would look weird. The last thing we needed was the guys sensing anything off between us.

Before I could voice my over-thought response, Finn saved the day by asking, "Is this the place?"

Sam directed his attention forward, taking in the two-story community center. "Looks like it."

"How long do we have to do this again?" Lincoln eyed the building with skepticism.

"Time's going to fly by." I nudged his shoulder. "You'll see"

"I'm holding you accountable if it doesn't, Naomi," he said. "Please, know that much."

I laughed. "I wouldn't expect anything less."

We filed out of the car. Lincoln and Henrik got into a new argument about the value of volunteering with Sam, once again, inserting himself in the middle. I listened, half-amused and half-keeping tabs on Finn. He lingered in the back of our group, his eyes trained on his phone as the rest of us talked. My phone buzzed, distracting me for a moment.

MidQuest: How's your morning so far?

Chai03: Awkward as all get out. Saw one of my roommates naked. And had to endure a forty min car ride with him after.

My cheeks burned at the memory. I rubbed the back of my neck as I waited for Mid's response.

MidQuest: He's probably more embarrassed by it than you.

Chai03: Doubt it. It was completely my fault... Now we're about to clock in volunteer hours. We'll be stuck in the same building for the rest of the afternoon. Pray, I don't make more of a fool of myself than I already have.

MidQuest: LOL, you'll be fine. Relax. Be yourself. I personally think she's incredible.

Chai03: Eh, she's alright. A 5/10 at best.

MidQuest: Come on, you're at least a 9/10.

I couldn't hold back an audible snort. I liked this teasing side of Mid the best. It's been a while since I've witnessed it.

Chai03: A 9/10? What happened to my other point?

MidQuest: You get docked when you call yourself a fool.

Chai03: Makes sense.

"Naomi," Celeste's gentle whisper pulled my focus away from my phone.

I looked up to find her manning the counter. Her parents liked her to work on weekends just so she could get out of the house. She obliged since she preferred to avoid most conflicts with her family. Plus, the desk got little action during the afternoon.

"Hey." I leaned on the counter to talk with her.

"How's it going?" She didn't look at the guys, but I knew they were who she wanted an update on. We hadn't been able to meet in person to talk about my living arrangements since I moved in. But I kept her filled in just like I updated Mid. She got the juicier details, for obvious reasons.

"Interesting." I gave her a knowing wink, which made her smile. "Tell you all about it later. Got the sign-up sheet? I'll explain to them how this works."

The guys got distracted in the main area of the lobby where there were posters for upcoming events and celebrity visitors, most of whom were athletes.

"Yeah, right here." Celeste's jaw visibly relaxed when I took the clipboard. "We already assigned them to classrooms since Sam called earlier. I think you should write your name next to Finn's."

I raised my brow as I looked at the paper. "English. You want me to tutor English?"

Celeste nodded. "You said you wanted to challenge yourself this semester, right? Plus, I can tell you're on a roll with him."

I snorted and then whispered, "I said we finally had a one-on-one. It's not what I'd classify as a roll."

She rolled her eyes with her good-natured smile intact. "Whatever. You just sounded happy about it. Like, happier than you've been in a while. A crush kind of happy. Which isn't something I've seen since you know who didn't show up for you know what."

I put on my best warning look. "Celeste."

"What?" She shrugged. "I'm only pointing out facts. You like him and he's a real boy."

I glanced over my shoulder to make sure the guys were still a good distance away. "Mid's a real boy, too. I don't like Finn. I mean, I do, but not in that way. And definitely not when I have unfinished business with Mid."

"Unfinished business? You sound like a ghost. Ever since you've met this guy, it's felt like a haunting. And not the good kind."

"I sound like a girl who can only handle one crush at a time. I'm not haunted, I'm patient. Focused."

Celeste narrowed her gaze. Instead of backing down like she usually did, she surprised me. My best friend grabbed a pen from a misshapen, handmade cup. She flipped the clipboard around and started writing before I could stop her.

"Hey," I protested when I saw my name next to Finn's.

"Sometimes, you're like me." She smiled, pleased with her handiwork. "Need a little extra push."

I scowled. "Not this kind of push."

"So...do we just go to whatever room calls to us or..." Lincoln appeared at my elbow. His question was for the both of us, but his eyes stayed on Celeste as he spoke. She met his curious gaze with a shy smile. An outsider wouldn't know by looking at her how hard this was for her. Her fingers were curled in tight fists at her side to keep from shaking.

"Naomi knows the rules," Celeste explained in a surprisingly steady voice. Days manning the counter did wonders to warm her up for social interactions. The effect never lasted long—unfortunately—but she took advantage of it whenever she could.

"She'll show you where you need to be, according to the chart." Celeste looked at me for the last part. "It's important you stay exactly where the chart puts you because it helps keep us organized. My parents run a tight ship. They don't like explaining to parents why their kid is being tutored by one person when the chart says it's supposed to be another."

She gave me a bright smile, which I returned in a flash ten times brighter.

"Okay…" Lincoln didn't know what was being said between us. But he was willing to stick around because he clearly wanted something else. "I don't see your name on the chart. Celeste, right? The Ables' only daughter."

Celeste's smile fell. Mine almost did too. Had I told him that? No. I never talked about Celeste to people because she hated people. I protected her from them as much as I could.

"That's correct," she said, carefully.

Lincoln smiled at her. "I thought so. Ran into your dad the other day at the house."

"Did you now?" Celeste eyed me, sending silent pleas for help. I shrugged because she was doing fine. Good even. And she was right. Sometimes she needed a little extra push.

"Yeah. He seems like a cool dude," Lincoln continued and shifted weight from one foot to the other, seemingly nervously. Wait. He was nervous? I spent a decent amount of time around this guy and had yet to see him nervous. Lincoln wasn't the type.

I glanced over to his friends, who were uncharacteristically holding back from joining us. When I sent them a look, they all tried to appear oblivious to what was going on.

"He's nervous?" I mouthed, which got me a nod and grin from Sam, a behind-the-hand chuckle from Henrik, and a lackluster brow raise—didn't expect anything more—from Finn.

I turned back to the conversation at hand with renewed interest and investment.

"Sure, I guess my dad's a...cool dude?" Celeste shrugged.

"He is." Lincoln cleared his throat. "But, anyway, your name's not on here and there's room in..."

"Third-grade biology," I read off. "Woah, and would you look at that? Lincoln, you're the only one assigned to that room."

"Am I now?" He studied the sheet, clicking his tongue in mock disappointment. "Such a lonely endeavor, enriching minds on one's own."

Celeste looked unimpressed with both of us. "I'm not tutoring this weekend. Besides, we have a floater for situations like this."

Lincoln's shoulders sagged. "That so?"

"Hm, is it —" I stopped short when she glared at me. I knew her limit. A little teasing here or there didn't hurt. But I never liked to push Celeste too far. "That's right, the floater. Besides, counter duty is important. Especially at this time of day. So busy."

My words seemed to echo through the near-empty halls.

"It is," she agreed with a smile. "Also, time is of the essence at this time of day."

She winced at her phrasing. I swallowed a laugh before adding, "We should get to our classrooms. Before we know it, the kids will be too antsy to focus on us."

"Right, of course." Lincoln tapped on the counter like he was trying to think of something more to say.

"Come on." I squeezed his shoulder and then said loud enough for the other guys to hear, "I'll set you guys up."

Celeste sent me a 'thank you' look as I gestured for the guys to start down the hallway.

"How did the extra push feel?" I teased in a whisper.

"Karmic," she said with an amused smile. "Good luck with yours."

Good luck, indeed. I was going to need it.

Chapter Eighteen

Finn

"Henrik," I said in a low voice when we entered the community center. He joined my side without a question, moving closer when he saw the serious look on my face. "Can I use my mystery whatever favor on you?"

He nodded, looking a little surprised. "Of course. What's up?"

"Uh..." I stuffed my hands in my pockets. My gaze strayed to Naomi for a second. She was at the front desk, talking with a familiar-looking girl who sat behind the desk. I had a minute or two before we figured out where we'd be heading for the afternoon.

"I could use your help and advice with some stuff...personal stuff."

He made a low, intrigued hum. "Don't get me wrong, I'm more than happy to help but...can I ask why you're coming to me?"

I blinked. "Um...I don't know. Naomi said that thing about you being straightforward. I can see that. Kind of remember that about you. I think it's part of the reason we're friends."

It took everything in me to not wince at my lie. I'm not sure why I said it. I wanted to reference whatever camaraderie we had in the past. There had to have been something we bonded over.

Henrik raised a brow, looking like he wanted to laugh. "Interesting. Very interesting."

My shoulders sagged because it sounded like he didn't believe me for a second. "What do you mean?"

He paused for a beat, studying me as if he was waiting for a punch line. Since I didn't have one, he seemed more than willing to deliver. "Finn, you've never asked me for advice in all the years I've known you. You don't trust me enough."

My forehead wrinkled. "Are you serious? Or just fucking with me? I can't tell these days."

"I'm not fucking with you," he said.

"So...are we even friends...or...?"

Henrik frowned, offended now. "Of course, we're friends, Finn."

"Then why don't I trust you?"

"It's complicated." He shrugged. Before he could explain, Lincoln started over to the front desk. Sam urged us to watch the impending train wreck.

"Look, I'll explain later. What do you need from me?" Henrik asked.

I hesitated a bit before whispering, "I need to practice a confession in front of you. And you need to give me...notes on my delivery techniques. No bullshit feedback."

Henrik looked confused. I needed the help of someone who was going to be honest, non-judgmental, and discreet about my situation. Lincoln would joke about the whole thing before he announced it to everyone who'd listen. Sam would question me until the end of time about why I kept this secret from them in the first place. I needed a more neutral, approachable party. Henrik was semi-neutral and hands down the most approachable.

"Like, a speech?" Henrik asked, trying to make sense of my strange request.

"Yeah, like a speech." I nodded.

"Cool. I'm down. Let me know when you're ready and I'm all ears."

I breathed a sigh of relief. "Thanks, buddy. I appreciate it."

He chuckled. "Yeah, of course. Happy to help."

"Everything good?" Sam whispered when we rejoined his side.

"Great." I offered him a curt nod.

He studied me for a second. "Perfect. By the way, are you ready to give up your phone next weekend? My contact's finally in town."

"Right." I nodded, remembering our deal. "I have a few messages to send and then, it's all yours."

"Exactly what I wanted to hear." He smiled and then nudged his chin in Lincoln's direction. "Check this guy out. Haven't seen him this bent out of shape in ages. Must be some girl."

I looked toward Lincoln but immediately got distracted by Naomi. It felt impossible to focus on anything else when she was in the room. Her dress clung to her waist today. The shade of yellow made her skin look more beautiful than usual. Her dark hair was piled at the top of her head, giving her more height. I desperately wanted to press a kiss to her perfect smile and play with the escaped strands of hair framing her face. I wanted to hold her close against me and to whisper words of admiration and lust in her ear.

If Lincoln was far gone, I was right there with him.

"Henrik and Sam are in room C." Naomi gestured to a room full of unruly children who couldn't have been older than six. Henrik took a deep, steadying breath. Sam nudged him forward.

"Relax, they won't bite," Sam insisted.

"No promises on that," Naomi teased and turned on her heel before either of them could question the validity of her statement. We passed two more rooms before we stopped again and she said, "Lincoln will be here with the third graders. There's only three, so you'll be able to handle it until Celeste sends the floater, right?"

Lincoln nodded while scratching his head. "Oh, yeah. I got this..."

"Call if you need help. We're right down the hall." Naomi gave him a warm smile, which he was too nervous to return.

She led me to the last room without saying anything. I tried not to steal too many glances in her direction, but it was difficult when we walked next to each other.

"And here we are." Naomi stopped in front of the open door. "English. Fun."

I noted the sarcasm because I could finally understand how to pick it out in her tone. "You don't like English?"

She laughed. "No... I wouldn't say don't like it. Hate is a better word."

"It's a very strong word, too."

"You would know, wouldn't you?" She pointed at me. "English major. God, I can't fathom."

"It's not too hard."

"Brag a little more, why don't you?" she joked.

"Sorry," I said, in case I'd truly offended her. "What I meant to say is, I think we're going to be a good team. You lead and I'll follow."

Her smile faltered as she took me in. I stared back, trying to figure out what I said wrong. One kid inside of the room called out a complaint while another threw back an insult. The heated exchange forced Naomi and me to redirect our attention. She fixed her face into its usual cheery glory and walked into the room. I followed, doing my best not to get distracted by the swing of her hips.

This classroom was the smallest I'd seen since we got here. It was only large enough to fit two long tables that were shoved on opposite walls. There were six kids, and they'd split themselves up with girls on one side and boys on the other. Though the space was small, large ceiling to floor windows facing the playground outside made up for it.

"Morning, guys," Naomi greeted. "I'm Naomi and this is Finn."

She glanced over at me. I didn't know what else to add, so I just gave them a nod of acknowledgment. They stared back at us with glassed over eyes—understandable considering it was ten AM on a Saturday. Two of the girls whispered to each other behind their hands. Their eyes met mine for a moment, but they quickly diverted their gaze.

"You take boys and I take girls?" Naomi asked.

I nodded. "Yup. That feels right."

She laughed under her breath. I felt my shoulders relax at the sound.

"Let me know if you need any help or tips." She leaned in a little closer as she whispered, "Kids can be a little difficult to keep on track. Also…"

"Also?" My forehead wrinkled when she bit her lip like she was re-considering what she was about to say.

Naomi scratched the back of her neck. "Try to be easy, you know? Chill. Not so…grumpy."

"Grumpy?"

"Yeah, you know, you frown all the time. Personally, it's grown on me, but it could intimidate the kids." She shrugged. I stood there, stuck on the 'grown on' part.

"Excuse me, Miss?" One of the whispering girls raised her hand.

Naomi's eyes flickered in her direction. "Coming right over." And then to me whispered, "Less grumpy. More chill."

"Less grumpy. More…chill." I repeated with a nod, even though it felt weird to say. I didn't like the word, 'chill.' People used it as if it was a neutral state. But even chill required effort. Practice.

As Naomi took a seat at the girls' table, I claimed an empty chair with the guys. One of them wore headphones and laid with his head in the crook of his elbow. By the steady rhythm of his breathing, I could tell he'd dozed off. I debated on whether to wake him and decided against it.

The other two boys had pencils in their hands. One drew doodles of warriors amid a battle in the margins of a copy of *The Hunger Games.* The other stared at the scarred side of my face like he was searching for answers.

I cleared my throat, unsure what to say. I was relieved when the kid staring at me spoke up, "I'm Darius. And that's Andy."

The artist looked up but quickly glanced back down at his drawing when he realized we'd made eye contact. The red on his brown skin crawled across his cheeks and down his neck.

"The sleeper's Eddie," Darius said, still staring as he asked, "What happened to your face, man?"

I raised a brow and touched the side of my face he'd gestured to. Most people went out of their way not to ask but still stared. Sometimes, I felt like that was worse than actually talking about it. I had so many scars that I didn't think about them much. I forgot kids aren't like adults. They don't avoid; they barrel forward.

"I was told this one was from an accident when I was younger," I said. "Around your age, actually."

Darius frowned. "What kind of accident mess you up like that?"

"Got in a fight with some older guys. One shoved me into a metal fence. Needed about forty stitches," I explained. Personally, I appreciated it when people were open with me. I hated metaphors and phrases that tried to smooth over rough edges. Whatever interactions I had here, I wanted to take an open approach. Especially since I was probably the first person they'd interacted with who had such visible scarring.

Darius's eyes widened at my explanation. Andy looked up after hearing my story. He spoke in a barely audible voice when he asked, "What are stitches?"

"How many guys were there?" Darius asked, simultaneously. His loud voice drowned out Andy's. "Cause you're huge. Couldn't you take 'em?"

I shook my head. "I wasn't big in terms of muscles back then. At least, not in the way I am right now."

I'd been an overweight kid until high school. My body still carried some extra weight, but my muscle mass evened things out.

"And stitches are when they use a needle to sew your skin together, so it'll heal properly," I told Andy. He sat up a little straighter, looking almost surprised I answered his question.

"They tore your skin apart!" Darius's voice was loud enough to be heard on the other side of the room. "Holy shit!"

"Hey." Naomi's tone was stern enough to make me feel like I needed to fall in line. "Indoor voice and respectful language, please."

The girls frowned in our direction. Naomi gave me a look that read, do you need help? I shook my head.

When Darius made a face at Naomi's scolding, I echoed her command. "She's right. No cursing. Don't look at her like that either, okay?"

He heaved out a sigh and sagged in his seat. "Fine. Sorry."

Naomi shot me an impressed look before refocusing on what she'd been doing.

"So, uh, what do you guys need help with?" I asked. Maybe starting the conversation off-topic was a mistake on my part. I'd need to steer it to the reason we were all here.

"A stupid paper," Darius mumbled and nudged his book with the tip of his pencil.

"It's about the Districts in Panem," Andy explained with his face down and pencil shading a sword. "Why they were made and what would happen if we had them today?"

"So boring." Darius rolled his eyes. "Then we gotta make a speech or something."

"It's a group project," Andy clarified and gave Darius an annoyed look. "It's a play, not a speech. We have to make different parts."

"Boring," Darius insisted. The two boys glared at each other, and I felt like I was back home, standing between my sisters in their latest battle.

"Finn." Naomi appeared at my side. She raised her hand like she'd been about to touch my shoulder. My body stiffened in anticipation of physical contact. She pulled back at the last minute, sensing my change of posture. She'd read it wrong. I wouldn't mind her touch in the slightest.

"Everything alright?" I asked.

She nodded with a smile. "Fine. Finally got the girls to tell me about the group assignment. Apparently, everyone here is a group member."

I glanced back at Andy, Darius, and the still snoring Eddie. Darius shrugged like the information had slipped his mind. Andy's skin turned red again. I couldn't tell if he was embarrassed at not telling me about the group assignment sooner or if it was Naomi's presence that made him nervous. It was probably a mixture of both.

"We should push the tables together." She moved her hands as she spoke. Her fingers looked graceful as she pointed at the kids, giving each one a specific command. They listened to her without protest.

Chairs scratched across the tile, making a deafening sound. No matter how many times Naomi told them to carry, they still dragged.

I stopped right next to her, doing my best to stay out of the way of the kids. I noticed Naomi was scratching her arm a lot and glancing at her phone every few seconds. After the fifth arm scratch in two minutes, I forced myself to go out of my comfort zone to ask, "Is something bothering you?"

She blinked, confused. "What?"

"You seem…" Anxious? I didn't know. The only thing I knew was she didn't seem like herself.

"Everything's fine." Naomi put on her usual smile. "Once we resume, do you mind taking the lead? I'm crappy when it comes to reading comprehension—always skimmed in my English courses. I'd feel weird giving them direction when you're sitting next to me."

"I'm sure you're fine." My words were supposed to be a comfort, but they looked to cause the opposite. Her fingers scratched at her arm again. If her dress didn't have long sleeves, her nails would've torn through the skin with how hard she pressed down.

"You should do it," she insisted. "I'm better at talking. I can guide the discussions."

"Okay." I nodded, not wanting to press her anymore. Before I could think about it, I reached forward to cover her scratching hand with mine. The second my palm made contact, she froze. Instinctively, my fingers curled around hers. I felt like I was on autopilot. No matter how much my brain urged me to pull away, I couldn't. Not without stopping her from clawing her skin.

"It seemed involuntary," I explained, and when she gave me a blank look, I continued, "You were scratching, and it looked like it hurt."

"Oh." Her gaze was locked on me, but mine strayed to my fingers covering hers.

My mind went down a road I swore I'd leave alone. I'd spent a long time trying to forgive myself for getting hurt the night we were supposed to meet. I tried to convince myself that she'd truly forgiven me. My heart ached thinking I could have met her so long ago. If I had, I'd already know what her scratching meant. If we'd seen each other that night, I wholeheartedly believe we'd be together. Even if she didn't want to be a couple, I'd have still wanted to be close friends. For her, I'd be someone who'd stop her from unconsciously hurting herself.

Naomi watched me, understandably perplexed at why I was still clinging to her like a man hanging on a cliff. That's how I felt most days. I went through life just hanging on long enough, hoping someone would peer over the edge and notice. When I met her eyes again, for a second, I thought I saw recognition. Whatever I saw quickly faded when Darius made loud kissing noises and the girls started laughing.

"Get a room," Darius teased with a wrinkled nose to exaggerate his disgust.

I released Naomi immediately. She rubbed her hand and turned away from me. For a second, I worried if I'd squeezed her too tight. I sighed, embarrassed for holding on so long.

"What did I say about respectful language?" Naomi started toward the table. She looked all business once more. "Come on, get in your seat. Let's get started."

Darius opened his mouth to make a few more teasing comments. I thought they were funny, but when Naomi looked pissed, I did my best to shut him down. For the remainder of the session, she didn't look in my direction. We sat across from each other, and she didn't glance at me once. Meanwhile, I was having a hard time looking away.

Chapter Nineteen

Naomi

Today was not my day. First, it was a nude Finn—which, okay, technically wasn't all that bad. Now, I'd embarrassed myself by mixing up words in front of fourth graders.

Reading out loud was never my forte. Scratch that, reading period wasn't my forte. The letters jumbled up so much I couldn't put together full sentences without stumbling. This continued until I was almost in middle school. By that time I'd been reading at a level so far below my peers, it was alarming.

I got lucky in second grade when an assistant teacher noticed I was struggling. In school, I was excitable enough to trick my teachers. Never underestimate enthusiasm as a stalling tactic. I've since learned to manage my dyslexia quite well. Audiobooks, text to speech apps, are lifesavers. But managing in front of people was something I had yet to conquer.

Queue my anxiety hives.

How embarrassing. Every few months I broke out in a terrible case of hives. From years and years of struggling, I discovered it was a mix of stress and poor diet. I wasn't conscious of any real stress since the beginning of the semester. I thought things were going well for the most part. My skin disagreed.

The hives spread across my arms like wildfire. Remaining calm felt vital yet elusive. At the height of my panic, Finn's hand covered mine and for a moment, everything paused.

His hands were so large and heavy. His touch was like a weighted blanket, made for comfort. My heart sunk the second he pulled away. I tried to shake off the lingering warm feelings as we resumed helping the kids. Never in a million years would I have thought Finn could be capable of being so...observant? Not only observant but tender with his concern. He was worried about me just like the night I cut my finger. The emotion in his eyes looked the same. He was ready to do whatever I asked to comfort me. He was ready to lean in and press his lips to mine.

I brushed my fingers across my mouth, imagining how they'd feel. Finn spoke to the kids in a calm and steady voice as I tried to come up with a list of reasons to not want him.

Number one was, of course, Mid. I needed to settle things with him. I couldn't give up on us, even if we were destined to be just online friends. At this point, I think that's all Mid wanted, anyway. He hasn't brought up voice chatting. He didn't reference the outside world as much as he used to. Shit, did I need to move on? Was Celeste right?

As if summoned, my friend poked her head into the room and announced, "Playtime."

The kids didn't need to be told twice. They tossed down their pencils and hurried to the front of the class where their jackets and shoes were.

"Where are we going?" Finn asked me as he watched the kids get loud and giddy.

I instructed them to form a line and once they did, led them out of the classroom. "To the rink. They skate for one hour, then get a snack before their folks pick them up."

Finn perked up, and it was the cutest thing ever.

"This place has a rink?" he asked. The tips of his ears turned red from excitement. I smiled at the reaction. He wore his beanie a lot, so his ears were usually hidden from the world.

"Yup. Most of the kids can't even stand up straight, but they love it."

"We're allowed to go on the ice, too?"

"Sure, if you want."

"Do you?"

I laughed. We rounded the corner to the rink. Our group of kids broke out in a sprint to where the extra skates were stored. The pre-teen girl in charge of divvying out the skates looked overwhelmed at the sudden rush.

"I'm going to pass. I enjoy having an intact femur." I spotted Henrik and Lincoln. They were already trying to help some of the little ones keep their balance on their blades.

"Right, that is preferable." Finn nodded. I assumed he'd leave to join the others. I started toward the stands to find a seat so I could watch from a safe distance. Instead of claiming a pair of skates, Finn followed me. He lowered himself onto the bench, making sure to leave plenty of space between us.

We were quiet at first, watching the kids tug on their skates. A few came by to ask for help with tying them up. Finn gave them a few tips on how to make tight knots that'd last the whole day. I followed his technique, trying to perfect my own knots.

"You're a natural teacher," I noted when the last kid left to enjoy the ice.

He stuffed his hands in his pockets. "Despite the grumpiness."

I smiled. "Maybe because of it. Grumpiness does cut through bullshit rather nicely."

"I like to think so," he agreed.

I gestured toward the ice. "You should join them. Maybe teach them a few non-bullshit hockey plays. I'm sure they'd love it."

He looked tempted by the idea but didn't move an inch. "I'd rather teach you how to stay upright."

My heartbeat quickened. It might've been my imagination, but his voice sounded deeper now. Lower too, which added a sense of intimacy to our conversation.

"Really?" I squeaked, in the least graceful voice possible.

"There's nothing like being on the ice. It feels like flying. All your worries just wash away. I noticed you might have some worries today."

There was a softness in his eyes. A kind of softness I'd never expected when I first met him. What changed? I know I shouldn't look a gift horse in the mouth, but this felt so different from the guy who used to avoid me like a plague.

"Will you join me?" He looked at me, dark eyes needy for a 'yes.' Damn, if he kept doing that, he'd get me to do whatever he wanted.

Slow down, girl. It's just skating. Not a date. He's still a moody roommate. And you're still hung up on a guy you've never met.

"I promise you won't fall." Finn sweetened the offer.

"You can't promise that."

"Okay, maybe not. But I can promise I'll do everything in my power to soften your fall. I have years of experience on the ice, so I know how to properly fall. I've caused too many not to know how a landing is done."

I swallowed. "Um...okay, let's give it a go. But I swear, one almost-slip and I'm outta there."

He nodded, his ears red again. I chewed my lip, trying not to smile too much. Finn asked for my shoe size before grabbing me a pair of skates. When he got back, he had a few pairs in hand. He kneeled in front of me and before I knew what he was doing, he untied my shoes.

"Oh...I could...thank you," I stammered when he removed my sneakers.

"First thing you should know about skating," Finn began, matter-of-factly. He spoke as if his fingers weren't gently gripping my ankle and coaxing my nerve endings into a state of panic. "It's vital you find the right pair of skates. And that's not always going to be your usual size."

I glanced over to see that, in addition to my size, he picked out two other sets for me to try on. My response got caught in my throat as he helped me slip my foot into the skates. He moved like helping me was second nature.

He tightened the laces with a firm tug. I pressed my lips together at the sight of his fingers readjusting the tongue of the skates. Who knew a kneeling man lacing skates could be so hot? Not me. I was glad I learned today, though.

"How does the fit feel?" Finn asked. His hands were still on my skate, but I couldn't feel the pressure of his fingers anymore. The veins on his skin were prominent. I tried my best not to picture him gripping other parts of my body, but damn, his hands would look ten times better around my neck.

What the hell is wrong with you?

I cleared my throat. "It feels fine. Good. Great, even. Wonderful, is a word one might use. All the positive adjectives."

He gave me a curious look. I laughed to show him I was fine, even though I sounded out of sorts.

"Stand up. Let's see how that feels." Finn pushed off the ground and offered me his hands.

I took a breath, accepting his support. He pulled me up effortlessly. His touch felt like a storm, familiar and new all at once.

As I wobbled like a baby deer, he stayed steady.

"Any pinching?" he asked, looking down at my feet.

I shook my head. "No, they're perfect."

And I think, in a way, you might be too.

"Great." He nodded in approval. "We'll skate for a bit. Then if you feel like they're getting too tight or loose, we'll switch them out."

I nodded, too caught up in the smell of his spicy cologne to form much of an opinion on my skates. Who cared about skates when a six-foot hockey player tended to you like a princess?

"Mind waiting a sec while I get a pair?" he asked in a low voice because we were a breath apart. I was about an inch taller than him with skates on, so I had to bend my neck to meet his eyes. Big mistake.

Up close, Finn's brown eyes were lighter. The scarring on his skin mapped across the temple down his chin like a winding river. This close, I didn't sense mystery in his gaze like I did from afar. A breath away, Finn looked like he couldn't hide a damn thing. He looked like he wanted me, and that sent panic through my bones. The itching was back with a vengeance.

"No rush," I told him as he helped me sit down.

As soon as he left, I grabbed my phone. My heart pounded a frantic beat in my ears as I opened my text thread with MidQuest. I was halfway through typing a message and I paused.

Did I really want to send this now? Was word vomiting necessary? Yes, I was attracted to Finn. I was about eighty percent sure he felt the same way. That didn't mean I had to make any immediate decisions about my relationships. In fact, I shouldn't make any decisions other than figuring out a new hive ointment.

I glanced at Finn and felt my head floating into the clouds. I needed to handle this because it was getting worse now that he was different. Finn was being nice, and I didn't know how to handle it. Quiet Finn was easier to manage. He didn't challenge me. He didn't make me question my focus. He didn't make me question what I really wanted now that there was stability in my life.

With a deep breath, I typed a message for Mid. Something less chaotic and more straightforward. I needed answers. We'd waited long enough. I'd given him time to think about us. I was tired of waiting and wondering and dreaming.

Today, I was nipping my crush in the bud. I'd put on my big girl panties and demand something solid. Finn was feeling more solid. I enjoyed that feeling and I wanted it to stay. I wanted to enjoy it with the right person.

Chapter Twenty

Finn

Chai03: I think it's time we try to meet IRL again. What do you say? I'm usually free on weekends.

I kept my gaze on my screen because if I turned around to Naomi, she'd read the sheer panic in my eyes. The girl manning the skates gave me a weird look when I mumbled a rushed 'thanks.'

Why was she asking this now? Since our first failed attempt, we both ignored the topic. I thought we mutually agreed to put it in a box and not open it until...we were ready. Until I was ready. I was getting there at my pace. I was working on becoming someone again—someone worth getting to know, someone worth growing to love.

My stomach twisted at the thought of telling her the truth. *Hey, we've already met. I live above you and we tolerate each other. Well, you tolerate me. Meanwhile, I pine. Hard.*

I took a deep breath at the fantasy. This panicking would have to wait. I stuffed my phone in my pocket and started back to Naomi. She looked up when she saw me coming. That perfect smile appeared. I felt a weight on my chest.

"Should I get one of those rail assistant things?" Naomi asked.

I shook my head. "No. You'll be fine. I won't leave your side."

She looked away. She'd been doing that a lot since we got to the rink, and it wasn't typical of her. Since meeting Naomi, I knew she liked eye contact. She never ducked her head like she was now.

I tried to run through what happened between the classroom and now that'd evoke a change of behavior. Maybe I said something wrong? I was doing my best to be less intimidating and thought I'd been getting better. Naomi was willing to spend extra time with me. I mean, we weren't exactly bonding on some existential level, but she wasn't coming up with excuses to leave. And that made me hopeful.

She let me hold her hand as we made it to the ice. I stepped on first and then encouraged her to follow. Her grip on my hand tightened tenfold. The strength in her thin fingers surprised me. Naomi's eyes widened a bit once she placed her first blade on the ice. Her whole body was frozen for a moment, stuck between safety and what she considered a risk.

"I think I changed my mind," she whispered when a few kids whizzed by. Her jaw tensed when she saw Lincoln and Sam moving by at racing speed.

"You good, Naomi?" Lincoln asked while turning around to briefly skate backward so he could catch her response.

"Oh, I will be," she called and added in a voice low enough for only me to hear, "once I get these dang things off my feet."

"Wait a second," I protested. "Just give it a few minutes."

She shook her head, coils bouncing back and forth. "Uh-uh. I've had nightmares about this exact moment."

"What happens in your nightmares?" I asked. Maybe discussing it would give her a sense of release. By the doom clouding her eyes, I think it did the opposite.

"I fall right as I get on my feet," she recounted while staring off into the distance. Her voice sounded far away as she spoke. "My body slams to the ground. There's a cracking noise—my spine, I think. And then, I try to get back up, but I fall again and this time it's my head cracking. The ice whispers, "*You're mine now.*"

I blinked. "Okay, very traumatic. I can understand the concern... Um, in your dreams, is someone else there?"

"No. Never. I'm alone." She met my gaze. There's something in her eyes I can't fully interpret. It's fear mixed with something stronger. I want to move closer but resist the pull because she's out of her element. She doesn't need the added stress of my attraction.

"The key to proving a dream wrong is to switch up the factors."

"I'm here," I continued. "So, there's one thing that isn't in your dream." She nodded but remained still.

"When you fall, where are you on the rink?"

Naomi looked over my shoulder toward the center. "Smack dab in the middle."

"We won't go to the middle," I promised. "We'll stay in the outer lane. You can hold on to me and the wall."

"I..."

I waited, but she seemed to be running out of excuses. "Naomi, once you get a hang of this, you'll love it."

She gave me an unconvinced look. "You can't promise that."

"I am a little biased," I confessed. "But once you find your center, as your blades touch the ice, it's the closest thing a human can get to magic."

The guys would jeer me if they could hear me now. But I believed it wholeheartedly. They did too, even if they didn't want to admit it.

"You must've never been to Harkin's Chocolate Factory," she joked. "Now, *that's* magic. If skating beats out all that chocolate joy, then I'd be in shock."

"I haven't experienced Harkin's, but from the sound of it, I'm interested."

"You should go," she insisted, brightening now that we were talking about something she enjoyed. "It's the real-life equivalent to Willy Wonka's factory."

"I'll go, if you come out here," I said.

Her mouth pressed in a firm line. I could see the dread return to her eyes. Naomi took a deep breath and shook out her shoulders before saying, "Alright, fine. You shouldn't be deprived of heaven because I can't woman up."

I steadied myself as she took a step forward. One hand in mine turned into two. She let out a small squeal and didn't take her eyes off her feet once. I dared to tug her forward.

"Wait, wait," she begged as she squeezed her eyes shut.

I stopped immediately. "What's wrong?"

"I heard someone blaze past and almost hit us," Naomi said in a rushed voice. She sounded like she was sprinting, she was breathing so fast.

"It's fine. They weren't going to hit us." I glanced around. It would be difficult to avoid getting close to the other skaters when there were this many on the ice. You can't tell kids to mind your personal bubble. I did the best I could to put my body between her and everyone else.

Her nails dug into my skin as we started moving again. She kept opening and closing her eyes like she couldn't decide which she preferred.

"You're doing good," I offered.

"Liar," she said with a nervous laugh. "You don't have to pretend. I'm a big girl. Tell me what you actually think."

"You really want to know?" I kept us going at a snail's pace. Her breathing seemed to even with every inch we moved forward, but her grip stayed the same.

"Of course, or I wouldn't have said anything."

"I find it interesting that someone as so graceful is stiff as a board right now," I confessed. "I'm curious if that's how you feel off the ice, too. Maybe you're good at hiding it?"

Her eyes flashed open, meeting mine. My chest tightened as I instantly regretted my words. I meant it more as a compliment, but as I played it back in my mind, it sounded mean.

I stopped us and moved, so I stood directly in front of her. "I... didn't mean that to come off as rude."

She blinked and stared. Shit. I'd done it again. Frustration boiled in my stomach as I tried to come up with some sort of remedy. It was times like these I wished I had some sort of psychic link with one of the guys. Any of them could smooth things over in a heartbeat.

"It wasn't rude," she said after several weighted minutes. "But it was very forward for a guy who I thought..."

I raised a brow. "You thought?"

"Didn't care enough to pay attention."

The tightening in my chest was back, but for a different reason. We were in rejection territory. She was onto how I felt about her. I needed to tread lightly if I ever hoped to stand a chance of getting a 'yes' when I finally asked her out.

"Maybe I was wrong about that," she continued in a lower voice. Naomi studied me like she'd put on a pair of long-lost glasses. I stared back, not sure if she realized she wasn't clutching my hands as hard. Her body was relaxed now that she had something else to think about.

"Would you describe yourself as shy?" she asked with a knowing smile. "Maybe even a little socially anxious?"

I frowned and let out a stiff, "No... not really."

Naomi laughed. The noise made my stomach jump. I wanted to pull her closer. To get a taste of her laugh. She always squinted when she found something entertaining. And she could make almost anything entertaining for herself. She lived her life looking at the world through half-closed eyes. It was beautiful.

How did it feel to smile that much? To laugh at the drop of a hat? Such a wonderful skill.

"There's nothing wrong with being shy," she finally managed.

"Of course not."

We were moving again. I don't think she noticed, and I wanted to keep it that way, so I forced myself to talk.

"But I'm not shy," I said with surety.

"You seem it." She was still watching me with newfound intrigue. "You avoid conversations like you're on a deadline for something."

"I don't enjoy small talk."

"Well, the rare chance you do talk, you keep your answers short. And a little abrupt," she said the last part lower as if she could offend me. Naomi could shove a knife in my gut, and I'd remain unbothered. She didn't know how much she already had a hold on me.

"Sometimes conversations feels weird to me," I confessed. "They're minefields."

"Shy people tend to say that. You know what?"

"What?"

"From this point on, I'm determined to get a genuine smile out of you...no, a laugh. You deserve a good laugh."

I snorted. "I smile and laugh. It won't be much of a win."

"I haven't seen you do anything but frown since I've met you. Maybe occasional winces, but that's on good days."

"Really?" I tried to think back to all our interactions. Surely, there had to be one time when we spoke where I gave her some sign I liked being around her? I had to have slipped up once. It was hard not to when she was around.

"Never," she promised.

"I suppose I haven't found much to smile about lately." Lies. White lies felt so easy and so dangerous, and they were piling up around me. There was plenty to smile about whenever I spoke to Naomi online or offline.

Nerves flowed through my blood when I remembered the text she sent. She wanted to meet, and I still wasn't ready. How was I going to put things off? Especially now that she was warming up to me. Which meant Finn was on her good side and, Mid might not be. Jeez. What a mess.

"We'll find something. I'll get you to smile for me, one way or another," Naomi teased.

My stomach flipped. Smile for her? Fuck. Whatever she wanted, I'd give it to her. I'm willingly wrapped around her finger.

Naomi's hand moved so our fingers intertwined. She was trying to reach for the wall again, so I didn't read too much into the change in hand placement. My thumb pressed against the back of hers. It took an insane amount of concentration for me to not trace circles on her skin.

"And it'll be genuine." She beamed at me. "I'll make sure of it."

"Sounds like it's shaping up to be quite a challenge," I joked. "You up for it?"

"Oh, definitely. There's not a doubt in my mind I'm the woman for the job."

Chapter Twenty-One

Finn

T he house was a goddamn mess. Not in the cleanliness department, of course. Naomi's skill and dedication were impeccable. We didn't deserve her.

It was the handywork that'd fallen through the cracks.

Our landlords skimped on the upgrades and weren't the best at keeping up with our growing list of requests. There were loose steps on the deck—one of which Naomi almost slipped on before I caught her the other day. The windowpanes on the front door were covered with a temporary screen. Our bathroom faucets leaked, and the door stuck. Most importantly, Naomi still didn't have a lock. So, I decided it was time to rise to the occasion.

I'd taken Aden's advice on approaching my memories. Instead of trying to mold into who I once was, I attempted to create him instead. Easier said than done, but my first step was leaning into what I wanted to do. Surprisingly to everyone around me, I wanted to fix things.

There was an unexplainable amount of joy in figuring out how to un-stick a lock or re-panel a window. Working around a house felt a lot like knitting for me. I got to construct something useful out of materials that might have otherwise been cast aside.

After watching videos on how to fix common house issues, I stopped by the hardware store to get a lock. As soon as I got back to the house and stood in front of Naomi's half-open door, I started feeling unsure about my decision.

"She's out, man," Lincoln noted when he caught me staring at Naomi's door. "Tutoring or something."

"Yeah, I know." I nodded without looking away.

"Okay…" He opened the fridge, grabbed what he needed, and stood at the counter to watch me. "Then what are you doing?"

"Thinking," I said.

"Thinking?"

"Yes, it's usually what people do right before they make a decision."

He snorted. "Ha. See you found your funny bone."

"That's what that was?" I tilted my head to the side. Huh, I suppose I did enjoy humor. The dry, sarcastic kind. Noted.

"I suppose I should have asked, what you're thinking *about*?" Lincoln rephrased.

"Putting a lock on Naomi's door." My skin burned a little because yeah, this felt weird now. Conceptually it was fine, but was it strange to buy an expensive-looking lock to place on her door? Would this be concerning to her? I didn't want to come off as overbearing.

"Hm." Lincoln nodded. "Nice."

I released a heavy breath. "It's weird."

"No, no." He chuckled a little, making me feel ten times worse.

"I'm returning this." I turned to go back outside. If I hurried, I could have my money back before she got home. It'd be like this never happened.

"Whoa, slow down." Lincoln caught me before I could get to the door. He wrapped his arm around my shoulders and turned me back toward her room. "I said it's nice. That's not a synonym for weird."

"Not a synonym, but potentially loaded with negative connotation."

"What? No. Look, you're thinking too much. You always have."

I sighed. "I guess some things never change—no matter how hard you hit your head."

Lincoln raised a brow. "Okay, *that* sounded loaded. You want to unpack it?"

"No. Definitely not." I felt my best when not taking part in deep discussions. I liked to save that for therapy and occasionally Chai—Naomi.

"If you insist." Lincoln shrugged, never one to push. "I think the lock is fine. Specific enough to get her to understand you like her."

"I am being pretty clear, right?" I winced at having to ask.

Lincoln laughed. "Oh, you are. If the puppy dog eyes weren't enough, helping her do even the smallest of things is. Nice save the other morning, by the way. Your reflexes are unmatched."

"That porch is a death trap. Her shoes keep getting caught on the wood," I grumbled. "I'm fixing those next."

"Wouldn't expect any less." Lincoln patted my back. "Finn, change the lock. It'll excite her and maybe relax you—for like a minute before you figure out what else you need to take apart and put back together."

I nodded and waited for him to leave before kneeling to see if I could tackle the project with ease. Taking the knob off was the easy part, of course. Putting on the new one took longer than I originally expected. By the time I tightened the last screw, it was dark out. I got so into the project, I didn't hear Naomi come in. Her familiar scent made me glance up.

She smiled, looking happy to see me. I could get used to that. I'd change a billion locks if it gave me an excuse to be in the same room as her.

"Hey," she said. "What's going on?"

I pushed off the ground, scratching my jaw. "I...changed your lock."

Her brows raised as she joined me by my side. "You changed my lock?"

"Yeah, it's..." I waved my screwdriver toward her door. "New. And changed."

She let out a hesitant laugh. "So I see."

We both stared at her door.

"Your crate is nice and all." I tried to fill the dead air. "But you deserved better."

Naomi nodded, not meeting my gaze. I watched as she stepped closer to touch the knob. Her fingers wrapped around the intricate handle.

"It's..." She chewed on her lip for a second. "Really pretty. Fairytale level beautiful."

"I got a salesperson to help me pick something out," I said, grateful for a topic to expand on. "I remember you said you enjoyed making your surroundings cute. It didn't feel right picking something common. We narrowed it down to three in the end and asked other customers what they thought. This model won out and also was my favorite of the bunch. I took photos of the other ones in case you didn't like it and wanted something else. I have them if you want—"

"Finn." Her soft voice made me stop short.

I took a breath. "Yeah?"

She stared at me with those beautiful brown eyes. I licked my lips, trying to do something about my dry mouth. Since it was the end of the day, she looked exhausted. There was a stain on her untucked work tee and one of her earrings was missing. I've never seen someone so beautiful.

"I'd never want another," she said. "This is perfect."

"I'm glad you like it." I nodded, not looking away from her. "Um...there are keys, too."

The box came with a matching set. I handed them both to her. My fingers brushed her palm during the exchange, sending a jolt through my veins. She'd stepped closer to take the keys. Her eyes never wavered from mine as she slipped them into her back pocket.

"Thank you, Finn." Her voice was low. Maybe she wanted privacy, or maybe it was because it'd been a long day. Either way, I adopted the hushed tone, too.

"No problem."

"Yes, problem." She laughed. "This must have cost a fortune. I want to pay you for the knob if you won't let me pay you for your time installing it."

"Actually, there was a sale going on, so I got a great deal."

"Oh?"

"Yeah. People named Naomi got one hundred percent off. So, I name-dropped you. Told them I knew one of the best Naomi's."

She snorted, and I felt drawn to the sound. I moved closer.

"Is that so?" she said through fading laughter.

"It is. She did almost break my nose when we first met," I teased. "But I figured out she was nice real quick. Hard-working, talkative, energetic, and kind. Definitely deserving of the sale. They seemed to agree."

She crossed her arms over her chest. "Show me the receipt, Finn."

"They ran out of ink, so I didn't get one."

"Not even an e-receipt?"

"Nah, my inbox is full. It would've bounced."

"You do know you left the bag on the counter, right?" She pointed over my shoulder. "The receipts flapping like a flag."

I turned around to find she was correct. My receipt was being blown by the AC, trying to show off every dollar I spent.

"It's not," I said and hurried over to the counter.

Naomi was fast. She almost beat me to it. I pressed my back against the granite as she took a swipe at the bag.

"Just tell me the number." She refused to back down. We were closer than we'd been since that night doing crafts. In the shuffle, her chest briefly pressed against mine. I bit my lip when I felt my cock stiffen. Naomi was none the wiser, still trying to reach behind me as I switched the bag from one hand to the other.

"Half. I'll settle for half," she promised while laughing. "Please?"

"It was free, Naomi."

"No, it wasn't."

"Fine, a gift then. A birthday gift." I stopped switching the bag around because she stopped moving.

Her smile faded a little. "Right."

"You can't pay for your own birthday gift once it's been given," I continued. "I've been told it's bad luck."

My forehead wrinkled when she looked down at the ground. "Hey, are you okay? If you really want to know that bad, I'll tell you. I just want it to be a gift."

"No, it's fine. It's a perfect gift," she whispered.

"Then, what's wrong? Your mood changed." I shook my head when she tried to smile. "Don't do that. Not if you don't mean it. You don't have to force yourself to smile around me. I don't need that to feel comfortable. Being around you, in any mood you're in, makes me...comfortable. I asked because don't you want to be comfortable, too? You can be sad if that's what you need."

Naomi opened her mouth, but nothing came out. She stared at me in shock.

"What do you prefer, Naomi? Don't smile," I said. "Just...what do you prefer?"

Her eyes got misty, and I felt like a proper jackass.

"Shit," I said. "I'm so sorry."

She brushed away a few tears. "No, you didn't do this."

"I think I did." I raked my hand through my hair, trying to think of something that'd make her feel better. Sure, I told her it was fine to be sad. And it was. I didn't want to cause it, though.

"You didn't, you didn't." Naomi shook out her hands. "It's...the lock and your voice and my silly birthday."

"What about it? I can try to fix it."

She sucked in a breath and pointed at me. "And that. Especially that."

I placed a hand on my chest. "What? That what?"

Naomi pressed her hands against her closed eyes. I massaged my neck as she scolded herself. As soon as she told me what I'd done, I'd draw up a plan within a few minutes. The execution might take longer, depending on the severity of the offense.

"I...I want to kiss you," she blurted. "Like, a lot right now."

My stomach dropped. Wasn't expecting that.

She let out a whimper of embarrassment. "You asked me what I preferred, and that was my first thought. I'd prefer it if you pinned me against a wall and kiss me."

I almost laughed because that'd been my dream for the past few weeks. Now that she voiced it, the fantasy felt more like a manifestation.

"What? Now you're looking weird." She held onto her stomach. "I made it weird. Damn it."

"It's not weird."

"I'm weird. You don't have to soften the blow. And don't kiss me."

I frowned, confused. "You don't want me to kiss you anymore?"

"No, I do. I have. I will. For a very long time, Finn, I will want you to kiss me."

"Good. That's good."

"Good?" She looked surprised. Before either of us could re-think another damn thought, I wrapped my arm around her waist, pulling her close. She braced her hands on my chest, gasping at my decision. Even after a long day, she smelled warm and felt soft. I brushed my nose across hers, soaking in being this close. Naomi's breaths were heavy as I moved a hand down her cheek to her chin. Her mouth parted when my thumb brushed her bottom lip.

My cock was straining now. Fully ready and willing to please the girl who was clinging to me like it was second nature. I tilted her chin up to expose her neck. She obliged, trusting, as I pressed a kiss on her skin. I could feel the sweet moan she released from her throat, vibrating against my lips. I kissed her again to get another feel of heaven. God, if kissing her neck did this to me, how was I going to survive her pussy?

"Finn?" she whispered.

I hummed against her neck in response. She sighed at the feeling, obviously entranced with vibrations like I was.

"Kiss me up here," she pleaded. "Please, kiss me on my lips."

I think I liked begging. I wondered if old Finn did.

Instead of giving in immediately, I walked her backward until she was against the wall. The smile on her lips was genuine, and I made myself a promise to remain worthy of nothing less.

"You said," I spoke in a low voice. The guys were upstairs. I couldn't hear any creaking on the floorboard in the hall, so we had time to enjoy this. "You wanted to be pinned against the wall."

I could see her eyes darkening as I lifted one of her legs to wrap around my hip. My hand remained on her thigh, holding firm to ensure she couldn't move. She whispered an expletive when I pressed harder against her. It was impossible for her not to feel my cock at this point.

"This pinned enough for you?" I asked, honestly curious.

She nodded and could barely get out the words, "It's perfect."

I pressed my lips against hers and tightened my fingers around her leg. I needed her to know how much I wanted this. Her mouth parted, welcoming me in like I'd been there before. Like I was coming home. I groaned when she bit my bottom lip.

Naomi tasted like she looked, sweet and heart-stopping. Once I had a taste, I couldn't go back, even knowing I was in dangerous waters. She didn't know everything she needed to know about me yet. We couldn't go far and still...I was practically dry humping her against the kitchen wall.

Her moans nearly killed me. When she started moving her hips in search of a sweet spot, I wanted to strip her. I tried to help her find some sort of relief by readjusting myself against her. The shiver that coursed through her body let me know when I found the right spot. She chewed on her lip, holding back a whimper as the button of my jeans rubbed her clit.

A creak on the staircase called us back to earth. Someone was coming down. I stole a few more seconds because I couldn't help myself. She was a Sun, and I was a frozen Earth, desperate for a change in season.

"Finn," Naomi pleaded between rushed kisses. "Should we...?"

"I know, I hear," I said, stealing a few more kisses before forcing myself to pull away.

As soon as I let Naomi go, she hurried to readjust her shirt. The guys' voices were closer now. In a second, they'd be in the room smelling the heat in the air because they were sharks.

"I should go," she said. "Sorry, I don't..."

I nodded, letting her know it was fine. "No, go. I understand."

She didn't want to be seen with me. Plenty of reasons. None I could confirm, but I wondered if she was embarrassed. It was silly and insecure for me to think, but once that thought burrowed in my mind it wouldn't leave.

"I'll...see you." She pressed her fingers against her bottom lip as she spoke, as if her touch could undo what I'd already done. But from the look on her face, that was impossible.

I winced at the thought of her walking away right now and feeling regret. "See you."

"Thanks again, Finn," she whispered. "Really. For everything."

She disappeared into her room before I could answer. I braced my hands against the kitchen counter, willing my heart to stop racing and my cock to get over it. Neither happened in a timely manner. I don't know why I even hoped they would.

Chapter Twenty-Two

Naomi

I never thought he'd kiss me. Sure, I asked. But never in a million years did I think stand-offish, grumpy Finn Howard would want to touch me, let alone have my body begging for an orgasm. And yet...

It'd been a week since our kiss. The weirdest days I've ever experienced because my body felt like it was on some Finn-specific drug. My skin burned to be touched and kissed. Any time I closed my eyes, it was Finn's face I saw. I heard his voice and felt his fingers, encouraging me to open up and enjoy his attention.

I spent my nights touching myself in a dissatisfying attempt to calm down. Days were spent avoiding him. I couldn't be alone with Finn because I didn't know what other erotic request might fall from my lips. I already appeared desperate when I asked him to kiss me.

But he did it. And he liked it. You felt that.

I did. There was no denying his excitement. That kiss was so much more than lust. For me, it felt like a step forward. Away from pining over MidQuest and keeping my social circle small. Kissing Finn was me opening up to having a connection. A relationship with him—sexual or romantic—was a risk I wasn't sure I was ready to take. I don't know if I could survive another heartbreak. Another huge disappointment could end me. I'd been doing so well this semester. I'd gotten stronger after everything that happened with Mom, finally standing on my own again.

Heartbreak could undo everything. It could weaken me to the point where I needed help. And I was done asking for help.

Instead of arguing with myself throughout the weekend, I committed to streaming instead. When I wasn't doing schoolwork, I was online, entertaining strangers who'd never see past my tailormade persona and username. In the eyes of my followers, I was the always happy and excitable Chai. I loved it. Being her was the best decision I could've made.

Mid popped in and out of the stream a few times to take care of some moderator duties. He didn't say much and still hadn't addressed my question about meeting sooner than later. I felt awkward about interacting so didn't reference him by name out loud. Ignoring him was far easier than ignoring Finn. Oh the joys of the Internet.

On hour five of the stream, I finally decided to step away and tackle a few chores.

"I'll be back online later tonight," I told everyone. "Need to adult for a bit. Stretching my legs is probably healthy, too."

My laundry bin was overflowing, so I used a garbage bag to carry the excess. Before opening my door, I listened for voices on the other side. It was an unusually quiet day in our house. Normally by this time, the guys were in the living room arguing about which TV show they were going to watch on the flat screen.

When I opened the door, my hand lingered on the knob. Seeing Finn's gift every day made me feel ten times worse for avoiding him. The thoughtfulness in the gesture was something I never expected. He'd been so nervous when presenting it to me, too, which made the moment sweeter.

I shoved down my emotions and willed myself to stay on task. As I tiptoed out of my room, I noticed Sam asleep on the couch. He snored softly with an arm over his eyes. I focused on being extra quiet as I made my way through the kitchen and into the laundry area.

I pulled out my cheap detergent and started separating my clothes. My mom used to get on me if I didn't separate my delicates. She enjoyed keeping things as nice as possible since we couldn't afford to replace items on the regular. I hummed to myself as I separated, remembering a tune she taught me when I was six years old. I needed to read her email soon. And visit her. I dreaded both, but it had to be done. Maybe a weight would lift if I got it over with?

My car was currently in the shop so I'd have to take the bus to the cemetery. I tried to map out the route in my head. At one point, I could recite every bus stop in the county. Mom worked late nights, so it was vital I knew how to get around on my own. I hadn't ridden public transport in ages, though, so my memory about the best routes was fuzzy. I got so distracted trying to figure out if it was the number seven or eight bus I needed to catch on Elden Street, I didn't notice I was no longer alone.

Finn lowered two sacks of clothes, pausing at the door. When I looked up, he pulled out one of his earbuds. My stomach flipped at the sight of him. Despite my embarrassment, I felt a genuine smile appear on my face. His response was a polite, curt nod.

I know he insisted he wasn't shy, but his similarities with Celeste were uncanny. I hate that I judged him for it when we first met.

"Need to get by?" I asked with a little extra energy in my tone. I wasn't okay, but I was addicted to pretending I was. I knew that if I smiled enough, I could trick my body into thinking everything was fine. It always worked if I waited long enough.

Finn looked like he was about to refuse but nodded instead. "Yeah...thanks."

"Of course." I pressed against the washer, trying to make myself as flat as possible.

Finn grabbed both bags, one in each hand. His muscles flexed as he lifted them. I turned my gaze forward so I wouldn't stare.

The laundry room was more of a closet, added on by the Ables as an afterthought. Thankfully, there were two washers and dryers, so the guys and I rarely waited for a turn. But we were starting to find ourselves in traffic jams—like now.

Because Finn was such a large person, flattening myself against the washer did little. He avoided knocking me with his laundry bags but wasn't as fortunate with his body.

A spark ran down my spine when his hip brushed mine. I chewed on my bottom lip, recalling how solid he felt kissing me against the wall. Finn cleared his throat once he got through and remained quiet as he unloaded his bag.

"So..." I scratched at my cheek as nerves bubbled in my stomach. One of us needed to rip off this band aid. Might as well be me since I caused this. "I was thinking about my promise."

Finn paused for a second. "Your promise?"

God, why did his voice have to sound so deep? And why was his cluelessness so attractive? Couldn't he be average? Boring, even? What I'd give for a boring roommate.

"You've already forgotten?" I asked, trying to keep my tone teasing. "I promised to find something that makes you smile."

He stared at me like he was searching for something specific. I shifted my weight from one foot to the other. I wondered if he practiced this dark look. It felt like he was glaring into my soul.

"I didn't forget," Finn said, finally. He tossed a detergent pod into the washer and turned it on. The water started drowning out some of his words as he said, "You've just seemed a bit—"

"Alright, party people! Gather round for the rules of the night!" Lincoln called from the living room. I heard Sam's loud protest over the noise of the washers. Finn looked unimpressed with the interruption.

"We could pretend we're not here," I sounded like I was joking but I truly wanted us to stay. "So, you can finish whatever it was you were about to say."

Finn shook his head. "It was nothing. We should go. He's going to keep calling until we answer."

My shoulders sagged, but I nodded in agreement. Finn picked up his bags. He nudged his chin toward the door, wanting me to exit first.

When we entered the living room, we found Lincoln standing in the middle of the space, looking giddy as all get out. Sam was glaring at him through half-closed eyes. He pulled a pillow over his face when he saw us enter the room, as if he couldn't take seeing any more people.

Henrik stood behind one of the couches. He looked up when he saw Finn and me exiting the laundry room. He gave us a smile that seemed to make Finn stiffen. I raised a brow, wondering what unspoken communication had exchanged between them.

"Must we do this now?" Sam said, voice muffled by the pillow.

"We're four hours away from this place being crowded with locals, so yes." Lincoln walked over to pull the pillow away from Sam. He earned himself a burning scowl.

"Locals?" Henrik asked.

"Yeah, they're more fun," Lincoln explained with a grin.

"You guys are having a party...tonight? It's a Sunday," I said as I scanned the room. How much damage would a party set this place back? Just yesterday, I got the kitchen floor literally sparkling—Henrik took photos and everything. But after tonight, I'd probably be scrubbing Cheeto dust out of the couch cushions into next week.

"What's wrong with Sunday?" Lincoln asked.

I shrugged. "Nothing. It's just, no one wants to wake up hungover and have to sit through a two-hour lecture."

"Well, that's why I've invited mostly locals." Lincoln beamed like he'd fixed the problem easily. "And the rest of the hockey team, of course. Because they're not complainers...unlike present company." His gaze landed on Sam, who rolled his eyes in response.

I laughed. "Okay, well, I'm sure non-students don't want to roll out of bed and into their nine to five hungover either. Everyone has a version of Monday responsibility."

"Agreed," Sam said around a yawn as he stretched out. "And why do you keep saying locals like they're some mystic beings? You just went down to the bar and told that hot server to bring her roommates, didn't you?"

"Why are you guys acting like this isn't a thing we all can enjoy?" Lincoln asked. "We go through the same thing every year. Except this year, *we're* in charge of keeping the tradition strong. Go Mendell Hawks and all that shit."

"And all that shit, yes," Henrik teased.

Lincoln didn't seem phased at the exorbitant lack of enthusiasm in the room. He was still smiling from ear to ear with excitement. I commended him for it and would've joined in if I didn't have skin in the game.

"Guys, I promise you, it's going to be great. We have a fucking pool. A beautiful maid..." Lincoln's voice faded when I gave him a look. He quickly corrected himself. "Who's going to act as our guest of honor, of course. No serving drinks unless she wants to."

I pretended to think about it. "Hmm. Yeah, I don't want to."

Lincoln held up his hands. "Fair enough. I'll serve drinks."

"What does the guest of honor get?" I probed.

"Honor?" Lincoln shrugged. "What else is there?"

Sam scoffed. "We're giving him shit because we're tired, but the party will actually be fun, Naomi. Beginning of season parties are a Mendell tradition. You should stick around. We promise to give you more than honor."

"Lincoln streaked last year. So, you might get your retinas burned out." Henrik sighed at the memory. "But, other than that, the company was decent. The rest of the guys on the team are more well-behaved than these geniuses."

"It was a truth or dare," Lincoln defended. "Everyone knows truth is for cowards. I'm no coward."

Sam pointed at him. "Remember that later. You guys heard that, right?"

Henrik wore a mischievous grin. "I won't forget it."

I smiled, warming up a little to the idea of seeing these guys let loose. I believed that to really know a person, you had to see them drunk. Which is why I turned to Finn, ready to ask if he'd be joining. I could tell by the pained look on his face the answer would be a no.

"You're not coming?" I asked, trying to keep my voice low so the guys wouldn't overhear. Lincoln had ears like a hawk, though.

"What? Of course, he's coming." Lincoln threw his arm over Finn's shoulders. "He's guest of honor number two. The main reason I volunteered to host the first party of the semester. We're celebrating his recovery."

Finn shook his head but didn't protest out loud.

"Recovery?" My interest was piqued. "From what?"

Lincoln looked at Finn like he wanted permission. Finn didn't protest him sharing the information.

"He got in a pretty rough fight last year," Lincoln explained, sobering a little. "Was in the hospital for a while. But now he's back. Ready to reclaim his spot at the top, right?"

Finn nodded and made a small noise of affirmation. I raised a brow, surprised. I opened my mouth to question, but Lincoln was over the sidebar. He wanted us to get into action.

"Sam, you're on pool duty. The cold will help you stay awake," Lincoln directed.

Sam sighed. "No promises about the awake thing. But, I'll scoop out as many leaves as possible before then," he murmured as he got up.

"The net's in the shed," I called after him. He flashed me a peace sign before disappearing out the sliding door that lead to the backyard.

"Henny and Finny are on snack run duty," Lincoln instructed.

"Actually," Henrik interrupted with a raised hand. "I have a thing."

Lincoln's smile fell. "A thing?"

Henrik gave Lincoln a wink. "Yeah. A thing."

Lincoln wasn't charmed in the slightest. "Okay. How long is your thing?"

Henrik shrugged. "Twenty-three or thirty-four."

"What is that? Minutes? Hours? Miles? Brunch orders?"

"Bunch orders?" I asked under my breath.

"It's one of their many things," Finn whispered. His voice made my heart flutter. I hadn't realized how close he was standing. "Don't ask, you don't want to know."

"Maybe forty-seven." Henrik shrugged.

Lincoln gave him a disbelieving look. "Fine. Whatever. Just don't be late. This is supposed to be a bonding opportunity for everyone."

"I will be home in time for bonding," Henrik promised. He smiled at Finn and me before exiting the room.

"Alright, that leaves you two for snacks…" Lincoln twisted his mouth to the side when his gaze fell on Finn and me. "I would go too, but I have to see a guy about a rooster and another guy about some brownies. So, you good?"

Translation, did Finn want to spend that amount of time with me? The closest grocery store was a twenty-five-minute drive with decent traffic.

Finn nodded. "Yeah. I can do that. Is that okay with you?"

They both looked at me. Lincoln with praying hands and Finn with a tight jaw. I suppose I could push off my stream for an hour or so. It would be healthy for me to participate in an offline activity. And maybe work on breaking apart the ice with Finn.

"Give me a second to grab a jacket?" I asked Finn.

"Of course," he said with a—I dare say—almost smile? I grinned up at him because I was getting closer to that moment. I could feel it in my bones.

Chapter Twenty-Three

Finn

N aomi wouldn't let me touch the shopping cart until she wiped it clean. She was a stickler for disinfectant. I watched her hurry around the cart, scrubbing the steel with a wet wipe. The air smelt of alcohol and lime by the time she was finished. Her wipes were homemade and she seemed excited about how well they cleaned. I loved the pleased smile on her lips when she finished. She looked so satisfied.

"Sorry about that. I only get like this when I'm grocery shopping." She glanced in my direction, looking a little sheepish. "I go a little overboard but...well, this entire process makes me uncomfortable. So many surfaces and so little wipes, you know?"

"Why didn't you say before? I could've come alone." I grabbed the cart's handlebars and started toward the grocery store's entrance. The place was crowded today. It'd probably take us an hour to get out of here with how long the checkout lines were. On a typical day, that would've annoyed the shit out of me. Today, it felt like a small win. Longer lines meant more time with Naomi. It gave me more chances to see if our kiss was a step in the right or wrong direction.

She'd been avoiding me for the past week. I think. I couldn't be sure because I'd been doing the same. The longer I held off, the longer I had to make sure my confession to her was perfect. It gave me too much time to ruminate on every decision I'd made up to this point.

"No one should have to go to this store alone. It's chaos incarnate." Naomi stayed close to my side. She grabbed hold of the cart too, placing one hand next to mine. I glanced down, enjoying the closeness. I don't think her helping me steer was a conscious decision. Naomi seemed too taken with fruit displays and signs for clearance items to notice her grip on the steel bar.

"Ooh, should we get some gluten-free options?" She pointed down one aisle. "Any of your teammates have intolerances?"

I shrugged. "Probably. I don't know."

"Let's do it. It can't hurt." She guided me down the aisle. As we walked, she rambled about her favorite gluten-free and dairy-free snacks. I listened, staying quiet as she talked. No matter what Naomi talked about, it'd be a shame to interrupt. She could give a five-hour lecture on the rise of lactose intolerances, and I'd happily give her my full attention. Listening to her talk on stream didn't hold a candle to hearing her in person.

"Of course, we'll get some of these as well." Naomi grabbed a few boxes of my favorite brand of cookies. "Can't forget the Sun Chips either. Garden salsa, right?"

I raised a brow. "Yeah, that's right...I'm surprised you remembered. The guys still think I like Chex Mix."

Naomi smiled. I might've imagined it, but I may have caught a bit of shyness in her eyes. She turned away before I could confirm.

We continued down the aisle. Naomi did most of the picking while I nodded in agreement. Eventually, I worked up the courage to ask,

"Would you be interested in coming to our game next week? It's the first of the season and it'd be nice to have you rooting for us in the stands."

Her eyes lit up. She rejoined me at the cart and it took every ounce of my willpower to not cup her cheek and taste her sweet lips. Her hand claimed space on the handlebar again and the outer edge of her palm touched mine.

We'd kissed for heaven's sake, but just that light touch was more than enough to make me lose focus.

"I'd love to," she said. "I still won't know what the hell's going on. You've all been so patient trying to teach me, but it doesn't stick. It's probably better if I experience it firsthand for myself. Maybe I should watch a documentary or something to prep? Understanding the history of something always provides a solid base."

I watched her tap her bottom lip with her index finger as she considered.

"The history of hockey is interesting but prerequisites aren't necessary to enjoy the game," I assured.

"Prereqs don't bother me. I like going the extra mile. It's why I'm good at trivia. I collect random facts about things I have no need for."

The determined look on her face made me want to kiss the wrinkle off her brow. I could practically see her wheels turning, fitting yet another thing in her jam-packed schedule.

"You don't have to study hardcore or anything," I said, hoping she wouldn't spread herself thin.

Naomi waved her hand. "I know it's not vital, but I want to learn. When I meet someone new and they're into something I know nothing about, I try to learn as much as possible. Especially if said person loves it. You love hockey. I find it helps speed up the process of getting to know someone if you understand the things they love."

I froze. That was probably the kindest thing I've heard anyone say. Naomi continued, not even noticing how touched I felt by her interest.

"If you're open to sharing, I'd like to know more about what you love, too," I said.

She stopped scanning the shelves for party-size bags of chips. "Oh...um..."

"Was that the wrong thing to say?"

"No, no. I just wasn't expecting it."

"Why wouldn't I be curious about the things you love?"

"I don't know. Usually, I'm the one with all the questions. With most friendships or relationships, by the way. I come up with the topics or plan the time we spend together."

My forehead wrinkled in disapproval. "So, you're used to people not reciprocating? Not remembering your favorite brand of chips or researching your interests."

She let out a guarded laugh. "I suppose."

"Sounds like you've been hanging around the wrong people," I said.

"I don't know. Everyone has a role, right? It's like you and the guys."

"How so?"

We'd stopped walking down the aisle at this point. There were only a handful of people on the other end, so neither of us felt self-conscious about getting in the way of more active shoppers.

"Lincoln's the energy. If not for him, you guys would probably spend most of your weekends at home. Sam keeps you guys on track and accountable. Henrik's the realist. He's honest and doesn't let anyone forget who they are."

I nodded in agreement. "And me?"

She smiled. "You're the grump who reminds everyone to think for themselves."

"Sounds like I'm a riot," I joked.

She laughed. "You're not, but there's nothing wrong with that. I've never met someone like you. That's why I'm excited to know more."

She released a sigh. It was barely audible and sounded like she'd been holding it for a while.

I leaned close, and she followed my lead. My fingers brushed across the back of her palm. She made a small hum of approval when my lips hovered mere inches from hers. I hadn't planned on doing this again until we talked about everything. Until we talked about who I really was and what I wanted and what that meant for us. But, when our mouths touched, I was a goner. The awkwardness that lingered from days of avoiding one another washed away. We kissed one another like our time was running out, and maybe it was. Maybe this was all I'd ever get—small, stolen moments. My stomach twisted at the thought because it wasn't enough.

"Um, excuse me?" a small girl interrupted us. Naomi pulled away from me in a flash. I swallowed an annoyed groan.

"Sorry, yes?" Naomi's voice sounded high as she smiled down at our interruption. The kid couldn't be any older than seven.

"Can you get that for me?" She pointed at a pack of sugary cereal on a top shelf behind us.

I grabbed the box. "There you go."

She pointed to another box. "And that one, too."

Okay...

I reached for her next request. When she gestured to a third box, I couldn't help but ask, "You sure your folks want you to have all this sugar?"

Her cheeks went red, and her lips spread in an amused grin as she accepted the last box. "No, but I cry, so they give it to me."

I raised a brow and Naomi burst into laughter as the girl giggled. We watched the mini master manipulator skip on her merry way.

"Unbelievable," I muttered.

Naomi was still laughing as she said, "Come on. We probably need to speed this up. Those check-out lines are only going to get longer the later it gets."

I nodded, ruefully agreeing. Naomi didn't seem interested in circling back to the position we'd been in before. She even moved to the front of the cart now. She still rambled but kept her distance, so we weren't close enough to touch again. I listened, doing my best not to convince her to abandon this shopping trip altogether. Tonight was the night. She needed to know about Mid and I needed to show her I could be so much more than just a grump.

"There you are." Henrik had slipped back into the house unnoticed. "Ready to practice?"

I'd secluded myself in a corner of the living room. The music was too loud, thanks to Sam's speakers. The house was too crowded, thanks to Lincoln's flexible invitation list. There were more than locals here. Everyone and their mother seemed crammed into the house. We'd taped off the upstairs with strips of Christmas wrapping paper Naomi found in the garage. That seemed to keep people off the second floor for a few minutes. But, from my position, I could see someone broke through. The wrapping paper was now discarded and trampled under the foot traffic.

Henrik sensed my mood and gestured to my cup. "You should get something stronger than that. You only like parties when you're drunk."

"Figured." I nodded and took another sip of my cranberry ginger ale. I'd asked for a cup when Naomi explained it was her favorite flavor. It wasn't too bad, but Henrik was right. I'd need more of a kick if I was to survive the night.

"It also might help if you talk to her." Henrik leaned in to whisper that part. I stiffened and he patted my shoulder. "She seems to work wonders on improving your mood."

"We've spoken. I'm just giving her some space now."

"Really? Seems like you've been avoiding one another. But what do I know?"

I scowled. After our shopping trip, I expected things would go back to normal. Our normal, at least.

My gaze strayed toward Naomi. She leaned on the kitchen island, listening to something Lincoln was saying. I watched them interact, getting jealous of how easily it looked for the two of them. Lincoln never second-guessed, moving close to her. He did this with all women and used space as a game. He touched her arm or tugged on her sleeve to get and maintain her attention. My grip tightened around my glass when he played with one of her curls at one point. He wrapped the black spiral around his finger, and she didn't seem to mind in the slightest.

How the hell did he do that without feeling an intense emotional connection? Just standing next to her felt paramount to me.

"He's doing what he does best," Henrik said in a voice meant to calm me. "You know it's nothing serious. Link knows you like her."

"His best is pissing me off," I mumbled. It wasn't the flirting. Naomi wasn't mine. She could flirt with whoever she wanted. It was the ease of their interaction. How he made her laugh until she cried. I wanted to be able to do that.

Henrik nudged me toward the glass sliding door that led to the back of the house.

"Come on," he said. "I know a place where you can practice, and we won't be disturbed."

I followed him to the backyard, where fewer people were milling about around the pool. Sam had done a nice job of cleaning out the water. I figured out how to heat the pool, so a few people sat with their feet dipped in the warm water. When we passed by some of our teammates, they stopped us to say 'hi.' A few looked at me like they were waiting for something to happen. I stayed quiet, silently willing Henrik to finish up his small talk.

Most of the group was made up of freshmen and sophomores. I recognized Jack Whitfield amongst them. Like me, he didn't look happy to be here. But he looked even more unhappy when he laid eyes on me. Something about my silence seemed to offend him on a personal level.

His tone was icy when he said, "Must be a rough year for you, Howard. Lost a fight and a spot on the ice. I've been wondering why you bothered coming back at all. Not much left for you here."

I shrugged, trying not to read too much into his words. "I think there's plenty left."

He raised his brow, disagreeing. "That so? Stoll doesn't seem to think so."

"Who gives a fuck about what Stoll thinks?" one guy said. He had brown skin and long, dark hair that almost reached the middle of his back.

Jack frowned. "You'd be an idiot not to."

"Stoll's just one of many factors in contributing to your hockey career," Henrik said. I kept my gaze locked with Jack, confused about why he looked so pissed and and wanted to say more.

"Anyway, we'll see you guys later." Henrik continued our journey. I gave Jack one last glance over before following my friend.

"You know what that was about?" I asked once we were out of earshot.

"Nope. And I don't care either." Henrik glanced over his shoulder to look at me. "I'm not fond of department rumors. Gets in the way of what matters."

I nodded. Normally, I'd agree. But for some reason, I couldn't shake the feeling I was supposed to know more. It wasn't just because of Jack. Sam had my phone and still wouldn't tell me what he was looking for.

As I pondered, Henrik led me out the wooden gate surrounding the backyard. I snapped back to the present when he continued to the small patch of forest behind the house. If not for his pale skin, the night would have enveloped him like a long, lost friend.

"Where are we going?" I asked, pausing at the edge of the forest.

"It's not far," he promised.

I frowned at his non-answer.

Henrik laughed. "Come on. It'll be worth it."

Chapter Twenty-Four

Finn

Henrik knew exactly where to move on the unpaved path. As we made our way through, I did my best to step wherever he did to avoid tripping. When we emerged from the overgrown trail, I saw a clearing and the edge of a cliff in front of us. There were wooden benches with peeling paint and chipped sides, facing the view of the city. I could see Mendell's campus from here. The shining lights of the science building, the constant warm glow of the hockey arena. Even the broken campus clock tower wrapped in ivy was visible.

Henrik took a seat on the least grimy bench

"Whoa," I breathed, still standing to take in the city.

Henrik nodded in agreement. "I'll say."

"I didn't even know this was back here." I glanced around, taking in the forest at our back. The outside world felt far away. "I didn't know we were this close to a cliff."

Henrik leaned back, relaxing his shoulders. "Neither did I until last week when I needed some air. It's been my getaway spot."

We sat in silence, listening to the muffled sounds of the city below us and the party behind. My mind got a rare chance to quiet down. The stillness helped my ever-pinching muscles relax for a moment.

"So, let's hear this speech. I've been dying of curiosity," Henrik teased. "Don't worry, though. I've been mum about it."

I took a breath and turned to him. "I appreciate it. That's why I wanted it to be you. Before I start, you need some context."

Henrik nodded and crossed his arms over his chest. "All ears."

I cleared my throat. "This isn't something I like talking about much. I've kept it to myself for a lot of reasons."

He raised a brow, looking a bit worried.

"I haven't exactly been honest about what I remember. Or who I remember, after the accident."

Henrik nodded for me to continue.

"Basically, I'm not Finn from last year and I don't think I will be ever again." Something about saying that out loud lifted a weight off my chest. The more I spoke, the easier it was for the words to come. "At first, I pretended because I felt bad for not being him. Whenever I looked at people who knew me, I'd get this expectancy in return. You were all waiting for someone who'll never come back. It doesn't seem fair, but I need to start being honest."

"You don't remember anything?"

I couldn't make out the tone of his voice, and it filled my stomach with dread. "No. I've tried to look at old photos, read old emails, and listen to stories."

Nothing worked. And I was tired of chasing a ghost. Tonight, I ended it. It started here and would continue with Naomi.

"Maybe one day it'll all come back in a miraculous flood of realization. But I'm not counting on it. I want to make new memories, not hope for the old ones."

Henrik leaned forward, placing his elbows on his knees. "That's a lot to go through on your own, Finn. We've been treating you like nothing changed because we thought you were better."

"I am better. But I..."

"Feel like we're strangers," Henrik finished. "We kind of are."

"More or less. You're great people, and I still want to be your friend. But I can't pretend for the rest of my life, you know? I can't be him." I winced. "I understand if you all decide it's too weird to hang out or whatnot. After all, if you're strangers to me, I'm also a stranger to you."

He surprised me by chuckling. There was an understanding in his eyes that brought me relief.

"Finn, it's fine. Sucks like hell, but it's okay. We don't care what you remember. Stranger or not, I think some part of you is still there. Whether you end up remembering or not, you're still our friend. We still care about you."

"Thanks. I didn't realize how much I needed to hear that." I'd been terrified of losing Naomi. But now that I was talking to Henrik, I realized a large part of me would be devastated to lose the guys, too. Each day that went by, I felt more like a part of their circle. They accepted my moodiness and gave me space without asking for anything in return.

"Now that I know you don't remember, I feel like I should tell you something about our relationship," Henrik said.

I nodded, intrigued to gain extra insight.

"Like I said before, we were never as close as you were with Lincoln and Sam. Mainly because when we first met, you thought I was a thief. I was...that's a long story. The point is, you and I didn't start off on the right foot."

I let out an amused huff when he laughed.

"We did bond one summer, though. You helped me come out as pansexual to my folks." Henrik broke apart a fallen leaf as he spoke. He seemed a little anxious to have to tell the story again. "They didn't take it too well. So, you took me on a road trip to distract me. We got stranded because you didn't have an extra tire for the van."

I snorted. "That doesn't sound like me."

"Eh, it was back then. You were forgetful. Ironic, I suppose." He shrugged with a chuckle. "We got into a heated argument. By the time we got back home, we didn't speak for months. The guys kept trying to patch things over."

"To no avail?"

"Nope," he confirmed. "We got over it on our own. We always do. I've been surprised you haven't jumped down my throat recently. Now that I know why, I sort of miss it."

"Do you really? If I were you, I'd love the break."

Henrik shook his head. "Nah. But I guess this is a case of you don't know what you've got until it's gone."

My shoulders sagged. Sadness clung to my bones like a second skin.

"So, is this the speech you want to tell the guys?" Henrik asked.

I shook my head, trying to brush off the feelings of loss. "No. I want to talk to Naomi first. Before all this, I knew her. We met online and we were supposed to meet in person."

Henrik straightened. "You knew Naomi before this? Wait, was that the girl you were going to see after the game? The one you missed the party for?"

"It's her."

"Holy shit. Small world."

"Yeah, except she still doesn't know it's me."

Henrik's eyes widened. "Wait, please don't tell me you've still been messaging her."

When I was quiet, Henrik let out a disbelieving laugh.

"Well, damn. That's a misuse of trust," he said.

"Be a little more honest, why don't you?" I joked.

"Look, you came to me because you wanted no bullshit. Finn, you've been sitting on this for way too long. It's ridiculous."

I ran my hands through my hair. "I've been working on it. Working through everything. It's all been so overwhelming."

"Time to stop working and start doing, man. I understand you've gone through a lot, but at a certain point, your accident isn't an excuse."

"I know. It's... happening tonight. I'm pulling her aside tonight and telling her everything."

He seemed to approve of my decision. "Perfect. Let's hear it. What do you have to say to the girl of your dreams who you've been lying to for months now?"

I frowned. "Laying it on isn't necessary, Hen. I do that enough on my own."

"I think you need a hardass on the outside, too," he informed. "You like this girl, so fucking tell her. Let the chips fall where they may and move on."

I blew out a breath and tilted my head to the sky. God, he was right. It hurt to hear my inner monologue spoken out loud through someone else's words. Was this why we didn't get on in the past? We thought the same things, but he didn't hesitate to say them out loud.

"Come on. I'll pretend to be her." Henrik gestured for me to talk. "You should probably practice groveling. You do know how to grovel, right?"

I gave him a look. "I think I can figure it out."

He grinned at my dark mood. "We'll figure it out together. Good thing Lincoln likes long parties because I think we're going to be here for a while."

"You got this." Henrik gave my shoulder a quick squeeze as we re-entered the house.

I scratched the back of my head, anxious to find Naomi. This was as close to ready as I'd ever get.

The house was more packed than earlier. Almost everyone was gathered around the coffee table in the living room. Guys were on one end, girls on the other. There seemed to be a competition going on. Aderyn, a girl with an impressive set of muscles, challenged the guys to arm wrestling. And from the looks of it, she was winning.

Naomi was close by, eyes dancing with amusement as she watched one of the freshmen from my team get his ass handed to him. The girls cheered for their champion while the guys grumbled in defeat.

"Hey," I said once I made my way to her side.

Naomi turned to me with a wide smile. "Oh, my god. Have you met Aderyn? I didn't even know we had a women's hockey team until now."

I glanced back at Aderyn, who was gearing up for her next challenger. She and the other girls on the hockey team would occasionally scrimmage with us. I'd only spoken to her a handful of times in the weight room. She was tough as nails and easy to talk to. Even though she could crush egos, most of the guys enjoyed it when she came around.

"I have. She's cool," I said.

Naomi nodded. "I'll say. She almost convinced me to join the team."

When I gave her a questioning look, she held up her hand and added, "Keyword being almost."

"I could have you ready for tryouts."

She snorted. "I'm sure you could."

We looked up when another guy groaned in defeat. Aderyn accepted high fives from both sides of the room.

"You should take a turn," Naomi teased and poked her elbow in my side.

"Later," I said. "I need to talk to you."

She raised a brow, her smile fading. "Is everything okay?"

"Everything's fine. Can we go somewhere quiet?"

Naomi's eyes strayed back to the crowd. Lincoln was taking his turn against Aderyn.

"Of course," she said. We both started out of the room as the two began their match.

"Front porch okay?" she asked as we walked down the hall. There was an unmissable shakiness in her voice.

I shook my head. There was too much risk of being interrupted. I needed time to say my speech. Who knew how long my courage would linger?

"Follow me?" I started up the stairs, and she trailed behind.

Naomi's eyes went big when I welcomed her into my room. She didn't say anything when I closed the door behind us. I lingered at the door to take a deep breath. This felt like do or die. I either lose her forever or got the chance to be something more.

In the silence, Naomi looked around my room. She scratched at her arm as she took the surroundings in. The last time she was in here, she'd seen me naked. I pushed away the thought because that was not the kind of distraction I needed right now.

"Naomi—"

"Finn," she said at the same time.

My jaw tightened at how she let out a sigh. "What's wrong?"

"Nothing. I-I think I know what you're going to say," she explained.

"Really?" My heart pounded. Her knowing what I was about to confess seemed unlikely. Unless she somehow discovered I was Mid. But how? Sam had my phone, so she didn't accidentally see a text thread there. I hadn't told anyone about moderating for her. And Lincoln only called me by my username once.

My mind raced with possibilities as she continued, "Yeah. This is about our kiss."

I swallowed. "Well, in part."

She closed her eyes for a second. "I didn't mean to avoid you...well, no, I did. What I wanted to say was, I didn't mean to come off as rude. I needed some time to consider what it meant for us."

"I get it. Trust me." I stepped closer to her but kept my hands stuffed in my pockets to maintain control. "I was doing the same thing."

"You were?"

I nodded. "I thought you were regretting it and I needed space to deal with that regret."

Naomi shook her head. "No, I don't regret it. I'd never regret it."

Some of the knots in my stomach untangled. "That's good to hear."

"Just so we're clear, not only did I enjoy the kiss, but I would also like to do it more with you." She picked at a loose thread on her shirt as she spoke. Her eyes remained on mine, and I could see her nervousness. "But you should know something before we move forward."

"Naomi—"

"I like you and I probably shouldn't," she said. "Because honestly, you're scary sometimes."

I winced. "I scare you?"

"Not in an 'I'm fearing for my life' kind of way. But I thought you hated me for a good while. After you kissed me, I wasn't sure if you felt like I did." She wrung her fingers. Her gaze flickered away at the last words. God, she was sweet.

"But I do have some baggage," she continued in a whisper. "I feel like you should be aware."

"Everyone does," I assured.

"Yeah." She laughed a little. "But mine includes this thing with a guy I haven't met before. I like him. Like a lot and I don't know what to do about it. It's only right that you know and understand. Whatever's between you and me I want to give it a proper shot. But I need to get some closure with him."

I swallowed because that was the most perfect opening one could ask for. When I opened my mouth to speak, Naomi continued,

"It's never my intention to string someone along. I'd understand if you would prefer to wait until I figured my stuff out before pursuing a relationship. Or maybe not wait and move on."

"I don't—"

"But I do need you to know that I'm serious about you." She looked determined. "I'm not going to avoid you again—"

"Naomi..." I held up my hand. She frowned at the suddenness of my words. "Sorry. I've been trying to tell you something. To confess. And the longer it takes, the more nervous I get."

"Oh, jeez, I'm talking your ear off. Great impression on a potential partner, I'm sure. Never letting you get a word in edgewise," she said, sarcastically as she closed one eye in embarrassment.

"You're fine. And if anyone could be the perfect partner, it'd be you."

"Well..." Her voice went high-pitched.

"You would be." My fingernails dug into my palm as I confessed, "I wish I'd been able to meet you that night. Then I could prove it to you for sure. That was supposed to be our beginning."

Naomi frowned. "Excuse me?"

I forced myself to march forward. There was no taking this back now. "You were nervous as hell. I'm sure I was too; I just didn't say it in the message thread. I was probably trying to be brave for you or some macho shit like that."

I wasn't supposed to curse during this confession. Henrik had stressed that part, but when I was nervous, it slipped out. I hoped she wouldn't hold it against me.

Naomi crossed her arms over her chest. "Finn, I'm confused."

"Last year, you and I were going on our first date. We still only knew each other as Chai and MidQuest. We agreed to keep it that way until we came face-to-face."

She stared blankly at me for what felt like ages before finally pointing at me. "You're MidQuest?"

I nodded, my jaw tight with fear.

She touched her chest. "My MidQuest?"

Despite still panicking, my heart warmed at the use of her possessive. "Yes, Naomi. Your MidQuest."

Chapter Twenty-Five

Naomi

My throat tightened. I stared at Finn, trying to piece together his words. A thousand questions flooded my brain, all overlapping so quickly that I didn't know where to start.

"Do you need space?" He moved away from the door, indicating I could leave if I wanted. "Time? Something to drink?"

I shook my head, still speechless as I battled with conflicting emotions. Finn stared, waiting for an answer I couldn't yet voice. He'd never looked so nervous. Stoicism had never been so far away. I felt bad for leaving him hanging but couldn't get my mouth to work.

"After the accident," he tried to continue in a shaky tone. "When I stopped responding, I was in the hospital, asleep for days because of a brain injury."

I nodded. MidQuest told me that much. Nothing too detailed. He said there was an accident, and he'd been unconscious. I didn't push him because it didn't feel like my place. Going through it once seemed traumatizing enough.

"When I woke up, I didn't remember anything about my life. Everything was gone." He cleared his throat, struggling to continue. "Since then, I've recovered a little. Nothing of true substance. Just things to do with feelings and muscle memory."

"You didn't remember me?" I asked in a low voice. "Anything about us?"

"No." His shoulders sagged. "My family tried to restore my phone and got most of the old apps back. I had the history of our chat. Our thread was saved, and I read through it to catch up. I watched some of the old streams hoping they would trigger memories. Nothing came of it though."

"So, you've been pretending this whole time?"

"Yes. Sort of. But I wasn't pretending to care about you," he said, quickly. "That part is real. It's never changed, Naomi. I've cared and wanted to tell you in person but, I'm not the guy you first started talking to. I thought I could become him. That's why I didn't want to tell you at first. I needed time to figure out how to be who you wanted. Except, I think that's impossible. He died that night in the parking lot. I can't get him back...and I'm not sure I want to now."

I raised a brow, shocked at the confession and sad at the lonely tone of his voice. "Why not?"

He hesitated for a moment, biting the inside of his cheek as he gathered his thoughts. "Because I'm here now. I've become someone else. And I want a shot at this life. I know this must sound weird and stop me if I'm confusing you."

"Don't stop," I urged him because he needed to say this. And I needed to hear it.

"It's selfish of me, but I feel like I've been given this chance." He blew out a nervous breath. "A do-over where I can be whoever I want. And what I want is to be with you."

My heart pounded against my chest. I could feel my eyes stinging from tears that I tried to blink away.

"You're the first and only person who made me feel safe since I woke up," Finn said. "I was terrified and alone and then I went into your stream and heard your voice and my body reacted. It knew you and trusted you instantly. I couldn't lose you. I know, I might lose you now. You deserved the truth regardless of what I was feeling. I just... needed time to work through everything. If I could take that part back, I would. But I don't regret a single message I've sent. No regrets about our kiss and the time we've spent together. Naomi, I'd never regret a second with you because everything was worth it. Just to see your smile...damn, your fucking smile. Sorry. I'm supposed to keep this clean."

I laughed then. Even though a part of me was still angry, I couldn't help it. "Why?"

He straightened his shoulders, relieved at my calm response. "Henrik recommended I not curse because it could come off as aggressive. And since I've already kept something from you for so long, he thinks it's best I am open and approachable. But you do have a fucking amazing smile. It doesn't feel right not to use stronger language to describe it."

I laughed again because he sounded like Mid. He always had, now that I think back. I didn't want to see the parallels. Didn't want to have to choose and lose one.

"Finn, I hate being lied to," I said, my smile fading. "It's something my mom did to me most of my life."

The color drained from his face. "I understand. It's...unforgivable. I don't expect anything from you, Naomi."

"It's forgivable," my whisper made him look up and met my gaze again. "Depending on the circumstances. The offender. And the right amount of time."

"Is it silly to feel hopeful about those words?"

I shook my head and dared to move closer. "It's not silly. Look, I trusted you. You were my person and when you didn't show up that night, I hadn't felt that alone in a long time."

I paused for a second because the tightening in my throat was back. As I tried to compose myself, Finn kept quiet, listening without looking away.

"And then, you showed back up in my life. But you didn't want to meet. I thought I was fine with it. That I could wait. I kept waiting for something and it felt like it'd never happen. Except you'd been here all along. I'm mad at you for not telling me sooner. I'm angry that you knew how I wanted to meet you but kept your distance. Most of all, I'm sad I couldn't be there for you during your recovery. You were anxious about coming back to school. I've been downstairs this whole time, wondering if I should avoid you for the rest of the semester. If I learned anything from losing my mom, it's that wasting time is the worst feeling. You can't fix that."

Finn pressed his lips together, giving me a solemn nod. I closed the remaining space between us. When I grabbed his hand, his skin felt warm. I brought his palm to my cheek and pressed it against me. His eyes softened with surprise and relief.

"You can't make it up," I whispered.

"I know. I'm sorry, Naomi." He nodded, stroking my cheek. "If I had to go to hell and back, I would. To fix this, I'd do anything."

"You won't do something like this again, will you? Lie to me?"

Finn frowned. "Never," he promised.

I pressed my forehead against his. "Good. You'll get a chance to prove it."

"Will I?" He cupped my other cheek, holding my face with both hands.

"Yes." I gripped his wrist, wanting to keep him close. "I'm not wasting any more of our time. Being with you still scares me and I don't know how much I trust you, but I still want to try. You're too important to me to not try, Finn."

He kissed me then. His lips felt hot and desperate against mine. A kiss wouldn't wipe away the pain, but it got pretty damn close.

Finn parted my lips with determination, trying to show me he meant business. I moaned against his mouth as he bit my bottom lip. When I needed to catch my breath, he moved to kiss other parts of my face. His teeth raked against my neck between licks and sucks. I whispered for him to not stop, and he whispered promises back.

"I'm going to give you everything you need, Naomi." He was out of breath. Finn forced the words against my skin between kisses. Every syllable felt like a tattoo. "Everything you want."

"I want you," I promised through a heavy breath. "Just you, Finn."

He paused, pulling back for a second. My brow furrowed as I met his gaze.

"What is it?" I asked.

"Nothing. You said want me and I couldn't help but think...which version?"

I laughed. "This one. The one in front of me. The one you're becoming. You might not be the same, but these past few months, I fell for you. I want your version."

When he kissed me this time, it was gentler than before. His touch made me feel safe. No, I couldn't give him my complete trust, but we were on the way to it. From how he handled me with such care, I felt like we'd get there one day.

Chapter Twenty-Six

Naomi

Celeste offered to do my makeup.

"It's a re-do date," I said. "So, I kind of want to do the same make-up I had on before."

My friend nodded with a smile. "You got it. I love a good cat-eye."

I sat on the pastel stool in front of her vanity and closed my eyes so she could get to work. This felt like old times. Her room had looked the same since middle school—save for switching out boy band posters with film prints. Celeste loved any and everything feminine and her frilly décor showed it. The air smelled of her trademark lavender candle. As I recounted Finn's confession, she listened with respectful hums.

"What are you thinking?" I asked, opening the eye she hadn't drawn on yet.

"I'm thinking you were quiet for days when he didn't show up the first time." She pulled away a little to look me in the eye. "I've never seen you like that."

I looked down, ashamed of the memory. "I know. But that's not happening again."

Celeste tilted my head back up so she could continue applying the liner. "I hope not."

"It only happened that time because..." I cleared my throat. This needed to be said. It felt like the longer I avoided it, the stronger the feeling got.

"I put so much faith in him and I hadn't done that since my mom, you know?"

Celeste's fingers stopped for a second. "I don't know. Not really."

"Right." I laughed, trying to lighten the mood. "Because I never talk about it."

"But you could." She pulled away again and kneeled in front of me. "You've listened to me complain about my anxiety a billion times. I'm in debt. Let me pay you back."

"Friendship doesn't work like that."

"It doesn't work like how you're going about it either," she argued in a firm tone. "You keep smiling and keep trying to make people happy, not taking yourself into account."

I pressed my lips together, trying to dissect the hardness in her tone. "Does that annoy you?"

It used to make my mom furious. She'd go on rants whenever I was positive on rainy days. But, once true darkness came around, she begged me to help her see the light. I learned how to be happy all the time just in case she needed a pick me up. The best practice I had was being happy for others, too. At this point, it was part habit, part gift, and part curse.

"No, God, no." Celeste shook her head, her features softening. "I'm lucky to have a friend like you. I don't think I would've survived this long if I didn't."

"Don't say that," I whispered as I remembered one of her more difficult patches.

"It's true." She shrugged, not seeming too bothered by the past. "Naomi, I love how you look at any situation and figure out how to shine through it. I've learned so much from you. But I wish you were comfortable enough to be sad and mad sometimes and show it to the people who care about you."

I nodded. "It's...a work in progress."

Celeste gave me a small smile. "I hope so. And I hope you know I'm here if Finn ever tries something like he did last time. Guys are nice and all, but we're going to outlast them. Metaphorically and literally—their life spans don't match ours."

I laughed, and she joined in. She pulled out mascara and gestured for me to look up.

"There you are," Celeste whispered as she pulled away. "Beautiful, as always."

She moved so I could get a good look at myself in the vanity. The acne scarring on my forehead was no more, my cheeks were a deep shade of red, and my lips a perfect nude. I looked like Naomi 2.0.

"It's perfect. Thank you." I grinned at my friend.

She wrapped her arms around my shoulder and pulled me in for a hug. "You're perfect. I just highlighted it. Now, go have the date you deserve. Take my car and call if anything goes wrong and I'll send one of my brothers to rough Finn up. He's not getting away with hurting you this time."

I laughed and hugged her back. "He won't. But thank you. It's comforting to know you have my back."

"Always." She kissed my temple. "Now, go show this guy what he missed the first time around."

A year ago, we wanted to meet halfway between our hometowns. It was an aquarium I used to go to on field trips as a kid. Mid said his school frequented the same place, and we joked about possibly walking past each other when we were kids. It was silly to think about at the time, but now it felt like it could've truly happened.

Finn was waiting for me at the entrance. I made such a big deal about how well he cleaned up that his ears turned red. I don't think I'd ever get over how cute he looked when he was nervous.

He wore black pants and a gray knit long sleeve T-shirt that hugged his form perfectly. His hair was swept out of his face, curling on the end like he used product.

"You look beautiful," he murmured in my ear when we hugged 'hello.' "I have something for you."

I stood still while he placed a small yellow flower behind my ear.

"The rest are back home," he explained. "Didn't want to leave them to wilt in the car."

My smile was so wide that it hurt my cheeks. "Thank you! Um, I'm Naomi."

Finn's eyebrows furrowed as it took him a second to catch on. "Right. And I'm Finn."

He offered me his hand to shake. As soon as I took it, he tugged me closer, so that we were a breath apart. He smelled like mint. There was a spark in his dark eyes reminding me of how much he wanted this. Wanted me. A warm feeling spread across my body.

"It's so nice to meet you, Naomi," he said in a low, honest voice. Then he kissed me.

My stomach jumped. I had not been expecting that this early. I responded instantly, feeling a hot need growing in my belly. We hadn't even made it into the aquarium, and I was ready for the next part of this date.

"A bit forward?" he asked when he pulled back. I could tell he was trying to conjure a look of guilt, but from his firm grip on my waist, it was obvious he didn't feel one ounce of shame. He shouldn't.

I shook my head. "I liked it. I enjoy knowing what people want."

"Noted," he promised with a devious look in his eye.

"What?" I asked, amused.

"Nothing." He kissed me once more, stealing the little oxygen I had left before pulling away again. "Ready to go inside?"

My eyes were still half-closed, and my head felt light as I nodded. I should take this slow and fall with less willingness, but damn, his kisses were addicting. His calm voice made me want to curl up against him and listen to him speak all day.

Finn led the way into the aquarium. We never let go of one another once as we toured the exhibits. I gushed about my favorite animals and rambled random facts. Finn listened intently, asking in-depth questions at all the right places. As I gushed about the sea otters, he nuzzled my neck and whispered,

"They remind me of you."

"Really?" My eyes widened because that was probably the most incredible compliment I'd ever received. "How come?"

"They always look excited and energetic." He glanced at the exhibit, where two scurried across the rocks to dive into the water. "Plus, they do that thing where they massage their cheeks."

"The grooming?"

He hummed and nodded. "You do that sometimes. But I think it's because your cheeks need massaging from all your laughing. It's adorable."

I tried my best to hold a laugh back here so I wouldn't prove his point. But there was no use. "That's the sweetest thing anyone has ever said to me."

Finn pressed a kiss on my forehead. "Want to see my favorite exhibit?"

I nodded, earnest and excited. He led the way up a dimly lit staircase. We passed by a group of kids who were squealing over an albino shark being fed by a diver. Finn glanced back at me with a rare look of excitement in his eyes as we neared the area with a large glass ceiling that looked up into a vibrant tank. The glass curved, showing off the various species existing harmoniously. I spun in a circle to take everything in. It felt like we'd been transported to the bottom of the ocean. The closer we got to the glass, the more a sense of calm set into me.

"I saw this on the map," Finn spoke in his usual quiet tone. I turned to him, making sure I caught every word. "And for some reason, it sparked a memory. I would stand right here..."

He grabbed my hand and led me to a dot on the carpet that indicated this was the center of the room. I smiled when he pressed his hand against my back. He wanted me as close as possible. We tilted our heads up to marvel at the water above.

"Stand right here and wish I had gills," he said while still staring up. "I wanted to swim to the bottom of the ocean so bad to see what was down there."

My hands were on Finn's chest. Instead of taking in the incredible view, I focused on him. Finn was so unlike me in every way. He loved sports and hated talking. Didn't know how to express himself most times. Could spend weeks in his own company. Yet we found one another and bonded. Even after a brain injury, he'd chosen to know me. My heart swelled thinking about it. After everything that happened, he chose me for a second time. I didn't realize how long I'd been staring until Finn squeezed my elbows and asked if I was okay.

"I'm good," I said.

"Is this too boring?" he asked. "The guys thought I should take you to drive go-karts or paintball."

I shook my head. "No, no. I don't want to be anywhere else but here, learning what little Finn wanted to be. A merman, you said?"

"I wanted gills...so, yes, I suppose I wanted to be a merman," he said, hesitantly.

I laughed. "Why are you blushing? There's nothing wrong with wanting to be a merman."

His skin seemed to get two times more red. "I'm not blushing. I don't blush."

"You're brighter than most tomatoes right now," I teased.

"No, I'm not." Finn kissed me as a distraction. I didn't mind it at all. When we pulled away, there was a smile on his face. My eyes widened.

"You know, I can tell when you're blushing, too," he whispered against my lips. "Your eyes get all wide and your skin's hot to the touch."

"Finn," I said, ignoring his statement for something more pressing.

His expression changed into one of concern. "What?"

"You smiled."

He frowned then, which made me laugh. "What do you mean?"

"You smiled at me," I gushed. "For the first time."

"I'm sure it wasn't the first time."

"It was the first time." I wrapped my arms around his neck. He chuckled at my excitement. And there it was again. A beautiful, perfect smile that lit up his entire face. The curve of it revealed a dimple in one cheek. His eyes wrinkled around the edges, revealing the genuine nature of the expression. This smile felt like it was made for me alone.

"You're so silly," he murmured and kissed my cheek.

"And you're so incredible."

Finn shook his head, trying to protest. I did a little dance in his arms and hummed a tune to celebrate the smile. This was momentous. We had to celebrate. Finn didn't agree but still enjoyed my little shimmy. He even stepped back to get a better look. It took a moment for me to realize he wasn't watching because of my silliness. He was blatantly checking me out. My skin warmed at the longing in his eyes.

"What?" I asked, even though I knew exactly what.

"Let's keep moving," he said with a determined look. "See what else there is to see before it's time to go?"

"What's on the agenda after this?" I blinked, trying to look innocent.

"I have a few ideas. We'll workshop them and decide together."

Chapter Twenty-Seven

Finn

I knew I had a long way to go in gaining Naomi's trust. But, she didn't make me feel self-conscious of that, which I loved about her. There were no double-meaning remarks about our friendship online. During our date, she never once made me feel like I needed to be someone else. The pressure in my spine even dulled for a bit when I got to completely relax in her presence.

Naomi hadn't lied when she said she wanted to be with *my version* of who I wanted to be. The acceptance came so easily for her, yet still felt revolutionary. It took every bone in my body to hold back from touching her constantly. I longed for her to know how I felt about her. The only way I knew to show it was physical.

We went to get food after the aquarium. She taught me how to mix three different sauces that took greasy cheese sticks to a whole new level. I couldn't keep my eyes off her the entire time. Any second I got the opportunity, I stole kisses. What she said the night of my confession stuck with me. Time wasted was a horrible loss. I didn't plan on making the same mistake twice.

Naomi dropped off her friend's car at the end of the night. I drove her home and walked her to her bedroom door like it was a proper first date. But, instead of saying goodnight, she welcomed me in.

The guys would be out for the next few hours at a hockey game in the next town over, saying they needed to scope out the competition. I think they wanted to give Naomi and me some space. I was grateful for their thoughtfulness.

She hurried around her room when I crossed the threshold. I watched in amusement as she tried to straighten up wayward clothes and scattered notebooks.

Naomi laughed shyly. "I'm the maid, but my room's a mess."

"You don't have to worry about it," I assured her while lingering near her desk. The old wooden desk held her laptop, a few sets of headphones, her rainbow keyboard, and a mic. I smiled thinking about her streaming in front of the screen. A part of me worried I'd never get to see her face-to-face, and now here I was. I was in her personal space. My stomach twisted a bit at the realization because, yes, I was here, but that also meant I could fuck this up. There was a huge chance I could ruin what we had.

I turned toward a still buzzing Naomi. She was stacking the books on her nightstand. When I got close enough to feel the heat of her body, she turned around.

Her shoulders relaxed when I cupped her cheek. "Hey."

"Hey."

"Everything okay?" She searched my eyes, already attuned to my mood swings.

"I'm kind of freaking out." It felt like growth to admit something like that out loud. Especially to someone I wanted so badly. When she stepped closer, I sighed at the feel of her soft body pressed against me.

"Don't freak out." She brushed her nose against mine. "There's nothing to freak out about."

I made a noise of disagreement and kissed her. She let out a sweet moan against my mouth. The sound made my body buzz with desire. My cock stiffened, more than ready to fuck her until neither of us could think straight.

"Can I show you what I've been dreaming of since we met?" I asked.

"Since Chai and Mid met, or me and you?" Her eyes remained closed as she spoke. I kissed her eyelids and then moved to her nose, mouth, chin, and neck.

"Me and you," I whispered against her perfect skin. She smelled like cinnamon, sweet enough for me to form an instant addiction. I'd fantasized about this moment so many times, but imagination couldn't hold a candle to her flame.

"Sit on the edge of the bed," I told her.

Naomi chewed her lip at my order. She lowered herself onto the white sheets. I kneeled in front of her. My hands wrapped around her waist, tugging her forward so that only half of her ass was on the bed. Her soft hips were like clouds underneath my touch. I did my best not to squeeze too hard. Sometimes, it felt like I didn't know my strength. On the ice, that was a good thing. I could crash, shove, and knock into whomever. Here, I needed to be careful.

I could feel her heart beating as I trailed kisses down her chest. She arched toward me, fingers sinking into my hair. My teeth grazed her nipple over her dress. She let out a pleading whimper that made me leak pre-cum. Shit, I wanted everything from her. Every small sound and furrowed brow. I wanted to hear her scream and feel her scratching at my back as I drove into her. The plan was to make her come as much as physically possible hoping each orgasm was more mind-numbing than the last.

I pulled down her sleeves to expose her breasts. I hadn't realized she'd been braless until now. The sight of her bare breasts made my body ache. The groan that released from my throat sounded so animalistic I thought it might scare her. Naomi wrapped her legs around me in response, indicating there wasn't any fear.

"I want to taste you," I said in a low voice. "Here, first." She shivered when I circled her brown nipples with the tip of my thumb. "Here." I trailed my finger down her belly. "And of course, here. That work for you?" I asked as I grazed my hand between her thighs.

Naomi nodded quickly with excitement when my finger added a minuscule amount of pressure on her clit. I nearly lost it as I felt her soaked panties. She was drenched for me. I could smell the sweetness pooling in her pussy. My mouth watered to get a taste, but I needed to savor this. Who knew if she'd want me again? I was going to make every second count because it could be the last. If I could make Naomi come, I was going to make sure it lasted as long as possible and was too incredible for her to forget. I wanted her to crave me as much as I craved her. I wanted her to long only for me because I'd never get on my knees for anyone other than her. Only her. I'd worship only her.

When I took her nipple in between my lips, she tightened her legs around my waist. Her areolas were large compared to her small breasts. I licked every inch, trying to elicit a reaction from the nerves. As I tended to one breast with my mouth, I used my fingers to play with the other. She was very vocal, whispering 'pleases' and 'thank you's' when I did what she asked. Naomi liked being treated with care. She didn't want twists or pinches. She responded to the softer licks and the vibrations of my moans. I enjoyed every second of showering her breasts with the attention they deserved. They fit in my palm perfectly. I could completely cover one with a single hand.

"You're good at that," she praised as I sucked on her nipple. I looked up to meet her gaze. As our eyes connected, a heavy sigh fell from her lips. I flicked my tongue out, circling it around so she could get a better look at what I was doing. She bit her lip at the sight of me teasing her. If she liked that, then she'd love what I had in store for her.

Her dress slipped down her hips. I followed its lead, kissing my way down her stomach. She had stretch marks on her hips. I traced the marks with my tongue and playfully nipped at the softer parts of her body. I've never seen someone so fucking sexy. Naomi was small on the top and larger further down. I could spend a lifetime exploring her curves and angles and it wouldn't be enough.

"Lift for me, gorgeous," I instructed as I tried to remove the dress completely. Naomi pushed herself up, allowing the dress to fall to the floor. She was in nothing but panties now. The pink cotton was ruined with wetness. I could feel my cock pulsing at the sight.

"Can I see you, too?" she asked.

I nodded. "You can have whatever you want."

She smiled when I removed my shirt. I'd never been the most chiseled guy. Extra fat appeared all over my body. Naomi's eyes widened as she took me in. I chuckled a little at her expression. She looked pleased, and I was glad she enjoyed the sight. I removed my pants but kept my boxers on because I wanted to focus on her now. I could wait. Right now, she needed to come.

"Relax," I whispered as I kissed Naomi's belly. "Lie back and enjoy."

She sighed and remained sitting up straight as she ran her hands through my hair. "I want you to enjoy it, too."

"You don't think I'm going to enjoy the hell out of eating this pussy?" I raised a brow at her. "Of making it mine for the night? Naomi, I'm going to take everything you have to offer me. After that, I'm going to fill you up like you wouldn't imagine. I have so much in store for you."

Naomi's eyes have never been this wide. She had no words. I've never seen her speechless. I chuckled at the sight and decided I kind of liked being on the other end. Now, I was talking her ear off while she listened in awe.

"My cock has wanted you since the night I broke open the bathroom door. It's been torture smelling you every time I take a shower." As I gave my confession, I rubbed tiny circles around her clit. "Fucking torture. I gave in a few times and jacked off in there."

She moaned at my words. "You fucked your fist while thinking of me?"

I nodded. "I imagined your sweet mouth on my tip, sucking me dry."

"What else?" She encouraged while sneaking a hand between us, under my boxers, to grab my cock. I closed my eyes for a second as my head spun, feeling her touch. Her fingers pumped up and down. She used my pre-cum as lube. I had to grip the bedsheets to remain focused. What had we been talking about? My fantasies. Right.

"Me inside you, giving you every inch. Finishing on your ass..." I trailed off when her grip tightened on my shaft and her other hand squeezed my balls. Damn. She knew what she was doing. My ears rang.

"You plan to finish on me?" she asked with a sweet smile.

"If you let me," I said in a thin voice. Naomi's hand job would be the death of me if I didn't put an end to it soon. This was supposed to be about her for now.

"I'm going to let you."

Her mouth found mine. We parted our lips, tongues clashing as she fisted my cock.

"One condition," she said when she pulled back.

"Anything, anything." I was hers. Completely hers. The feeling of utter devotion should have frightened me, but I've never been more thrilled.

"Let me finish on you first," was her request.

Chapter Twenty-Eight

Naomi

I had this fantasy I'd never shared before. I'd felt too embarrassed to explain it to my partners. But after hearing Finn tell me he masturbated in the shower, I felt like he was the perfect person to explore with. He knew me better than any of my past boyfriends. There were so many sides of me only Finn got to see. And so many sides of him he felt comfortable enough to only share with me. We were a haven for one another.

As expected, Finn didn't blink an eye when I pulled my dress back on. I told him to lie on the bed and he followed my instructions.

"Are you comfortable?" I asked. "It might be better without a pillow."

Finn tossed the pillow to the side in a heartbeat. I laughed at the eagerness in his movement.

"Tell me if you want to stop," I reminded him.

"I won't need to." He shook his head and gestured for me to crawl on top of him. "You might not realize this, but there is nothing hotter than having a woman like you want to sit on my face. I keep wondering what I did in my other life to deserve this."

I laughed at the wide smile on his lips. My grump wasn't stoic in the bedroom. He offered me smiles and praise without faltering. There wasn't a moment I felt unwanted. Finn was open with his desire for me. God, it felt good to be the object of his affection. You'd think I was the hottest woman in the world from how he touched me.

My fantasy was born from years of consuming regency romance films. The balls and manners weren't what made me fall in love with the era. It was the dresses. Thick, long, and perfect for hiding someone if they were going down on you. I stumbled across one film by accident where a woman was face-sitting. Her dress stretched across her legs, hiding her partner's head from view as she rode his tongue. In the past, I'd mounted pillows to mimic the visual. But nothing came close to the real thing. The second Finn's mouth captured my clit, I felt a jolt go through my belly. This was the feeling I'd longed for. He gripped my ass, tugging me down, so I wasn't hovering but properly sitting.

"I... I don't want to suffocate you," I said between breathy moans as I tried to push myself up on my knees.

Finn's response was to pull me closer. He squeezed my ass as if to say, *it's worth it*. The hair on his cheeks tickled my inner thighs. I leaned my head back as his tongue circled my clit in long, constant strokes. He took his time. Finn sucked on me like he was willing to let me fuck his mouth for the rest of the week. I gasped when his hands spread my ass cheeks. He massaged them and the sensation sent a hot pulse throughout my pussy. My walls clenched and, as if sensing it, he slipped two fingers inside of me.

"Oh, my God, Finn." I grabbed onto my headboard to steady myself. My pussy squeezed around his fingers. I could feel cum dripping onto his warm tongue. He licked up every drop with determination. My heart hammered in my chest as I experienced the hottest sensation of my life. I was sitting on the face of a six-foot hockey player. He was eating me out like he wanted nothing more out of life. When I ground my hips, he moaned into my pussy. My wide movements make my clit brush against his nose. Finn didn't mind getting his entire face into the mix. His grip stayed firm, and his fingers continued to pump in and out of me.

As my hips sped up, so did his tongue. He pulled his fingers out so I could widen my stance. Most of my weight was on him. His hands locked my legs around his head. Finn wanted this as much as I did. He wanted to drown between my thighs.

"Finn," I begged. "Please, make me come."

He didn't hesitate. Finn took my clit between his lips and his tongue circled the sides. He paid attention to how my body reacted to his rhythm and channeled his focus maintaining that speed. I came hard in his mouth. My body shook so much that I could barely keep myself upright. Finn held onto me, refusing to let up for a second. My thighs were weak when he coaxed me through my first orgasm and then into my second. I couldn't hold back a scream as the second climax overtook me. This one was far more powerful than the first. He refused to let me shy away from it, wanting me to see this through to the end.

I was near tears when I finally slipped off him.

"You okay?" Finn asked, breathless and covered in my wetness. He licked his lips like he couldn't get enough.

I grinned at his question and gave him an excited nod. "I'm incredible. So...incredible."

He smiled, and I pulled him close for a kiss. I didn't mind tasting myself on his tongue. In a way, it was hot knowing he'd been down there so long.

Finn's dick strained through the fabric of his boxers. When I spread my thighs and rubbed against his shaft, he pulled back to make sure he understood what I wanted.

"You said you were going to fill me," I reminded him with a coy smile.

"I did." He nuzzled my neck before whispering into my ear, "Like you've never been filled before. And then, I'm going to come on your ass. That's my fantasy."

I moaned, arching my back at the thought of his cum leaking on my skin. "Show me."

Finn nipped at my chin, earning a laugh from me, and then pulled away to grab a condom from his pants. When he came back, his face looked more determined than ever.

"Spread yourself," he instructed, as he rolled the condom on.

I widened my thighs as I was told, only to earn a shake of his head. When I frowned in confusion, he took my hands and guided them to my pussy.

"Nice and wide so I can watch every inch go in, Chai," he said in a dark voice.

My body shivered at the sound of my username on his lips. This wasn't any fantasy. This was a fantasy created with the online me in mind. He wanted to fuck me long before we met based on my voice and our conversations. It made this moment feel even more intimate.

I did as I was told and used my fingers to spread my pussy for him. He took his time, teasing me with the tip at first. Finn possessed both length and girth. I swallowed with anticipation when I laid eyes on his cock lining up with my entrance. As he pushed himself in, my walls squeezed around him.

"Damn," he breathed, steadily moving his cock in. "You're squeezing so tight."

"Mm." I moaned as my eyes fluttered shut, enjoying his achingly slow entrance. Once his base touched the lips of my pussy, I chewed on my bottom lip to revel in being filled. Finn began pumping himself in and out. The skirt of my dress rode up my hips because of his movements.

"You feel that?" he asked between kisses on my neck. "A perfect fit."

"Did you think it'd be any different?" I teased and gasped when his thrusts turned rougher.

"No. I knew it was you."

My eyes opened at the seriousness of his tone. He stared down at me. Lust still dominated his gaze, but when he kissed me, I felt like a princess. It took the right kind of guy to fuck you like you came from the streets but kiss you like he was your knight in shining armor. Finn Howard was that guy. When he pulled away from our kiss, he refused to show my pussy the same tender love and care my mouth received.

"There you go." His hands squeezed my hips and pulled me closer. "Take this cock like I know you can. I'm going to make sure you remember me, gorgeous. Make you so sore you won't forget."

"I'd never forget," I promised as he forced his cock deeper.

"Never," he agreed, and started massaging my clit. The sensation of being pounded into while my clit got the attention it longed for, made me see stars within seconds. I grabbed at Finn's thick arms as I climaxed. He looked pleased with the marks my nails left on his skin. We were branding each other in ways we might regret later. Our marks wouldn't be easily hidden, but damn, the pain mixed with pleasure felt necessary.

When my orgasm subsided, Finn pulled out of me and flipped me onto my stomach in one quick motion. I forced my ass into the air when I realized what he was doing. He slapped my butt cheek hard as he removed the condom. His warm cum spilled onto my lower back and down my ass. Finn's hand gripped my hip, holding me still as he came. I moaned at the feeling of him emptying himself on me. My fingers found my clit, rubbing it to the sounds of his orgasm. Another climax overtook me as Finn released every drop. I hadn't realized what a turn it would be having cum on me. My body shook from the pleasure.

We collapsed onto the bed. Finn buried his face in my hair. He snaked his arm around my chest. We lost all track of time as we laid like that and tried to recover. I was half asleep when he stirred.

"Don't go," I whispered, reaching for his arm to wrap it back around me. "Stay here tonight."

He kissed my temple, smiling at my request. "I want to get you cleaned up and comfortable first."

I relaxed back onto the sheets. Finn pulled on his clothes and listened to the door before going outside. He wasn't gone long before returning with a glass of water and a warm washcloth. I drank the water without stopping as he cleaned my skin with careful strokes.

"They aren't home yet. You can use the bathroom if you want while I make us a snack," he said.

I nodded with my eyes half-closed. "That sounds perfect."

He kissed my nose. "Good."

By the time I got through my nightly routine, Finn had made me a cup of tea, a bowl of fruit, and cheese toast. He laughed at the wide grin on my face when I took in the spread.

"My favorite late-night snack," I said with a skip over to the bed.

"Get comfortable." He nudged his chin toward the bed. His tone meant business, but the glint in his eye said otherwise. "I want to get a head start on the massage."

I wiggled my brow. "Massage?"

"Yeah, I know I said I wanted you to be sore, but..." He gave me a shrug. "Not that sore. I think I was a little rougher than I'd intended."

"Not at all." I shook my head as I crawled into bed. "But I won't turn down a massage."

He chuckled and joined me in the sheets. The rest of our night was quiet. We ate snacks and watched gaming streams while he massaged me all over. One thing led to another, and he went down on me again, making me moan his name over and over.

After I came back down from my sexual high, I decided he deserved a massage. He relaxed into my touch more than I thought he would.

When I mentioned it, he said, "I have had chronic back pain ever since my accident. Massages help."

I paused for a moment. "Chronic? Why didn't you say something sooner? I just sat on your face and had you on your knees for like hours."

He laughed. "And I adored every second of it. Don't worry. Sex distracts from the pain most of the time. And even when it doesn't, I still enjoy myself."

"Still, you should speak up if it ever gets too much. If a position is too strenuous or—"

"Naomi," he said in a firm voice and then turned so we were face to face. "I'm fine."

"I just want to make sure you're taken care of."

He grabbed my hands and brought them to his lips. "You have taken wonderful care of me tonight."

My cheeks warmed. Finn grinned and continued to kiss my fingers.

"You need to tell me these things." I squeezed his hand. "So I can keep taking wonderful care of you."

His eyes lit up at the request. "I will. Only if you promise to do the same."

I pulled him in for a kiss. Finn smiled against my lips, chuckling at my eagerness. I'm not sure I'd ever get used to that sound. It was better than the world's greatest symphony.

"Deal," he said when I finally let him up for air.

Chapter Twenty-Nine

Finn

When Whitfield slammed into me, it felt like a semi. He'd held his stick firm to cross-check me. I did my best to recover quickly, forcing myself to regain speed after losing all momentum. The shoulder he'd forced against the boards screamed in protest as I pushed through the pain.

"Howard! What the actual fuck!" Benson, our newest right-wing player, yelled. He was a transfer from a school upstate and all he did was complain about his decision to become a Mendell Hawk. Half of the team wanted to punch out the bastard's teeth. He was good, though. Mouthy, but good.

Sam righted my wrongs. He stole the puck back from Whitfield and started to the opposite end of the rink. He scored, making Lincoln curse as the puck went right between his legs and into the net. This was supposed to be a friendly match. But friendly and hockey didn't mix well. Especially when half the team was stressed about the upcoming game.

"You might want to go take a seat, bud," Whitfield mocked as he skated past me. "Let the actual players get ready for showtime."

My jaw tightened. "How about you try to win without the penalties? Bringing a gun to a knife fight isn't as impressive as you think."

Whitfield chuckled and shook his head as he continued forward.

It'd been this tense all morning. Our next game was against one of the best teams in the league, the Westbrooke Angels. I was nowhere near impressing Coach enough to expect playing time. When I wasn't doing schoolwork or hanging out with Naomi, I was on the ice with Sam. He'd dedicated copious amounts of time trying to help me get back to the level I was before. Now, it looked like those hours were a monumental waste. I wanted to drive my fist into a wall at the realization.

"Where's your head?" Sam stopped in front of me, looking just as frustrated. "In bed, with Naomi?"

"Shut up," I warned. Sure, these last few days I've been distracted. But Naomi wasn't my problem. In many cases, she was my solution. I hadn't felt a moment of peace until we started opening up to each other. Every second with her reminded me of how good life could get.

"Am I wrong?" Sam continued. "Because your dribbling's worsened. You can't initiate a breakout to save your life. And you're letting Whitfield—a scrawny son of a bitch compared to you—shove you like a rag doll."

"He plays dirty," I reminded him.

Sam shoved my shoulder. "So did you once."

I pushed him back. "Back off."

"Or what?" he taunted, getting close enough so our visors clashed. "What are you going to do, huh?"

My blood boiled. I could tell from the look in Sam's eyes he wasn't going to let this go without a fight. This wasn't about my fumble. He'd gotten my phone back to me and found nothing useful on it. After that, he seemed to have it out for me. Thought I was hiding something. I couldn't even get him to tell me what he was looking for. Our agreement was null when his search turned up empty.

"Get out of my face, Sam," I said through gritted teeth. "I might not be as quick to throw a punch as I was before, but I can still teach you a lesson."

"Boys!" Coach Haynes finally intervened. Most of the time, he let us figure out our own issues. When it seemed like there was no resolution in sight, he'd step forward. "Off the ice, *now!*"

Stoll was at his side again today. The closer it got to game time, the more he hung around. Even though I didn't have much of a reference, the time he dedicated to our team felt unusual. He watched with a hard look when Sam and I went to the sidelines. Neither of us said a word to Coach as we started toward the locker room. Haynes's pensive glare was enough to let us know we were done for the day.

The second the locker room door closed behind us, Sam threw his helmet across the room. It banged across one of the metal benches before tumbling to the floor. I watched, calm as he snatched his gloves off and tossed them toward his helmet. He started ranting about Coach and the new players. As he paced, I lowered myself onto a bench to watch and listen.

Sam looked unhinged. He scratched at his neck as he spoke. The mood rubbed off on me, transferring like an airborne virus. I tried to use a breathing technique Aden recommended, but it didn't work.

"This isn't about what happened out there," I said in a stiff voice, still pissed at how he'd gotten up close and personal. "So, calm the hell down and tell me what's bothering you so we can fix it."

"Fix it." Sam laughed humorlessly. "God, fix it? What if it isn't broken, Finn? I mean, look at you."

I frowned when he stopped pacing to gesture in my direction.

"You're fine. Better than fine, you're in a dream state. Wrapped around a woman's finger. Fucking like mindless—"

"Don't bring Naomi into this." My order was laced with a dark warning.

He pinched the bridge of his nose. "Fine. My point is—"

"What?" I pressed.

Sam paused and went over to lock the door. When he turned back, his eyes were wide as his secret spilled out. "We're poker chips to them, Finn. I came down here because Mendell was the only school that seemed willing to do what it takes to win. Come to find out, we get benched when we cross a certain threshold. Be good, but not too good."

I shook my head. "I'm not following. Slow down or maybe speed up. Just get to the point, please."

The air felt thick with Sam's anxiety. I think I knew what he was getting at, and my stomach twisted when I got confirmation.

"Stoll, the greatest AD." Sam scoffed. "Savior of dying programs. Champion of the poor and weary. He's got a whole betting system that works like a well-oiled machine. Probably makes thousands, moving his chess pieces, pretending he's God. And he's such an idiot, but no one can see it. Or maybe they do. I know Haynes does, he just doesn't say anything. Stoll must have something on him."

"Slow down, slow down," I urged, struggling to keep up. Sam seemed to have reached a breaking point. "Just...the betting thing. Tell me about the betting thing."

This was what he'd been looking for on my phone? I had known something about this before the fight. Had evidence apparently. But, of course, I couldn't recall a goddamn thing. How in the world did I get evidence on a guy I barely spoke to?

"He benches players strategically." Sam took a seat across from me, moving his hands as he spoke. "Rich donors probably place their bets alongside unknowing gamblers. We lose, they win."

"How...how do you know this?"

Sam rubbed his eye in frustration. "Stoll helped me out my first year here."

I raised a brow when Sam hesitated.

"I...got into some trouble. Didn't tell you guys because I was supposed to be better, you know? A leader. The captain."

The embarrassment in his tone was unmistakable. I nodded for him to continue. He looked grateful I didn't push him to tell me how he fucked up.

"He not only got me on the right path, but he also found me more scholarship money out of thin air...or what I thought to be thin air at the time."

"Stoll was trying to win you over," I figured.

"Yeah." Sam nodded. "But I can't prove that. I feel it, you know? Like, every time he looks at me, he's going to ask me to pay back a debt. I think he's in charge of who goes on and who stays off the ice during certain games."

"This is mostly speculation, Sam." I wanted him to ground himself a little more. But, for the most part, I understood where he was coming from. Haynes would often stop us during breakthroughs in practice. He'd pair us off in mismatch groups, not paying attention to chemistry and sometimes even positions. It was like he wanted chaos on the ice.

Sam sighed. "That's why I haven't told anyone. You all will think I'm losing it. Maybe I am, you know? Maybe we're not that great of a team?"

"No, I...I didn't mean it like that. I meant it's going to be difficult to prove."

"I know. Which is why I need the Finn of last year to do it." Sam pushed off the bench to start pacing again. "You don't remember a thing? Not even the small amount of information?"

"I'm sorry." I shook my head. The familiar feeling of guilt was back. Sam sucked the back of his teeth. I felt useless but I pushed against the feeling this time. I couldn't keep apologizing over something unfixable. Maybe the fight was my fault. Maybe I had it coming. That part I'd take responsibility for, but the rest needed to be let go.

"And you won't go to a doctor again? Do a CAT scan or something?" Sam looked hopeful.

"No," I said. "I feel strong, Sam. Better than I have in a while."

He opened his mouth, but I spoke over him.

"Not just because of Naomi. Because I'm starting to feel okay with who I am today. Going back to the hospital, getting those tests done, just the thought of it...my body goes into a panic, remembering trauma that my brain's trying to protect me from."

Sam's shoulders sagged. He looked sorry and ashamed. "Finn, I didn't realize it was still that difficult for you."

"It's fine. I'm moving on. I understand everyone who knew me before misses who I was. Sometimes, I get so caught up in mourning my loss I forget you all lost someone, too."

"We didn't lose you, Finn. Thank God." Sam's voice was finally back to its normal, low cadence. He was calming down.

"No, you did. It's time we face that fact. I know it's hard to let go. I've struggled with it for months now. But I'm not wasting any more time hoping someone I didn't know comes back to claim his life."

Sam chuckled, even though there was a sadness in his eyes. "You sound like a body snatcher."

I laughed too. "That's how it felt at first."

"Sounds terrifying."

"It was." I went quiet for a moment. "I was scared out of my mind."

That was before Naomi. Before gripping a hockey stick. Before realizing I could rebuild. Aden was right before, I was never no one. I was just someone new. Different and hopefully better. Definitely braver.

"We're going to figure this out." I took a breath and stood up. "Whatever evidence is lost, we're going to find it again. I'm going to find it and help you prove your theory."

Sam raised a brow, shocked and relieved. "You sure it's not too much for you?"

"I don't know why I chose Mendell. I have an inkling it had a lot to do with staying with you guys," I said. "You're my family. I'm going to help make sure we get what we deserve, so our futures are exactly what we want them to be. I don't know much, but I know you guys should be out there with the best because *you're* some of best."

"You sound like the old Finn now." Sam let out a heavy sigh. "A bit more levelheaded, though. I like it."

I smiled. "Thanks. Me too."

"This isn't some weekend project. It'll take time and effort," Sam warned.

"I'm not afraid of putting in the work. We're going to catch them in their lies and then we're going to become the best team in the league," I promised. "We win, they lose."

I knew something was wrong with Naomi the second I stepped into her room. It wasn't the clay that gave it away—I hadn't seen that yet. Her smile didn't come easy when she met my gaze.

"How was practice?" She popped up from her desk chair and hurried over to greet me. "I'm so excited to finally see a game."

I pushed away the drama with Sam. There was no use in troubling the already troubled Naomi.

"It was fine." Before she could pull away from her welcome home kiss I asked, "Look at me?"

Naomi froze and blinked. "What? What's wrong?"

"You tell me." I rubbed her dangling earring between my fingers. "You're crafting."

She made a face. "I craft when I just want to make something, too."

"Naomi. Our promise."

"You're right...okay, come look at this." She sighed and walked back to her desk. I followed, standing behind her as she opened a screen with her inbox pulled up.

"What am I looking for?" I asked, scanning through a multitude of junk mail. It amused me how well she kept the house in order while everything in her personal life was in disarray.

"That." She pointed to two emails, both from the same sender. "My mom. Her email came early."

"Right." I nodded. "Your birthday."

"My birthday," she said in the most lackluster tone imaginable.

I massaged her shoulders and rested my chin on her head. "Are you going to read them now?"

"No... maybe. I don't know. I haven't even gone to see her since... you know. It feels too weird. All of this feels too weird."

"You don't have to," I whispered. "You can take your time."

"I need to do it sooner than later." There was determination in her voice. Pressure.

I shook my head. "Not necessarily. Yes, you should face it eventually to get some closure. But what's wrong with waiting for now?"

"Because I need to get over it. I need to get rid of h—" She stopped short. My forehead wrinkled when she covered her face with her hands.

I couldn't begin to imagine the heartache that came with losing a parent. Sure, I wasn't close to mine, but they were still there, willing, and able to help me if necessary. Outside of Celeste, Naomi didn't have many people. I kneeled in front of her and rubbed her back as she hid. My body went cold seeing her in pain. I knew it was impossible to take that from her, but I still wracked my brain for some solution.

"Take your time," was all I could offer for now.

"I'm fine." She waved a hand as she sat up straight. There was a small smile on her lips. I wouldn't call it fake. Naomi's smiles were never fake. They were careful constructions created from years of practice.

"You're not," I murmured. "Talk to me. This is about more than the emails."

She shook her head, not meeting my gaze.

"Naomi, I want to be here for you, but you got to let me in." I massaged small circles on her knee. "You deserve to be happy. I can tell when you're forcing it."

She met my gaze, confused. "What?"

"I see you do it all the time."

Naomi winced, embarrassed. "It's easier. I'm not trying to be fake. The smiling comes easier for me."

"I know, and I didn't say that to make you feel bad."

"I...carry a lot of guilt sometimes. When I'm not happy, I feel guilty," she explained.

"Why?" I asked, curious and concerned. Looking at Naomi struggling to find the words felt like looking in a mirror. I knew that struggle intimately. She was trying to escape who she truly was underneath.

"Is it because you don't think you deserve to be upset?" I guessed.

She shook her head. "I don't know. Maybe? It's more like, I don't think I can handle it. The anger and frustration and rage. Finn, I've pushed it away for so long, it doesn't feel right. Or even earned."

I tilted my head, thinking. "You believe emotions need to be earned?"

Naomi nodded, looking down at her hands. "Yes, in a way. Nothing's happened lately for me to be upset. Everything's been good."

"You can be angry about things that happened forever ago. There isn't an expiration date on how you feel. Even on the most perfect days, you're allowed to be upset."

Naomi's jaw clenched. I wrapped my hands around hers and brought them to my lips. She watched as I kissed her fingers.

"Can I take you somewhere? A place I went after my accident when I wanted to let off steam?"

She nodded, looking eager. "Yeah. I'd like that."

"You'll have to keep it a secret," I teased.

The corners of her eyes wrinkled when she smiled this time. "Of course. It's safe with me."

Chapter Thirty

Naomi

Anxiety hives formed along my arms and across my chest. I slipped on a long sleeve shirt to cover everything before following Finn to the van. My body felt like it was in danger of being swallowed by guilt. Not just because of Mom, but because I was dragging Finn down with me.

I couldn't help glancing in his direction every few minutes. I searched for any sign of annoyance. There was none. His brow was unbothered, and his shoulders remained relaxed as he drove us down a road that led outside of town. The muffled hum of the radio made the van feel isolated. Like we were the only two people left at the end of the world. I leaned back in my seat to stare at the overcast sky. I wasn't used to giving in to moodiness but seemed prone to it today. Instead of thinking of what to say, I leaned my head against the headrest and let the silence settle between us.

It's scary how easily something as simple as an email flipped a switch in me. As soon as I saw my mother's old address, I felt a dead weight on my chest. The email reminded me of how I once was—and probably still am—in the running for the world's most horrible daughter.

I hated this feeling. It was cold, dark, and too similar to the life Mom chose to lead. The warmth of happiness felt safer and more stable. I wanted to fight my way back to it but didn't have any energy left.

We drove for an hour. I was dozing off when Finn pulled onto an unpaved road. Rocks crunched underneath the tire, making the van gently rock. There was a brightly painted welcome sign shoved into the grass that read, Windmill Camp.

"My uncle owns the place," Finn explained when I sat up straight to get a better look at the rows and rows of cabins. They weren't big but looked well maintained, with rocking chairs on the porches and flower pots hanging from the windowsills.

"During the summer, it's a camp for kids who are interested in playing college sports," he said as the van slowed to a crawl. "And during the off seasons, he tries to rent out the empty cabins. Not many people come because, besides the college, Tinsel doesn't have much tourist appeal."

I unbuckled my seatbelt. "What are we doing here? Saying hi?"

Finn shook his head. "No, you don't want to say 'hi' to my uncle. He doesn't enjoy company."

"Not the friendly type, huh?" I teased, earning myself an amused grin.

"Maybe it runs in the family." Finn opened his door, and I followed his lead. We'd parked right outside the only cabin with lights on inside. I waited as Finn sent a text.

"If we're not making small talk, then why are we here?" I asked once he shoved his phone back into his pocket.

Finn held out his hand for me to take. I raised a brow but grabbed hold.

"I need you to have an open mind and trust me, okay?"

"Okay..."

"And also, don't take this the wrong way."

My stomach twisted, and my elbows itched. "You're making me anxious. Show me or tell me something because I think I'm about to burst."

"You're angry."

I shook my head. "No, no. Of course not. I don't get angry. Upset, maybe."

And even being upset felt weird. The word felt like an ill-fitted top, not communicating who I wanted to be.

Finn didn't look convinced at my denial. "Maybe you're both. You're allowed to be both. I happen to be an expert at both. We're here, so I can show you how it's done."

I laughed. "We're here so I can be angry?"

Finn nodded and led me away from his uncle's place. We passed a few cabins before venturing to the back of one. There were outdoor lanterns lining the pathways, giving us enough light to see where we were stepping. Finn stopped in front of a large stack of logs and a row of axes.

"This is giving me slasher film vibes," I said while glancing toward the forest only a few feet away. "I don't do cabin in the woods or axes. I'm the prime candidate for being the first kill. I satisfy a trio of requirements."

Finn's forehead wrinkled as he took the bait. "Trio?"

"Black, a woman, likes sex." I counted on my fingers.

"Oh, I see." He nodded. "Don't worry, I'll protect you."

I stuffed my hands in my pockets. "Famous last words."

Finn laughed.

"By the time we're done here, you'll be the scariest thing within a fifty-mile radius," he said.

Now Finn had my undivided attention. I watched as he picked up a small ax and move one log to the chopping block. He lifted the handle in my direction and waved it a bit when I didn't reach for it.

"You want me to chop wood?" I took the ax, surprised at how it felt heavier than it looked. "Do I look like a wood chopping girl? Have you seen my wrists? Wait...don't answer that."

He looked amused when I tugged my sleeves down to cover my weak wrists.

"I have seen your wrists," Finn confirmed. "But I promise you, this isn't as hard as it looks. You're just going to have to scream."

My eyes widened. "Scream?"

Finn nodded, excitedly. He was getting a kick out of this. I've never seen his face this animated. The corners of his mouth looked as great going up as they did going down. My body heated at the warm smile because he saved this one for me. I was sure of it. He made me feel so worthy, even on my dark days.

"Yes, scream, yell, and swing." He gestured to the log. "Preferably in that direction."

"I'm confused. You drove me all the way out here to chop wood for your reclusive uncle?"

Finn considered my words. "Yes, and no. Uncle Aaron will appreciate the work, but I brought you here, so no sees you get mad. Around everyone else, you feel like you have to be Miss Sunshine. I've seen another side of you. It doesn't matter what you say or do here. Nothing will change what I think about you—how much I care for you."

My throat tightened. Damn, did he have to be so straightforward? I was already melting in a lava pit of guilt, then he caked on more rubble.

"Get mad and swing," he instructed. "I know it sounds silly, but trust me, it works."

"Finn, I..."

"What happened with your mom?" he interrupted my protest. "Tell me why you can't read the email."

My vision was blurry now. "It's complicated."

"Well, good thing we have a hundred acres of land and all night to figure it out. Now, just try. For me, Naomi, please try."

There was a squeeze around my heart. An invisible string that only Finn controlled. "She hated me."

"Hated you?" There wasn't any judgment or disbelief in his voice, and that did wonders in terms of making me feel like I could share my truth. Most people would tell me she didn't really hate me. They'd say that mothers couldn't hate their children, as if they knew everything there was to know about life.

I shut my eyes for a second and nodded. "I wasn't part of the plan. Mom got pregnant at seventeen and got kicked out of her house."

"Must have been hard for both of you."

My hands gripped the handle of the ax. "It was, but it didn't have to be all the time."

"How come?"

The ax was starting to feel lighter. I tested the weight in my hands, feeling the urge to draw back and hit something. So, I did. The metal slammed into the wood. Somehow, it didn't make a dent, but it still made me feel better. Putting my negative energy into something helped my chest feel less tight.

Finn walked slowly, stopping when he was across from me.

"She didn't accept help from anyone. Whenever her mom sent money, she burned the checks," I said. "We lived off one meal a day for a year and she refused to cash the checks. She told me it was my fault we couldn't use the money."

Another swing. A small chunk of wood chipped off. I rolled back my shoulders and tried again.

"Whenever she did make money, she donated most of it to this religious group." I huffed at the memory. "They told her she'd find happiness in the next life if she gave them everything in this one. Spoiler alert—they were scam artists. Even eleven-year-old me could figure that out."

Finn nodded, remaining still and expressionless.

"So, for most of my life, she refused to smile. Said her happiness was in heaven because this earth was meant for suffering. She had to pay her dues and I...I was one of those dues. I was penance."

His jaw tightened at my words. "She lived angry. And you live happy."

"To show her it's possible," I said, anger coating every word. "If she's watching from somewhere, I want her to see that everything she did to us was a waste. It's vindictive of me, but I want to prove I can be content without anyone's help. And I'm always trying to prepare for the possibility that I'll...end up alone like she was. If I do, I want her to see that it's possible not to waste your life away."

Finn frowned. "But she wasn't alone. She had you. Doesn't sound like she appreciated it, but she wasn't alone. You won't be either."

"You can't guarantee that." I hit the wood again. "A part of her is in me, and that part scares people away. I know I can get too talkative and smiley and it's overwhelming."

Finn shook his head, but I knew it was true.

"At this point, it's my armor. I need to be my good thing in case it's all I have left. My mom died angry—at me and the world. I can't do that. I want to be happy. So, I stay happy to survive. Stay happy and push forward."

He moved close to me, standing just out of arm's reach. "Naomi, happiness will still exist in your darkness. You don't have to push away the anger because you think it'll consume you. You are not your mother. I've known you long enough to say with surety, anger will never consume you."

My jaw tightened when he reached out to touch my arm. I wanted so much to believe him. So much to trust in what he told me. I sighed as he pulled me closer, so we were face to face. His hand tucked under my chin, holding me in place to look at him.

"Be everything," he urged. "You can be everything. You're avoiding anger because you want happiness, but in a way, you're doing exactly what she did. Blocking away a whole other side of you."

"What if it doesn't stop? And I become like her, always upset?"

He shook his head. "You'd never become like her. I've seen how much you care about people. I've heard how excited gaming makes you and I've felt how warm it is to be in your presence. You're always patient with people. You are bigger than one emotion."

I let out a deep breath. "I hate that...I hated her. And loved her. That part makes me want to scream. She had so much control over my emotions, and she barely listened to what I had to say. I'm embarrassed that a woman who barely knew me can make me so mad in a heartbeat. Even now, an email sends me in a spiral. I should be better than this."

Finn pulled me into his chest. I wrapped my arms around him and squeezed tight. His shirt was damp with tears by the time I pulled away. Finn brushed at my cheeks, trying to help me clean up.

"Scream," he dared.

I frowned. "What?"

"Right now. Don't think about it. Just scream."

This felt so unnecessarily dramatic. My emotions never happened on a sliding scale, but tonight, that changed. Finn stepped back, giving me space. My cheeks burned at the thought of yelling into the night like some banshee. He seemed to sense my shyness and turned around. I laughed when he covered his ears after saying,

"Get mad Naomi Lewis. No one's watching."

I placed a hand on my throat, wondering if I even had the ability to produce something so loud. As I closed my eyes, it helped me feel less self-conscious. Finn drove all the way out here so I could scream, so the least I could do was give it a shot.

Actually screaming was less awkward than the buildup. A few birds in the trees nearby fled in a hurry to avoid whatever drama was brewing. My throat opened to let the sound out and, with it, pure anger. What'd been building up for hours in my muscles was released. The tears were back, paired with the scream like it was a matched set. I've never angry cried before and it was quite possibly the most therapeutic thing I've ever done. Pressure I didn't even know that'd been building in my lungs, vanished. God, how long had I been carrying around this weight? I thought happiness lightened the load, but pure rage demolished it.

Finn turned around when I was finally quiet. I laughed at the impressed looked in his eyes.

"You did good," he said, laughing too. "Far louder than I expected."

I rubbed my throat. "I haven't cried in years. And I haven't screamed...ever."

"This is good then," he assured.

I snorted. "You're a bad influence. This was the plan all along, wasn't it?"

Finn raised a brow.

"Find a happy girl and make her scream?" I teased. "Make her grumpy like you."

"More or less," he agreed with a bright smile.

I snorted at the pleased looked on his face. "Well, you've succeeded. And what got you most of the way was your uncle's ax. I know I'm weak, but I don't think this thing could chop through butter. It's infuriating."

Finn laughed, holding onto his stomach. I smiled. I was right. All cute guys held onto their stomachs when they laughed. It was a law of the universe.

"I purposefully picked the dullest of the bunch."

"Why?" I asked.

"The added frustration helped send me over the edge the first time I came out here to do this. Thought it'd work on you too."

It was my turn to laugh. "So, you have me trying to cut wood with a crappy ax so I could reach my breaking point?"

"I wanted you to feel like you could rage. Vent and hit things, you know? Everyone should be able to hit things...in a controlled environment, of course."

I smiled and looked down at the ax. "I suppose you're right. Your form of therapy has some merits. I do feel lighter. The swinging was cathartic."

"I'm glad." He kissed my forehead. "Would you like to swing some more, or should we head home?"

"How about neither?"

Finn looked confused.

"Let's not go home yet. I have an idea. You said there are a hundred acres here, right?"

He nodded, still not following. "Right..."

I smiled. "Let's go find some to borrow for a bit. I know another therapeutic way to let off steam."

Chapter Thirty-One

Finn

Naomi placed her hand on the headrest behind me as she lowered herself onto my cock. We both released low moans as our bodies connected. I battled the urge to roughly lift her up and down on top of me. Instead, I clung to her waist, letting her control the pace.

It'd been her idea to drive further onto the property. We were still close enough to see the dimly lit cabins in the distance, but far enough to have some resemblance of privacy.

Naomi's beautiful body shuddered against mine as she began grinding back and forth. I gripped tight to the back of her panties, trying to make sure the fabric remained pulled to the side. The tight gray shirt she kept on showed off the curve of her small breasts. Her nipples poked against the fabric, practically begging to be teased. And what was I, if not willing to give Naomi everything her body desired.

A desperate moan fell from her mouth when I sucked on her covered breast. Her fingers curled against my scalp, holding me close enough to feel the pounding of her heart. On top of me, with her fingers in my hair and pussy around my cock, she was in complete control. The speed and pattern of our fucking were all up to her. I loved it. Being at her mercy was as content as I've ever felt.

"I wish you could see how incredible you look," I murmured while peering up at her.

Since we were both tall people, Naomi's head grazed the top of the van as she rode me. I'd let the seat back to give us space, but there wasn't much room to work with. Limited space made this even more fun. Without an inch to spare, we only had one another to hold on to and nothing to come in between.

"These thighs," I continued while running my hands up and down them. "The stretch marks, the curve of your breasts, the hair on your pussy. You're heaven, Naomi."

She kissed me, trying to hide the shy smile on her face. I parted her lips, wanting to claim her mouth with the same force her pussy was currently claiming me. She whimpered against my probing tongue. The convulsions of her body made me leak precum. I reached for her clit, rubbing tight, hard circles around the swollen bud. Naomi tore her mouth from mine to scream with pleasure. Her juices soaked my fingers and dripped down my cock. Every grind of her hips sent me closer to the edge.

"I need to see you come," I begged. My thumb continued to circle her clit. "Come on this cock, gorgeous."

She pressed her forehead against mine and a moan slipped through her parted lips as she climaxed. "Holy crap, Finn."

God, I wanted to satisfy her like this forever. I wanted to be the one she could be every part of herself with. The anger, desire, and pure happiness. There was not one side of her I didn't love. Every part of my being was hers and would do whatever it took to make her mine.

My orgasm came shortly after Naomi's. Her walls squeezed around me so tightly that I could barely think straight. This woman was better than oxygen itself, which was why I tried to drown in her pussy when we went to the backseat next. Naomi came twice on my tongue. Both times, she pressed her hands on her breasts, pushing them together, forming tiny mountains. The sight of her playing with them nearly sent me over the edge. I fisted myself as I watched her come. When her pussy had stopped trembling and she noticed me masturbating, she wanted me in her mouth.

The second her lips touched my cock, I willed myself to think of something, anything, that didn't involve the woman before me to make this last. It took a few tries, but Naomi got most of me in her mouth. I felt the back of her throat pressed against my tip. My heart hammered in my ears as she moved up and down. I now knew what perfection felt like. Naomi hummed around my cock as she sucked me. The vibration made me grip the car seats, a poor attempt at warding off my climax.

"I'm close, Naomi," I said in a hoarse whisper. "Better move back if you don't want cum all in your pretty mouth."

She didn't move away. Instead, she swirled her tongue around my tip as if to say, *bring it.*

"You sure?" I forced out. Speaking coherent sentences was getting harder with each second. Naomi's nod and eye contact were all the permission I needed. I came in her mouth as I stared into her eyes. She swallowed some but let most of the excess drip down her chin. The sight was the most erotic thing I've ever witnessed. She pulled away when I'd fully spent. I tugged her onto my lap, encouraging her to curl up against me. Our heavy breaths and the sound of crickets filled the air. The dark night pressed against the van windows. I stared up toward the stars, thanking whatever god was listening for helping me find Naomi.

"Thank you," she whispered into my chest.

I rubbed her back, thinking maybe I said my thoughts out loud for a second. "For what?"

"For wanting more from me. Not just the good stuff, but every part."

My arms tightened around her. We stayed like that for hours, holding onto one another like nothing else existed but us and the stars. For a few moments, nothing did. My body never felt lighter. And the smile on my face never came so easily.

We woke up in my bed. My legs were tangled in the sheets as I reached over Naomi to turn off my alarm. She stirred, hugging my torso.

"Are you leaving?" she asked, voice heavy with sleep and disapproval.

I kissed the top of her head. Sometime during the night, she'd wrapped her head in a silk scarf. The scarf now fell around her shoulders. She'd be upset over the matter—I'd seen this happen once already—so, in my sleepy haze, I tried to tug the scarf back up her head. She murmured a thank you when I successfully got the fabric to cover her braids.

Note to self: buy a silk pillowcase. That would make her more comfortable sharing my bed.

"I have a tutoring session," I whispered to her.

"That's my line," she joked, and opened her eyes.

"It's with my sister," I explained, kissing her forehead. The sun reached through the blinds, painting perfect lines across Naomi's skin. I traced those lines with my lips, enjoying the warmth. She sighed under my touch. I could feel myself getting hard against the softness of her belly. Before I could make a move, my alarm went off again.

I cursed under my breath. Naomi laughed at the hardness in my brow. She tried to smooth it with soft pecks and whispered promises for later. I loved this part about us the most. We tried to balance one another. I tugged her one way, and she tugged me another. We met in the middle.

"Go tutor." Naomi playfully shoved my shoulder. "I'll keep quiet."

"I could do it downstairs," I offered.

She yawned and shook her head. "And have the guys interrupt you every other minute? You won't get anything done."

I chuckled. "You're right."

"Usually am." She wore a smug grin, which I kissed until it dissolved into something far more lustful. I ruefully pulled away with a groan when I heard my video chat pinging. Naomi laughed as I hurried to tug on a pair of sweats and a T-shirt. I winked in her direction before turning on my laptop to accept the call.

"I thought you forgot." Denver looked annoyed as soon as her face came up on the screen. The second she got a good look at me, her eyebrow raised.

I cleared my throat, realizing I still wore an uncharacteristically happy look. "I didn't. Just needed to get ready."

My sister eyed me with suspicion. "You're usually up and running somewhere by this time. Who is she?"

In my peripheral vision, Naomi paused as if she was already in the web cam's frame. I glanced in her direction to see her mouth, 'sorry' when the floorboards creaked under her feet as she tried to tug on her clothes.

"I'd like to meet her...if she's dressed, of course. Not trying to make this awkward or anything," Denver said.

"You already have," I mumbled and then flashed Naomi a questioning look. My sister would go on about this until she got her way.

"Is this okay?" Naomi whispered, coming closer.

I smiled and nodded. "Of course. Come here."

She accepted my invitation, eyes growing wide when I pulled her into my lap. It made perfect sense to have her this close. Having Naomi crouch uncomfortably was out of the question. I placed a firm, possessive hand around her waist. I couldn't remember if I'd had a girlfriend before. And if I had, I didn't know if I ever introduced her to my folks. So, this felt like an important milestone in which I needed to show Denver I wouldn't accept any judgment. My family was free to complain and talk about me. If it happened with Naomi, it'd get shut down in an instant. As long as I lived and breathed, no one would make her feel like she had to act a certain way to be accepted.

"So, you're the reason my brother's face has stopped looking like a statue?" Denver asked with a teasing smile.

I shot her a warning look.

Naomi laughed. "Yeah, I suppose so. I'm Naomi."

"Denver. How long have you two been together? Or is this a fuck buddy thing? No judgment either way. I thought he was too afraid to start another one of those."

Naomi shifted uncomfortably in my lap.

My expression clouded over. "I'm not afraid to end this call—"

Denver held up her hand. "Relax, I'm only teasing. Glad to see you're finally getting back to normal. Maybe now you'll stop pretending not to remember family dinners?"

"I'm not..." I started in a hard tone, but Naomi's gentle hand on my thigh made me relax a little. "Pretending."

"Right." Denver nodded, obviously not believing me. She thought I was pretending solely to get out of coming home. And I probably would have maintained some sort of ignorance to keep space between myself and my family. Obligation felt like a knot in my stomach, twisting tighter any time I thought of interacting with them. Before, I didn't know if this was normal. Now, I had a strong inkling it wasn't. Sometimes, you don't click with people even if you were related. It'd taken me half the semester to realize that the guys and Naomi felt like home. Nothing else made me feel safe like they did.

"I heard something about tutoring," Naomi swooped in when silence lasted for a second too long.

"Finn fancied himself a know-it-all when he promised to help me study," Denver explained. "I figured I'd put his brain to good use."

Denver held up a textbook with calculus written on the front. I winced at the sight while Naomi's eyes brightened.

"I'm actually a math major," she said with excitement in her voice. "And I happen to be a tutor at the school, so maybe I could be of some help?"

"No, it's fine," I said at the same time Denver gasped, "Oh, yes, please."

My jaw tightened at the pleading pout on Denver's face. She clasped her hands together as she begged for my girlfriend to sacrifice her morning.

"She's got enough on her plate," I said with a shake of my head.

Naomi looked at me with an honest smile on her lips. "It's fine, I don't mind."

"I do," I whispered.

"Come on." Naomi teasingly shook my shoulder. "I can spare an hour. Besides, shouldn't you be prepping for your game?"

She had a point. I'd woken up far later than I originally planned. By this time, I was supposed to be showered, dressed, and have my bag packed for the drive.

"Let me help. You already look exhausted, and you just got out of bed." Naomi insisted in a voice too low for the mic to catch. "I got this."

"You sure? You don't have to do this."

"I want to do this." She stood and shooed me away while Denver cheered.

"An hour tops," I warned loud enough for Denver to hear. "You're not stealing too much of her time."

"Yeah, yeah, relax. You always make such a big deal about everything. She's helping me do a math problem, not build a skyscraper."

Naomi chuckled while I rolled my eyes.

"I've started a timer," I said. "Not a second more."

Chapter Thirty-Two

Naomi

Denver was sweet. A little nosy and a little rough around the edges, but sweet. Finn didn't seem to share my thoughts. He grunted when I expressed my opinion, and seemed desperate to move on.

"You don't go home on the weekends like the guys do sometimes," I said. It was supposed to be a question but came out as a statement. There was no use in pretending I didn't know he hung around the house every weekend. We'd started this semester avoiding one another since neither of us left campus. Back then, it felt like bad luck. Now, the idea of having him all to myself was thrilling.

"Nothing for me there," Finn said. He stood in front of the mirror hanging on his closet door. I watched from the bed as he struggled to put on his tie. The hockey team always wore suits during away games. It was quite a sight to witness a bunch of rowdy guys in black ties. Why did simple dress pants make even the meanest-looking guy look charming?

I pushed off the bed to help him. He didn't even bother protesting when I took over.

"Do you know what you're doing?" Finn asked with an amused twinkle in his eye.

"No." I shrugged while fiddling with the tie. "But it can't be that hard to figure out."

He snorted and waited for me to realize my error. I sighed when my fourth attempt at making some sense of the fabric failed.

"What kind of sorcery do I have to learn?" I huffed and got out my phone to watch a quick video. Finn kept reaching for my ass as I tried to follow the instructions.

"Stop distracting me." I laughed and swatted his hand away. "I'm trying to make sure this is on right while also learning more about you. You're not sad about not spending much time with your family?"

He wore a ghost of a smile as he said. "Why would I be sad about that?"

I shrugged, not meeting his gaze. "Seems like something most people would be sad about."

"I'm fine." He brushed the back of his hand across my face. I shivered in response. "Are you? Sad about not being around your family?"

"I don't know my mom's side of the family, so there's nothing to miss there. Same for my dad. The only thing I knew about him was that he left before my mom had me. I'm glad he did because I don't have to regret anything about a failed relationship."

He pulled his hand away from my ass and remained quiet for a moment. I finished the tie, giving it one final adjustment before stepping back to view my handiwork. It wasn't bad for a first attempt.

"I'm not sad because, much like with your family, I don't know them," Finn said in a low voice. "And anytime I'm with them and try to get to know them, they want me to be someone different. I'm not him anymore. I don't want to be, and they don't want to let go."

I nodded. "Have you told them that? That you're ready to move on?"

"I tried."

"Maybe they need to be reminded a few more times before they let up?"

"Unlikely." He didn't look too torn up over the matter. "My family's the kind that talks at you. I learned that much from being carted around to every doctor imaginable. No matter how many times I wanted to stop and rest, they kept at it. I stayed in the hospital until we couldn't afford it anymore. At first, it made me sad—for not giving them what they needed. Then, I got angry. You know that night you ran into me with that door was the first night I'd been away from them. I felt quite liberated until I tasted blood."

I laughed and quickly pressed my hand over my mouth. He chuckled at me. I didn't resist when he pulled down my hand.

"You can laugh," he said with a smile.

"I really shouldn't." I traced the bridge of his nose with my finger. "It looked like it hurt."

"Terribly," he assured. "But I can't think of a better way to have met you. Ever since that moment, you've felt like a force in my life, pushing up against me. Demanding me to do something. Feel something."

My shoulders sagged. "Is that a bad thing? It sounds like what your family does."

He shook his head quickly. "No. Nowhere close, Naomi. I like the pressure you bring. It's healthy and exciting. It feels like...love."

My eyes widened. Finn's ears turned red. He let out a shaky laugh and stepped away. I could hear my heart in my ears.

So, he had an inkling of how strongly I felt? I hadn't necessarily been trying to hide it but wasn't sure if I was ready to say it out loud.

"Finn..." I picked at my nail, watching him put a few more things in his bag.

"Point is," he said without looking back at me. "I feel like the guys and you are my family. I'm content with that. So, I don't need my folks as much. I get to choose, and you all feel like the best people imaginable to pick."

I chewed on my bottom lip, trying my best not to smile too wide. Being his choice felt good. Hell, it felt amazing. A few months ago, my elation would've startled me. I would've been scared out of my mind to care this much. But Finn felt right. Seeing him content allowed me to do the same. No, I didn't have a biological family around. But Celeste was a better sister than I could ever dream of having. It felt wonderful to have a choice about who was and wasn't in my life.

Finn cleared his throat. "Um...so, I'll see you at the game, right?"

"I'll be there. Cheering you on and trying to keep up."

He came close enough to touch me again. I relaxed into him as he pulled me in for a kiss.

"You'll take the van?" he asked when he pulled away.

I made a face. My car was finally out of the shop, but still wasn't the most reliable ride.

"Naomi," Finn warned and then pulled out his keys. "You're taking the van. From the second I saw your car, I hated the thought of you in it."

I took the keys. "I thought it was me you hated back then."

"Never." He shook his head, amused. "No part of me could ever hate you. I was intimidated. You're a very intimidating person, you know."

"Says the six-foot hockey player with biceps like boulders." I poked his arm.

"It was your beauty. And grace." Finn wore a teasing grin at the word 'grace.' He's saved me about a million times from falling on my face on the front porch.

I pinched him. "Oh, shut up."

"Manners, too. You're always so nice to me, Naomi Lewis. In public, at least. The nicest people are usually bullies behind closed doors, in my experience."

"You're so full of it."

He laughed, grabbing my hand as I reached to pinch him again. Before we could launch a full-on war, Sam called from downstairs,

"Alright, assholes! Ready or not! Time to fight for our lives."

Chapter Thirty-Three

Finn

There was a change in the line-up. Jack was out, and I was in as a starter. No one complained about the last-minute shift. Not even Jack—who'd usually have a field day with this sort of thing. During the bus ride, he went straight to the back and put on his headphones to block out everyone.

I didn't know the plays as well as the others and confessed as much to Sam in a low voice once when we got off the bus.

"I know. That's why you're in." Sam gave me a knowing look. "Relax and prove them wrong. Okay?"

"Right." My stomach clenched. He made it sound easy. Like keeping up with a bunch of guys who were well on their way to becoming NHL athletes within the next year was going to be a cakewalk.

Breathing felt more difficult when my blades hit the ice. I couldn't make out much of the crowd behind the glass. Everyone who wasn't in gear looked like a blob of some sort. This was my first big game since my accident. I wanted to throw up.

"You got this. Don't overthink it." Lincoln bumped my shoulder with his before claiming his spot in the goal.

"All in." Henrik stretched his hockey stick out, knocking it against mine.

I repeated his mantra, "All in."

I blew out a breath and closed my eyes for a second to block everything out. I wasn't out here because I'm good. Coach put me out here because I was more likely to fuck this up for us. My grip tightened on the hockey stick as I willed myself to remember I'd screwed up enough times this semester. I had it out of my system now and, statistically I was more likely to have improved. At least, I hoped that was how statistics worked. Naomi would know. She'd probably have the perfect thing to say right now. Something wildly positive and bright like, do your best and it'll work out. I smiled thinking about her.

Sam lined up for the face-off. He glanced in my direction once and nodded to make sure I was good. I gave him a nod back because what else could I do? Bailing wasn't an option—well, maybe it was, but I wouldn't be able to forgive myself. This felt like a hurdle I needed to get over so I could regain my confidence. If I got through this, I'd be on my way to performing at the level I needed to.

The referee stood in the middle of Sam and Westbrooke U's center to drop the puck. As soon as it hit the ice, everything became a blur as both teams scrambled. Sam was always clear when indicating which plays he wanted to run. My execution didn't start great, but the further we got into the period, the more my body got used to the adrenaline.

Midway through the game, I started feeling more comfortable than I'd ever been during practice. No matter how hard the body checks were or how messy the fight for the goal got, I kept control of my anxiety. Soon enough, the twisting of my stomach dulled to a barely visible ache. Unfortunately, my back couldn't say the same. Still, I pushed through the pain. I needed this, and so did the rest of the guys on the team. We needed a win for morale and to prove that even our weakest links could be strong.

During intermission, Coach Haynes benched me. A rookie took my place while I fell into a spot next to Jack. He said nothing at first, offering me a water bottle. I took it, grateful for the cold liquid to soothe my dry throat.

"That was better," he mumbled.

I thought he was referencing our team. My eyes were still trained on the guys in the rink. One of Westbrooke's wing players—a fucking beast with the speed of a cheetah—almost scored. Lincoln blocked it, earning a roaring cheer from Mendell's side of the crowd.

"Coach wasn't expecting you to pull through like that," Jack continued. He leaned forward, placing his elbows on his knees as he spoke in a low voice. It would be near impossible to hear him over the cheering crowd and our yelling teammates unless one was sitting right next to him.

"No?" I looked at Jack now.

He grinned. There was no humor in it. "You're a good possum player. On and off the ice."

"Possum player?" I raised a brow, considering the label.

"You play dumb until you can't anymore," Jack explained with a shrug. "I like to do it, too. You think I don't know why you were out there and not me?"

It was hard to keep my expression neutral, but I managed. So, Jack knew about the attempt to sabotage our scoring tonight? Maybe this conspiracy wasn't as much of a well-kept secret as Sam and I thought.

"I know why." Jack looked back on the ice.

"You going to do something about it?" I dared, wanting to make sure we were talking about the same thing.

"Maybe." He shrugged. "Not now, though. You fucked up for good this time. There's no use in making a fuss now."

I followed his hand as he gestured toward the scoreboard. We were in the lead by three. I'd assisted on at least two of those goals.

"Timing's everything," Jack finished. He cupped his hands around his mouth, yelling encouragement to our teammates currently making Westbrooke's defense work their asses off. I smiled at Jack's words, making a note that maybe he wasn't one hundred percent jackass. A ninety percent jackass could come in handy.

Half the team went to a local bar to celebrate our unpredicted win. Naomi met me in the bar's parking lot. She laughed when I swept her off her feet and spun her around for a hug.

"You were so good," she gushed and waved two small Mendell flags back and forth. Her wide grin was infectious.

"He was alright, I suppose." Lincoln slapped my back. "For a guy who could barely dribble a puck a week ago."

I frowned at his jeering, which only made him want to continue.

"Amazing," Naomi insisted and waved her flag in Lincoln's face. "Everyone was! And we won!"

Henrik laughed at her enthusiasm. "Come on, first round on me. You said you like to see people drunk, right?"

She nodded, her eyes bright with anticipation. I smiled as she bounced on the balls of her feet. Naomi didn't know what she was in for. These guys fell apart when they consumed the right amount of alcohol. The singing would start, and she'd beg it to stop.

"You heard the man! Drinks on Henrik!" Sam announced. He already had a beer in hand but shockingly didn't yet have a girl in the other.

The rest of the team cheered. Naomi slipped her hand into mine as we made our way inside. The place was crowded with typical weekend traffic.

Since we were in enemy territory, there were quite a few Westbrooke Angels fans around. They gave us dark glares as we claimed booths and spots at the bar.

"You really okay to hang around for a bit?" I asked when I pulled Naomi close to me, so she stood between my legs. I chose a spot at the bar to keep close to the guys. They needed a babysitter when it came to drinking and I assumed the role since I'd given up drinking.

"I am," Naomi assured me as she wrapped her arms around my neck. Her fingers played with my tangled, wet locks. I took a quick shower before we left the arena because I knew we wouldn't be going home until early tomorrow morning, and I still wanted to hold my girl close before then.

"Who did this for you?" I rubbed the smudged Mendell green and gold on Naomi's cheeks. She looked like a proper fan with her flag-waving and painted face.

"The girl's hockey team. I ran into them before the game," she explained. "It's cute, right?"

"Very." I tightened my grip around her waist, kissing her cheeks and then her mouth.

The guys around us started whistling and cheering like the childish bunch they were. I blocked them out and continued to kiss her. Naomi smiled against my lips, distracted by my teammates. I could feel her heart racing when I placed a hand on her back to hold her close.

"Relax," I said with annoyance in my tone when my friends continued to pester us. "Don't you guys have anything better to do?"

Naomi kissed my forehead, trying to urge the wrinkles to disappear. I hummed at the effort, redirecting my attention back to her.

"I like when you kiss me like that," she whispered. "Makes me feel like I'm yours."

"You are mine," I murmured, and massaged circles on her hips. "Aren't you?"

Naomi nodded, looking pleased. "And you're mine?"

"Without a doubt." I playfully nipped at her neck because I wanted to hear that beautiful laugh. It's strange to think that was something I only heard through my computer speakers at one point. A mic could never do justice capturing her delicate pitch. Nothing came close to watching her lean her head back as she giggled.

For the rest of the night, I tried to be social because Naomi insisted. I'd much prefer to slip into a booth and escape with her for the rest of the night. The guys on the team seemed to appreciate her presence, though. Lincoln and she led the charge in drinking games. Henrik downed Naomi's drinks for her when she said she couldn't take another sip. I watched them all, smiling more than I thought humanly possible for one night.

The longer we stayed out, the more crowded the bar got. I paid little mind to the newer arrivals. My team and Naomi took most of my attention. At some point in the night, I got separated from Naomi. Lincoln was throwing up in the parking lot. Henrik needed help with keeping him sitting upright.

"He's back!" Lincoln cheered when I waved a water bottle in his face. "Finn, the Destroyer of Greates is back."

I sighed and opened the bottle for him to have easier access to the water. "Drink, asshole. You'll get alcohol poisoning."

"I should have followed you that night," Lincoln lamented between gulps. I was still holding the bottle, pouring the liquid into his mouth. Henrik laughed at the sight. Henrik was a humorous drunk. Any and everything was funny to him.

"I would have had your back," Lincoln continued, and then grabbed my collar to pull me closer.

"Whoa." I winced at the smell of his breath. "Relax, would you?"

"Tonight, I'll stay by your side," he slurred before letting go. "The Greates are upon us, but I will remain faithful."

I snorted when he fell back onto a small patch of grass. Henrik's laughter multiplied. I smiled a little because I suppose the entire ordeal was a bit silly.

"Ever faithful." Lincoln punched the air with his fist. "Hoorah."

"I think it's huzzah," Henrik teased.

"Huzzah," Lincoln tried again.

I rolled my eyes and gave the bottle to Henrik to finish off. "Watch him. I'm going to get everyone else. We need to get out of here."

Henrik nodded. He took his new job seriously and flopped onto the grass next to Lincoln. They both started laughing at how the stars looked in the sky. I glanced up, shaking my head. Everything looked perfectly normal. They'd gone off the deep end for sure.

When I went back inside to round up whoever I could find, I realized instantly something was off about the crowd. It hadn't escalated to shouting yet, but by the time I pushed through the throng of people, I heard Sam's slightly raised voice. He wasn't too drunk to speak coherently. As he stood in front of Naomi, he looked sober. He blocked her from a pair of guys who were roughly the same height and possessed features similar enough to indicate they were related.

"Hey, are you alright?" I asked, grabbing onto Naomi's arm, and pulling her into my chest. She was shaking, eyes wide with fear. My jaw tightened, and I was instantly ready to hurt whoever did this to her.

"It was...a misunderstanding. Can you stop Sam?" Naomi begged. My friend refused to back away from the guys as they stepped closer to him, too. This wasn't deescalating anytime soon.

"Go find Henrik and Lincoln in the parking lot," I told her.

She shook her head. "I don't want to go unless you're leaving too."

"Naomi," I warned.

Aderyn appeared by our side and offered, "I'll get her outside."

I nodded my thanks and gave Naomi's hand a squeeze before letting her go.

"What happened?" I asked Sam, who looked pissed.

"Hey!" the bartender yelled. "If y'all wanna fight, take it outside."

We ignored him. On one side of the room, there were Westbrooke Angels shirts. The blue outnumbered green five to one. Sam was currently staring down the two guys who didn't sport a color for either team.

"Look who it is," one guy leered when he saw me. "The dickwad that can't take a punch."

I frowned. "Do I know you?"

He scoffed and looked at his brother. "Fucking hell, the nerve of you Hawks. Think you own the world after a few easy wins but curl up in the fetal position once you're going up against a Greate."

I paused, studying them closely. Everything I knew about my accident had been relayed to me from second-hand accounts. I had to watch security cam footage of the attack. Four guys against one. Winning my case in a court of law had been easy. Of course, the accused weren't pleased. Alex Greate had been suspended from the league until further notice. I had a restraining order on him. Not on his brothers, though. Both of them looked more than ready to avenge whatever cause they stood for.

"What happened?" I asked Sam in a low voice.

"Came in here threatening us, asking where you were, and then harassed Naomi," Sam explained without taking his eyes off the two.

I cared little about the other stuff. Once Naomi was mentioned, my fingers curled into a fist.

"Take. It. Outside." The bartender warned before any of us could throw a punch.

The Greate siblings exchanged knowing smirks. My jaw tightened. I didn't like how they'd come in here ruining what was supposed to be a good night. And I especially didn't like the idea of letting them go after messing with Naomi.

Not much thought went into swinging the first punch. Or second and third, for that matter. Fighting on both sides broke out like a faulty dam. The bar was flooded with shouts and screams and warnings from all around.

I pinned one brother underneath me. After getting a few hits in, I felt Naomi's grip tugging me off the guy on the ground. For a moment, I was out of it. I swung and didn't let up until there was someone else's blood on my knuckles. The sight of it broke something in my mind. A memory rushed back so quickly, I got a headache.

Much to Naomi's relief, I pushed off the guy and backed away.

"Let's go." She pulled me through the brawling crowd, unaware of my current epiphany. "They're calling the cops."

I numbly followed her out of the bar. We bumped into Lincoln and Henrik at the exit. Both of whom urged us to hurry along the side of the building, going the long way around the parking lot.

The police were already here. Their blue and red lights flashed as they parked at the curb.

Naomi shushed the guys as we all crouched behind a bush a fair distance away from the bar.

"What the hell happened?" Lincoln hissed, ignoring Naomi's glare.

"I know where the photos are," I said to no one in particular.

"What photos? What do photos have to do with this?" Henrik asked, while staring at a group of people who were currently being dragged out of the bar.

Lincoln and Naomi looked at me like I'd lost my mind. On the contrary, I'd found it. Or, at least, part of it. I remembered that night now. What happened before the game, during, and after. I remembered where I put the evidence.

"I need to get to my laptop," I said, sounding loopy even to my own ears.

"What the hell, Finn?" Naomi hissed. She looked beyond upset. If I didn't know any better, I'd say she wanted to clock me as hard as the Greate brothers had. "What is wrong with you? Why would you do that? After everything that's happened...I...what the hell?"

I frowned, confused by her anger. "I was trying to defend you."

"Defend me?" She shook her head. "By punching the shit out of a guy in front of a hundred witnesses? Not to mention starting a fight with the guys who wanted you in the hospital in the first place?"

"Would you have preferred I walk away?" I challenged, getting pissed. I didn't like the idea of anyone messing with her or even thinking about messing with her. So, if I got the opportunity to shut something down before it escalates, I will. I didn't see the problem, but from the dark look in her eyes, she did.

Naomi stared at me like she didn't recognize me. And that hurt more than getting knocked in the gut.

"I would have preferred you not risk getting hurt again," Naomi said in a lower voice.

My anger faded when I saw the worry in her eyes. She wasn't arguing because of morals—though I'm sure she'd stand against the violence. She was arguing because she'd been afraid for me.

"What if you hit your head again, huh?" she asked, her tone desperate now because she thought I wasn't listening. "What if this time you didn't wake up? There are only so many times someone can injure their brain before they start to see permanent damage. And you just spent an hour slamming into guys for fun in the rink! Yes, Finn, I would have preferred you walk away. I would have preferred you consider that some people love you and would rather see you awake and not lying in a hospital bed somewhere!"

I pulled her in for a hug. Despite Naomi's stiff stance, her fingers curled around my shirt to hold me close. Lincoln and Henrik exchanged confused looks.

"Is this some kind of foreplay?" Lincoln asked.

I frowned at him and gestured for them to turn away. "Shut up and go see if you can spot Sam."

To Naomi, I whispered, "I'm sorry. I thought I was helping you. Defending you."

She shook her head, pulling back so she could look into my eyes. "I don't want you to do that if it means getting hurt in the process."

I held my hands up, trying to prove to her I was fine. "I'm not hurt. Look. I'm fine. Everything's fine. I'm not going to hit my head, okay?"

She sighed. "I don't want you to forget again."

I nodded and pressed my forehead to hers. "I know, I understand. But even if I did—which will not happen—I'd still be here for you."

"You can't promise that." Naomi lightly knocked her fist against my chest, a hollow attempt at scolding. I could already tell her anger was fading as quickly as mine.

"I can't," I agreed. "But I've fallen in love with you twice now. I think it's safe to say I'd do it again."

She let out a low laugh. The smile didn't quite reach her eyes, but she looked like she was on her way back to her normal self.

"I'm proud of you," I whispered.

She raised a brow. There were still fights going on outside of the bar. Lincoln and Henrik were currently whispering to one another about how to get back to the van without being noticed. I tuned everything out for a moment to focus on her.

"You got mad at me, and you didn't hold back," I told her. "You weren't trying to be happy."

Naomi smiled as she considered my observation. "You're right."

"It was quite good. You yelled and everything."

She touched her throat. "That part hurt."

I laughed. "You'll get used to it after some practice. Soon enough, you'll be doing it for fun."

"You know what I'd like to do for fun?" Lincoln leaned over to break up our conversation. "Not hang out in a bush that smells like piss all night. What do you say?"

Naomi wrinkled her nose. "Is that what that smell is?"

"Unfortunately," Lincoln confirmed.

"You're right," I agreed, and let go of Naomi so we could focus on making an escape plan. "How do we want to do this?"

Henrik pointed toward a chain-link fence that surrounded most of the area. "Stick to that. The lampposts' lights don't reach out that far. We'll circle around and eventually get to the van."

"Sounds like a plan to me," Lincoln said.

Naomi grabbed my hand, fingers intertwining as she nodded.

"Alright," I agreed. "Let's do it."

Chapter Thirty-Four

Naomi

E scaping the parking lot unscathed was a feat, but we managed. Somehow, Sam had made his way to the van before we did and was waiting for us to unlock it.

"This night's unbelievable," Sam said as we all piled into the van, ready to put some distance between us and the bar. As soon as we were on the road Finn said something about "having the photos" to Sam. Sam cheered so loud that Finn rolled the windows down. I laughed when the still drunk Lincoln and Henrik joined in with Sam's whooping. Like me, neither one of them knew what Sam and Finn were so excited about but that didn't too much matter. We all celebrated regardless.

"It's a start." Sam clapped Finn's shoulder.

"It is," Finn agreed and gave me a smile that said he'd explain later.

The ride back to Mendell didn't feel as long as it did on the way there. We made it back to our house in one piece.

Despite it being late—or early, depending on how one looked at it—we were all still wired from the events of the night. I wanted ice cream. Lincoln seconded my motion. So, instead of falling into bed like we should have, we piled back into the van and went to NicMart to raid the shelves.

I convinced Finn to venture outside of his safe strawberry option. He picked up a limited-edition flavor thought up by some kid who won a contest. He wasn't too impressed with the mash-up of six different flavors, but gave in to my pleading because I pouted.

"He's officially whipped, folks," Lincoln announced to the two strangers beside us at the gas station. Neither of them looked impressed.

Finn pretended to be annoyed at Lincoln's declaration. The tips of his ears were red, and I kissed his cheek, only making them redder.

We ate our ice cream while walking through the dimly lit campus. The guys started singing a sea shanty they had no business knowing. I laughed, pretending to know the lyrics as well. Outside of the fight at the bar and my argument with Finn, this would, hands-down, be one of those nights I'd label the best in my college career. I kept glancing over at Finn, trying to gauge his enjoyment. He wasn't going to be like the rest of us and suddenly find pleasure in doing random, silly things. That was okay. We loved him for it. But I wanted to know if his time spent doing nothing productive brought some form of enjoyment. By the amusement in his eyes, I'd say it did.

"Guess what?" I pulled on his hand, putting some space between us and the guys. They continued to sing, almost drowning out my words.

"What?" Finn smiled at me, wiping a bit of ice cream off the corner of my mouth. My cheeks warmed when he licked it off his finger.

"I read the emails. My mom's emails," I said. "Right before the game, I decided I wanted to read them."

His expression changed to something a little more serious. I kept my smile intact.

"How do you feel?" he asked, leaning closer to make sure I knew he'd comfort me if I needed it.

"Good. Better." I took a breath, and my smile wavered a bit. Not because I was upset. In fact, I hadn't felt this light and truly happy for a long time.

Now that the emails weren't looming over me, I felt like I opened a door leading me outside. Now, I had the entire world to explore.

"She apologized." I stirred my melting ice cream as I spoke. "Not for everything, but for the big stuff. Mainly for blaming me."

Finn nodded, searching my face in case I was hiding my true feelings. "That's good. Right?"

God, I loved him. He was so patient. I'd argued with him earlier out of fear, and he hugged me. Now, I was talking about my dead mom, and he was doing his best to listen and understand.

"It is. I'm not ready to forgive, but I think this will help me get closer, you know?"

"I'm happy for you, Naomi." He reached for my hand, pulling it up to kiss the back of my palm. "If you need it, we'll go back to the camp. As many times as it takes."

I laughed. "Definitely. I still have to at least make a dent in one log. I've convinced myself if I do, I might unlock a new level of self-discovery."

Finn chuckled. "I know you will."

We started walking again but kept our pace slow so we wouldn't catch up with the guys. They were still singing and jumping on benches to dance.

"You'll still be my mod after this, right?" I asked.

Finn raised a brow. "What made you ask that?"

"I don't know. I just thought about our argument back at the bar and realized now that we're in a relationship, there might be some more of those in the future."

"Probably." He shrugged, unbothered by the possibility.

"That doesn't make you nervous? It doesn't worry you that our relationship could complicate things during streams?" I probed. It sure made me anxious. I didn't argue with people. That was most likely because I tried to keep a smile on my face. But now that was changing—for the better. I was going to stand up for myself. I was expressing emotions, other than happiness, thanks to him.

"No." He squeezed my hand. "No matter how mad at me you get, I'm not going to leave you hanging. We're a team, Naomi. A good one. No matter what happens between us, I'm going to be there for you. I know you'll do the same for me. No matter how big the argument is, we'll find a way to work it out. We'll find our way back to each other."

My chest warmed with so much joy I thought I'd burst. He was right. We'd find our way back to one another. We'd proved it this semester. Despite everything standing between us—including our own personalities—here we were, walking through our college campus, hand in hand, with melted ice cream, a group of silly friends, and the entire morning ahead of us.

I bumped my shoulder against his and nudged my chin to the sky. "We officially stayed out all night. Sun's coming up."

"Very irresponsible of us," Finn pretended to disapprove as he looked at the sky.

"But fun."

He nodded and looked over at me. "Very fun."

I kissed him. Our lips were sweet and cold from the ice cream. Finn's arm around my waist kept me warm. I moaned under his touch and that made him smile against my lips.

Never in a million years did I think I could make a grump like Finn kiss me with a grin. But I had. I returned the smile and my heart swelled at the thought of this only being our beginning. This kiss reminded me that our brightest days were ahead.

THE END

Epilogue

Finn

"I can't believe you two hid this from us." Lincoln stretched out on my bedroom floor as he complained. "From me. I thought we were closer than this."

"Why are you making it sound like a personal attack?" I asked as I finished tying together the cords to all of Naomi's electronics. We'd moved her streaming set-up into my room earlier this week because now that it was the dead of winter, downstairs felt like a freezer.

"Nothing about our online life is a personal attack," I added.

"Yeah, well, not being included in some chapters of your love story makes me feel like I've missed out," he said.

Naomi laughed as she plopped down on my office chair. "Aw, Lincoln."

"Don't 'aw' him," I warned, only half-joking. "He'll develop a complex."

"Too late." Lincoln let out an exaggerated sigh. "Complex developed. I officially feel left out of this relationship."

"As you should," I grumbled, and handed Naomi her headset. She murmured a 'thank you' and I bent down to give her a quick kiss. My chest warmed at the feel of her warm lips against mine. I was tempted to beg her to cancel tonight's stream and kick Lincoln out immediately. But I kept my mouth shut. I could hold myself together for another hour or so.

"What are we doing in here?" Henrik peeked his head into the room.

Wonderful, more company.

"Watching Naomi stream to her thousands of followers she never told us about," Lincoln said.

"It's only a couple hundred," Naomi told them, looking a little shy about the number.

"You guys aren't doing anything but leaving," I said.

"Finn's her personal guard dog," Lincoln explained when Henrik frowned in confusion. I shot Lincoln a look. He backtracked and said, "Sorry, I mispronounced stream moderator."

"Oh, right." Henrik's lackluster response triggered Lincoln's sixth sense.

"You already knew?" Lincoln sat up to catch his response. "Did Sam know, too? Was I the last one to know?"

I pleaded silently with Naomi. She didn't want me to manhandle them out of the room, but damn, they were on thin ice.

"Relax," she mouthed, eyes bright with amusement.

"Probably missed it when you were talking so much," Henrik said.

"This space..." I gestured around my room. "Is a drama-free zone for my girlfriend to do whatever the hell she wants, alright? And right now, you two are f-ing with the vibe. I don't take vibe f-ing lightly."

"Holy shit." Lincoln clutched his chest. "He's actually a good boyfriend. Henrik? Are you seeing this?"

"Taught him everything I know," Henrik teased and instead of moving down the hallway like I hoped he would, Henrik claimed one of my bean bag chairs.

"Of course, he's a good boyfriend," Naomi said, beaming up at me. "Why would you expect anything different?"

"Because..." Lincoln gestured up and down at me. "Have you met him?"

My jaw tightened. "Naomi, you have to let me—"

"Alright, alright." She popped up from her seat before I could make any rash decisions. "Time to separate you two."

I let her pull me to one corner of the room while Henrik scolded Lincoln in the other corner.

"You are so worked up today." Naomi rubbed the side of my arm. "What's really bothering you?"

"Nothing. I just want this space to be comfortable for you and Lincoln's ruining it."

She shook her head. "Nope. I'm not buying it. You love it when we're all together."

"Do I?"

"You pretend like you don't, but I know you do," she insisted and kissed my cheek. "Stop being so difficult and tell me what's up. I can't have you two bickering in the background. My mic will pick everything up."

"Which is why you should let me kick them out," I said. Sam was now lingering in the doorway, listening to Lincoln's spiel about our streaming "secret." "It's getting a little crowded."

"You know I love when we're all together, too." Naomi's smile was wide and content. My annoyance faded at the sight of her happiness.

"Fine." I cleared my throat before continuing, "You're right. I... I might be a little on edge tonight."

Her expression changed to something more serious. "What's wrong?"

"I wanted to be alone with you because I have to ask you something," I explained. "And I'd prefer not to have an audience."

Her eyes went wide, on the brink of panic. "Is it something serious? Is something wrong?"

"No, no, nothing's wrong. It's not serious... Well, not a bad serious. Just your typical serious." I hadn't realized just how nervous I was feeling until now. My heart drummed quickly.

Naomi laughed at my rambling. "Finn, just ask me. They're not paying any attention to us right now. Besides, even if they were, they'd figure it out, eventually."

I frowned. "I guess you're right."

"Ask me," Naomi whispered, and stepped closer to create more privacy. She placed her hand on my chest, thinking her touch would be soothing. Instead, my heartrate picked up even more.

"Sorry." I let out a shaky sigh. "Didn't think I'd be this nervous."

She tried to press her lips together so she wouldn't smile too much. "I don't know if it counts for anything, but you always wear nervous well."

I chuckled. "Thanks."

"You're welcome."

"Okay, so, here's the thing," I started. "You and I have been spending a lot of time together, particularly in this room."

"We have," she agreed. "Wait, are you asking for more space?"

"No, no, the opposite," I blurted. "I think you should consider moving up here with me."

Naomi's eyebrows rose, but she didn't say a thing. I hurried on, hoping I wasn't scaring her.

"My desk is larger than yours," I explained. "It fits your streaming setup perfectly. And my mattress is ten times softer than yours. I know how much you love sunlight and mornings are so bright it's almost blinding in this room. If you moved up here, you'd have easier access to the bathroom. It'll be warmer, too."

"All very logical reasons," she agreed in a low voice.

"Exactly." I nodded, glad that we seemed to be on the same page.

"But you're leaving out a big part."

My shoulders sagged, disappointed I missed something. "What's that?"

"You. You're here."

"Is that an issue...?"

Naomi's smile was back. "No. It's the best part. I would have led with it."

I took a breath, feeling relieved. "I see."

"You sound like you're trying to convince me."

"I am. I want you up here."

"Because it's logical?"

"Yes, and... because I want to be closer to you. I've been making sure this room is as comfortable as it can be for you because I want you to stay."

"Finn, I'd stay if you had a tiny desk and brick mattress."

My stomach flipped because I was pretty sure this was the beginning of a 'yes.' "Really?"

She tilted her head to the side, considering. "Well, if the mattress was brick, I might suggest we sleep on the carpet instead. But, other than that, yeah. I'd want to be with you even if this room was the crappier room."

"So, to clarify, is this a 'yes'?" I asked.

Instead of answering, Naomi wrapped her arms around my neck and pulled me in for a kiss. I clung to her waist, ignoring the whistling from the guys behind us.

"You seriously thought I'd say no?" Naomi wondered.

"It always felt like a decent possibility," I admitted.

She laughed and kissed me again.

"Get a room," Lincoln joked.

"We're in it," Sam reminded him.

Lincoln laughed. "Oh, right."

"Can I kick them out now?" I pleaded in a whisper against her lips.

"Go for it," she permitted.

The guys didn't give me much pushback when I corralled them out of our room. But they continued to yell teasing taunts even after I closed the door behind them.

Naomi squealed when I picked her up and carried her to the bed. I kissed every part of her face, neck, and shoulders.

"You're going to be late for your stream," I said between kisses.

She laughed. "That's not an ask, is it?"

I shook my head and slipped my hands underneath her shirt. "It's not."

She moaned when my hands cupped her breasts. "I like it. You should boss me around more often."

"I plan to," I promised and captured her mouth again.

"What else do you plan to do?" she whispered when we separated for a breath.

"Whatever it takes to make sure you're happy with me."

She teasingly 'tsked.' "I thought you were going somewhere dirty with this, but you chose romantic."

"I can talk dirty to you if you want." I pressed kisses along her jawline. "I can do both. Which do you want?"

"Both. Everything. Every part you have to offer. Just like you want every side of me."

I smiled. "You have a deal."

"Perfect," she said, pulling me back to her for a kiss.

Bonus Epilogue

Naomi

F inn smiled when he saw me walk into the living room with my knitting needles in hand. "There you are. I was about to come looking for you."

"Your Padawan's making progress," I said.

"Come here, let me see." He gestured for me to join him on the carpet, pushing his schoolwork to the side. I claimed a spot between his legs and leaned my back against his chest. Finn held me close as I demonstrated the stitches I'd been practicing for the last few days.

"It's better, right?" I asked after getting through a couple of stitches.

Finn chuckled, voice low and soothing as he said, "Um... yes, but you should try to slow down a bit."

"I think this looks way better than my other tries." I paused and held up the square I knitted for both of us to examine. There were fewer lopsided holes in this attempt than in the previous test swatches I'd made. The light showed through those holes as I held it up to the ceiling.

"It does," Finn humored me, always the patient teacher.

I counted all the dropped stitches. "Only five this time."

He kissed my temple and then, placed his hands over mine. "Here, I'll show you a trick."

I smiled as his warm fingers guided mine. He did all of the work, wrapping the yarn around one needle and transferring the stitch over to the next. I watched in awe at how easily his hands moved. He once said his large hands weren't made for details yet he worked with my small needles and thin yarn so easily. Something so crafty didn't seem like it could be sexy but it was.

"See," he said, after finishing a row. His deep voice this close to my ear made my stomach flip. "It's simple."

I cleared my throat, trying to regain some sense of composure. "I don't think we have the same definition of simple."

When I attempted to start the next row on my own, I botched it up almost immediately.

"This was supposed to be a calming hobby..." I trailed off when Finn absentmindedly massaged circles on my waist. My shirt bunched up a little but not enough to get him to push the fabric aside for skin-to-skin contact.

"It is if you slow down."

I sighed, half disappointed in my lack of skill, half mesmerized by his touch. Was he trying to distract me? Because his voice sounded normal. Finn usually didn't know what he was doing to me unless I told him.

"But I want to be able to knit you a hat by Christmas," I said.

"Naomi, Christmas is in five days."

My shoulders sagged. "Exactly."

"How about you knit me a short scarf," he tried to solve the problem.

"I have to figure out how to stop dropping stitches first." I took a deep breath and willed myself to try again. Plenty of people learned how to knit. I wasn't some odd exception. I could do this. All it'd take was for me to implement Finn's advice of slowing down... which had been far more difficult to master than I anticipated.

"It can be a very holey scarf," Finn noted.

I gasped and placed a hand on my chest in mock offense. "Very holey? Excuse me, but I've gotten my dropped stitches down to five. There won't be enough holes for you to call it very holey."

"My mistake." Finn nuzzled my neck and placed apology kisses beneath my ear. "I'm sure the holes will be down to a minimum."

"Minimum," I agreed with a nod. "And, dare I say, simply one."

"A large effort that–" He stopped short when I tilted my head to look up at him.

"That?" I prompted. My breath hitched when he snuck a hand under my shirt, running his fingers across my stomach. After nearly two years of dating, his simple touch still sent my head spinning. Shouldn't my body have been used to casual contact by now? But no, nothing ever felt casual with Finn. It all held meaning. And the look in his eyes confirmed as much.

"That I have no doubt you will accomplish," he said, voice as low as a whisper now as he leaned in close.

"You're damn right," I teased.

He grinned. "I don't doubt you for a second. My scarf will be my most prized possession."

"It better be."

Finn leaned in to kiss me. I nearly dropped my needles but remembered the stitches would fall off and be almost impossible to put back on. So, I lowered my project to the floor carefully. Finn smiled against my lips in approval.

"See, I can slow down," I whispered when we pulled away for a moment.

"Very nice," he approved and gave me another kiss before adding, "But you still have more practicing to do. Good thing you have me as a teacher."

"Because you're a pro?"

"Because I quite literally can't get enough of you. Which means, you can get me to do any and everything you wish and I won't complain for a second."

"Any and everything?"

He nodded, hands tightened around my waist. I could feel his hardened cock straining against his pants.

"I think you're right. I do need more practice on slowing down," I said.

Finn cleared his throat, eyes flickering back to my knitting. "Okay... uh, I'll demonstrate a few more rows."

I laughed because he didn't understand what I'd been hinting at. His cheeks turned red and I gave them both multiple kisses.

"What?" he asked, his smile reappearing. I kissed the dimple it revealed.

"I wasn't talking about knitting, Finn."

"Oh... right." The red in his cheeks remained. He did what he always did, pulled me in for another kiss to distract me.

"That's what I need to get better at," he whispered against my lips. "Reading between the lines."

I shook my head. "I like how you are now. Don't change unless you want," I insisted. "Unless it makes you happy."

He tucked a stray curl behind my ear. "Do I make you happy? How I am now?"

My heart fluttered. "You do. So much so that sometimes I wonder if you're real."

"I'm very real," he promised.

"Good." I grinned. "Do I make you happy?"

"Unbelievably," he said without hesitation. "And thank god you're real. If you weren't, well, I don't think I'd want to know."

I laughed. "I'm real, Finn. You know what else is real?"

"Um... is this a read between the lines thing again?"

"A little." I brushed my nose across his. "Graduation. Something both of us have been avoiding despite how more real it gets every day. We should talk about it."

Some of the light faded from his eyes. "Right."

"Don't sound so excited."

"I'm very excited," he said in a flat voice.

I pulled back a bit to get a better look at him. "Have you decided what you're going to do?"

Finn was quiet and for a second, I didn't think I'd get an answer out of him.

"I'm going to sign with the Eagles," he said. "They're an amazing team and I think I'd fit in well there. Sam's thinking of signing too so that's a pretty big incentive, as well."

"Really?" I pulled him in for a quick hug.

Finn chuckled, seemingly relieved about my reaction. "I didn't expect you to be happy. I'll have to move three states away."

"Why wouldn't I be happy about you figuring out your next step? Playing for the Eagles sounds perfect for you."

"Are you ready to get rid of me?" he teased. "Is that it?"

"No, it's just... Well, I haven't applied yet but Amber U's math grad program is one of the best in the country. If I get in I wouldn't be from the Eagles' home arena. Amber U's campus is only an hour drive away from it. Forty-five minutes without traffic in the day time and almost thirty-nine in night time traffic."

"So, you've done a little research." Finn's eyes danced.

"Just a bit." I held my index and thumb a centimeter apart. "We could spend weekends together. You could move in with me during the off seasons. The rent is amazing down there. I'll work hard to get a grant.

Maybe we could get a dog! Or cat... you're more of a cat person, aren't you?"

"I can see us having both." He held onto me tighter, catching onto some of my enthusiasm. "We'll get both. And I'll pay for the rent. I don't mind a longer commute. I want you to focus on school and save your money."

My heart swelled and I shook my head. "Let's figure out the details later. We'll argue about rent and animals and commutes and whatever we want."

"Is it weird that I'm looking forward to arguing with you?" He pulled me close so his forehead pressed against mine. "I can't wait to do it all with you, Naomi."

"Me, too. We make a good team."

"The fucking best."

I laughed at the passion in his tone. "Yeah, the fucking best."

Also By Deanna Grey

Mendell Hawks

Team Players

Westbrooke Angels

Just Please Me

Just Fall For Me

Just Dare Me

Standalones

The Deep End

Printed in Great Britain
by Amazon

21170414R00161